Strawberries
and
Crime

Also available by Elle Brooke White

The Finn Family Farm Mysteries
Dead on the Vine

Strawberries
and
Crime

A FINN FAMILY FARM
MYSTERY

Elle Brooke White

CROOKED
LANE

NEW YORK

Copyright © 2021 by Christine E. Blum

Published in the United States by Crooked Lane Books, an imprint of The Quick Brown Fox & Company LLC.

Crooked Lane Books and its logo are trademarks of The Quick Brown Fox & Company LLC.

Library of Congress Catalog-in-Publication data available upon request.

ISBN (hardcover): 978-1-64385-578-3
ISBN (ebook): 978-1-64385-579-0

Cover design by Tsukushi

Printed in the United States.

www.crookedlanebooks.com

Crooked Lane Books
34 West 27th St., 10th Floor
New York, NY 10001

First Edition: October 2021

10 9 8 7 6 5 4 3 2 1

For nature, with respect.

Chapter One

As the last remaining dewdrop elongated and started to slip away from the strawberry that morning, life was beginning to stir on the Finn Family Farm. A black phoebe with its feathered, chimney-soot body and starched-white-shirt belly made a dapper entrance to all but the flies and other insects that it preys upon. Way up above, a flock of wild parrots announced their arrival with piercing Amazonian shrieks, signaling to the hawks that the competition for today's resources had begun.

On a farm, every living thing has a job, and they work together to maintain the equilibrium of the beating heart of the land. The ground beetles keep the snails in check; ladybugs help stem the aphid population; snakes regularly have mice on their dietary menu; and so on. A farm is a bucolic biosphere supported by a coliseum of natural gladiators. And this farm nestled in the hillside of the Santa Barbara Mountains in the town of Little Acorn is no exception.

* * *

"Horse!" Charlotte shouted for her friend from the kitchen. She stuck her head out the door to the back wrap-around patio and scanned the area. Her long red curls followed every turn of her head, a stark contrast to her peaches-and-cream complexion, made slightly less creamy now that she'd spent the past six months working mostly out of doors. Since Charlotte Finn inherited her great-uncle Tobias's produce farm and left her big-city job behind, her introduction to agrarian life could best be described as a "baptism by fire."

Thinking back, Charlotte can remember waking up her first morning, with a combination of excitement and trepidation, to the bright sunshine and crops of ripening fruit planted for all to see on the undulating hills below. But her jubilation for choosing a simpler, pastoral life soon burst like overripe fruit when she made the grisly discovery of a dead body impaled with a pitchfork, lying among the heirloom tomato vines. With the help of the farm's resident staff, they had followed the investigation trail to its conclusion. But most of the credit for solving the murder had to go to Horse, the farm's little pig, named so because he eats like one. It was Horse and his uncanny way of comprehending the English language that got him rooting out the important evidence that led the humans to the killer.

"Ah, there you are." Charlotte said as the pink pig, not so much a baby anymore, trotted into the kitchen. The gleam in his eyes and his apple-cheeked smile indicated that he hoped whatever mischief he was about to be blamed for would be trumped by his cuteness factor. Alice, who was preparing lunch, sandwiches for the crew working in the fields, was the first to fall victim.

"Go easy on him, Charlotte. If Horse is the culprit, then I'm sure that once you inform him of his mistake, he will never repeat it." Alice held up a dishcloth to her mouth to hide her smile.

Alice was one of the farm's caretakers, along with her husband Joe. When Charlotte moved to the farm, she hadn't realized how much she'd come to depend on them until they helped her solve a murder.

"That's what you said the last five times he did this Alice. I hope you haven't started to go soft on me. The Finn family does not tolerate thieves. Horse, look at me."

He sat on his chubby hind legs and tried to give Charlotte his most cherubic expression, head cocked to one side, eyes sparkling adoringly.

Charlotte's love for her porcine friend, along with a special ladybug named Mrs. Robinson, goats, geese, and a soccer-playing horse named Pele, had won her over to farm life, and she'd vowed to make a go of it.

Mrs. Robinson sat perched on Horse's shoulder, eying the situation. She flapped her wings several times to make sure that she'd be ready to take flight if things took a turn for the worse for the pig.

"Alice had set a bowl of hard-boiled eggs on the counter, to cool, early this morning. When she returned to prepare lunch, half the eggs had disappeared." Charlotte noticed that Horse took a nervous swallow at the news while she addressed him. Alice tried to stifle a giggle.

"I know that you've learned some special skills in your young life and that you are a very smart pig, Horse." Charlotte continued.

Horse beamed.

"As such, you knew perfectly well that those eggs were not left out for you. I can see by the mud tracks you left that you slid the footstool over to the counter to reach the bowl. Yes, you returned the stool to its right place against the wall, but you left telltale evidence behind. I suppose it's true that deep down every criminal wants to be caught."

Charlotte walked over to the footstool and knelt down next to it. Alice and Horse's eyes were fixated on her.

"Look what we have here: a couple of hoof prints. And what's this? Why it looks like there are fragments of eggshell caked to the stool as well."

As Horse hung his head in shame, his ears flopped down and covered his eyes for an added remorseful effect.

"Has Horse been caught pilfering eggs again? Or should I say poaching?" Samuel Brown, the resident farmer asked, snickering at his own joke. He'd breezed into the kitchen, grabbed a couple of apples from a bowl on the kitchen counter, and tipped his cowboy hat to Charlotte. "One for me, and one for Pele," he grinned as he headed back outside.

Tall and lanky, with stick-straight dark hair that he could often be seen brushing back with his strong farm hands, Samuel was the shy but resolute agricultural backbone of the Finn Family Farm. A bit of a loner, Samuel (Charlotte had to be told several times to stop calling him "Farmer Brown") was most at home with the crops he'd tended since he'd worked as a boy apprentice for Charlotte's Uncle Tobias.

He and Charlotte had gotten off to a rocky start when she took over the Finn Family Farm, and no one was sure back then, including herself, whether she'd stay or prepare for a quick sale and departure. The decision was, in a way, forced upon her when the murder victim was discovered on the land, derailing all prospects for turning over the property quickly. Samuel could have taken off for greener pastures, so to speak, but he stuck by Charlotte, seeing in her an innate love for the land despite her big-city life so far. Samuel had family living in proximity to the Finn Family Farm, but no significant love interest it seemed, at least of the two-legged variety. Charlotte and he had had their moments of entertaining the idea, but one or both had always pulled back in the interest of saving the farm from disaster.

Ultimately, and with a good deal of hard learning, everyone seemed to have settled into their proper roles and responsibilities. Samuel tended to the strawberry fields and a wide variety of tomato crops, as well as experimented with branching out into growing other categories of produce.

And much to his relief, Samuel had relinquished all financial responsibilities to caretaker Joe Wong, Alice's husband. Joe dealt with the distributors that brought the Finn produce to mass market, and Alice managed the more personal sales at weekly farmers markets and through the onsite Farm Shop. Joe's even-keeled temperament helped him greatly in negotiations—but he wasn't to be mistaken for a pushover. He and Alice considered the farm their home, as did Samuel, and all three would protect it with their lives. In fact, they had in the past—but that's another story.

Which left Charlotte free to ply her expertise as master marketer. She'd had the inspiration to design a "You Pick 'Em" program, providing visitors with baskets and guidance on how to harvest their own strawberries and tomatoes. The farm was saved from the constant burden of finding day laborers when the fruit was ripe, and the program had saved them money and helped expose a past distributor who was robbing them blind. This season Charlotte had high hopes for creating even more opportunities to take the farm to the next level.

The only farm resident refusing to stay in his lane was Horse, who wanted to have a hoof in every pie.

*   *   *

"While I understand that on a farm it is difficult to sleep past the chickens, I never signed on for rising with the roosters. What are you lovely ladies doing up at such an ungodly hour?"

Beau stumbled into the kitchen, one eye still stubbornly shut to the daylight. He was clad in a pair of cowboy-print pajamas. If it weren't for the fact that he was six feet two, Charlotte might have thought that the little boy from next door had spent the night. Beau and Diane Mason had grown up living next door to Charlotte and her family in a suburb outside of Chicago. Both sets of parents worked, so the three were often left to their own devices after school, spawning each of their unique personalities with the passing years. It also created a friendship and devotion between them that was as solid as the earth's mantle.

Beau, the youngest of the three, often described himself as being "Beau-dacious." A freethinker and creative spirit, Beau had never shied away from a chance to make his surroundings more beautiful. Which is not to say that he insisted on being an arbiter of taste—far from it. Beau loved life and could uncover the charm and allure in even the most mundane of creatures. "There's a lid for every pot, my Momma used to say, Char. But I prefer to think that in every living being there is an ingenue just waiting to be called to the stage. All they need is the right role."

While living in Los Angeles, Beau had been a successful event planner known for creating large-scale extravaganzas for the music industry, car companies, and sporting events. How he found the time to visit the farm so often baffled Charlotte, though she was ever grateful for the company.

"Beau, it's almost nine. The workers in the fields have been at it for three hours now," Alice playfully reprimanded him.

"Then it's a good thing that my day job is almost always a night job, or I'd be hard pressed to keep myself in such whimsical sleepwear."

"That's quite a sartorial statement, Beau," Charlotte said, eying a rider on a bucking bronco across his breast pocket. "Or should I call you 'Bonanza Beau'?"

"Yee-ha!" he replied.

"How about you get changed into some proper daywear for Little Acorn and accompany me to the Garden Center? I've got a long list, including some items that Samuel says he needs as soon as possible."

"Yes, boss, I shall return posthaste. Is my beloved sister still in blissful slumber?"

"Are you kidding? She was up and out to the construction site before I'd even brushed my teeth," Alice explained. "She's a woman with a mission now."

You couldn't ask for a more loyal, understanding, and wise person than Diane Mason, Beau's older sister and Charlotte's BFF, to be by your side. Where Beau was always ready not just to test the boundaries but to blow them up, Diane was more measured in her approach to life, both for herself and her loved ones. Charlotte worried for a time that this discipline would result in Diane missing out on some of the fun, but when Diane made it clear that cooking was her passion, Charlotte was overjoyed that she'd found her creative outlet. Up until recently, Diane had worked as a sous chef for an "impossible-to-get-a-reservation" L.A. restaurant and received great reviews for her own pastry creations. But more and more, Diane had longed to leave the often-cutthroat business of working in an impressively popular restaurant for a chance to build her own dishes and recipes across all courses of the menu. For the longest time, she'd kept these thoughts to herself, and when she'd finally decided to share her dreams, it turned out that everyone had already figured them out.

"Ah. But is the goal of the mission to complete the building or the builder?"

"Beau!" Charlotte and Alice shouted at him, and chased him out of the kitchen.

* * *

The town of Little Acorn proper hadn't changed much since the first settlers claimed it in the late 1700s. It was divided in two by a cobblestone street that wound its way for about four miles before emptying off into a wider paved road out of town. Within city boundaries lay everything that a rural community would require: a post office; the Little Acorn First Federal Bank; a small police station; the Hall of Records, which shares space with the public library; Stewart's more than ample General Store; and the tourist-beckoning, local artisan wine, cheese, and specialty shops. Though every building fit organically with the environment of the town, they all also displayed their own design characteristics that seemed to hint at the kind of commerce that was plied inside. Outside in front of Stewart's General Store were six white Adirondack chairs, because a visit is only partially about getting supplies and equally about catching up with townspeople. The First Federal Bank had a tin-and-copper-tiled facade that had originally been white, but as it aged, oxidation had created a sea-green patina. The color of money.

At the far end of Main Street, the Garden and Feed Center could be found, always bustling with farmers, weekend agricultural warriors, and those that practice Little Acorn's second-favorite pastime after cultivating the land: gossiping. Under duress Charlotte would admit that she'd used that town trait to her advantage in the past, to help solve a murder, of course.

"It looks like the entire hillside has gathered in the parking lot," Beau said as Charlotte pulled her vintage Buick Roadmaster station wagon into the Garden Center. She'd bought the car on the internet, captivated by its classic family-road-trip style that reignited memories of going to the lake cabin with her parents and childhood buddies Diane and Beau. When, upon arrival on the West Coast, she'd picked up the vehicle at the Los Angeles airport, it did not disappoint. Super-sized and all American, it was white with faux wood grain siding, sported a large sunroof, and had plenty of room for hauling farm supplies from town. Plus, the seats were large and soft enough to sleep on in case of an extended, overnight drive.

"They look too serious for run-of-the-mill gossiping. I wonder what's brought all these farmers together. Did Samuel mention anything to you, Beau?" Charlotte asked.

"Not a peep, and you know what a chatty Charles he is," Beau replied, making fun of Samuel's eschewing of idle conversation.

"We're missing something, boys. I don't need to tell you how urgent it is that we nip this in the bud," groused an older cowboy who looked as worn as the loose stones that covered the parking lot dirt beneath them. He'd puffed out his chest, perhaps to give himself more authority when addressing the ring of farmers around him.

"We haven't been sitting on our hands, Linc," said a much younger and more polished-looking man to the cowboy. "I've watched how much money my farm's owner has put toward this so far. He's hired consultants, sent samples off to labs for testing, and even installed electronic fences around the fields. Money is no object to Ford Barclay. If there's better technology for working on the problem, then we'd love to hear about it."

"We're dealing with nature here, Martin," Linc said in disgust. "The currency that it trades in doesn't come out of a wallet. No matter how thick it is." He spat into the dirt to punctuate his statement.

"Er, excuse me," Charlotte gently interrupted, causing all heads to turn in her direction.

"For those of you I haven't met yet, I'm Charlotte, owner of the Finn Family Farm. Is there some sort of problem you all are being challenged by on your farms? Everything seems to be going smoothly for once on mine."

The minute that last statement came out of her mouth, she regretted it. Charlotte prided herself in being able to hang with the big boys, and what she'd just told them made her seem naive or, worse, not in control of her farm.

"Like I was saying, boys," Linc continued, ignoring her, and after a moment of silence. "We need to compare notes on what we've tried so far. Javier, tell us what you've been doing."

"The usual stuff," explained the stocky farmer in the chin-strapped, worn straw hat. He was shorter than the others, but the muscles on his shoulders and the exposed forearms of his rolled-up chambray shirtsleeves were the telltale signs of heavy fieldwork. "Alternating watering patterns, organic and chemical pest control, soil additives—the whole nine."

"Let me guess: nothing stopped it," the well-dressed Martin said, shaking his head.

"Stopped *what*?" Charlotte's Irish temper could only be contained for so long.

"This blight that's destroying our young strawberry plant growth, that's what," explained a tall, barrel-chested man with a proud face that bordered on patronizing. He had a mop of blond hair that he kept mostly under control beneath a black and yellow ball cap emblazoned with a "Hoover Farms" logo.

"Destroying how?" *They are going to include me, dang it. I'm a farmer just like they are.*

"The triple threat, Charlotte: yellowing, browning and then withering," Linc replied, shaking his head sadly.

"Wow, we have no such issue with our strawberries, and I'd be the first to know." Charlotte defiantly punctuated her point.

"You calling me a liar, missy?" Linc glared at Charlotte, hairy nostrils flared, and got Beau's attention.

Charlotte didn't respond immediately, something that she'd practiced over the years to get the upper hand in a confrontation. By her keeping silent, her opponent felt compelled to keep talking, thus revealing more about himself. Charlotte also wanted a moment to physically assess her competition. Linc was a cowboy through and through. He wore a beige brimmed hat, a white shirt under a leather vest, and well-broken-in blue jeans, and he had an impressive white beard. He looked to be anywhere between seventy and ninety years old. His weathered face was a road map to a life spent outdoors, and his scarred hands broadcast his years of manual labor. Charlotte was about to relent and show him some respect when his temper flared up at her ignoring him.

"Another pretender, that's what you are. All of you—you don't know the first thing about cultivating the land. About listening to the sky, the winds, and the sun. That's how honest farming is done."

Linc turned his attention to the barrel-chested blond man. "Like you, Boyd. All that's important to you is being the biggest and the best. What are you, up to being the fourth or fifth largest produce farm in the county? I've heard the reports predicting a very robust strawberry season; I'm sure you've salivating over them. Greed is the culprit here, if you ask me. Someone is using sabotage, plain and simple, to destroy the competition."

With that statement voices were raised all around the circle of farmers, with Charlotte stuck in the middle of the melee.

"I'm going to remind you, Linc," Boyd said in a raised voice so all could hear, "that my people caught a couple of your farm workers roaming around our strawberry fields without permission late last year. Can you explain why, Linc? I had Security question them at the time, and all they could say was that they thought that our farm was open to the public. Now where would they get an idea like that? And what was so interesting to them that had to trespass on my property? I don't suppose that you put them up to it?"

Linc lunged for Boyd, and the second that Beau saw some fists go up, he rushed in to try to diffuse Linc and extricate Charlotte from the situation.

"Linc, I'm sure that you didn't mean to accuse anyone directly. Let's just step aside and calm down, sport, okay?" Beau tried to ease Linc away from the group.

"Get your hands off me, pretty boy! I don't take orders from your kind. You need to leave this to the farmers and go back to your cushy home in the city, where you belong!"

Linc gave Beau one firm shove on his shoulder as he pushed past, sending Beau to the ground with a thud.

"Beau!" Charlotte screamed, reaching down for him. "Don't just stand there—help him up," Charlotte commanded the group of staring farmers. "You all should be ashamed of yourselves, acting like brawling hooligans. I know your mommas brought you up better than that."

This was Charlotte's best method for controlling the unruly.

Talk to them like their mothers would. It gets them into line every time.

"I've never seen this much anger in Little Acorn," Charlotte continued, addressing the men. "No doubt, it's only a matter of time before my strawberries fall victim to the scourge—all the more reason that we need to work together."

"Forget what Linc said, Charlotte. He's just a cranky old man." Ford Barclay's agriculturalist, Martin, tried to assure her.

"He's right about one thing, Martin: we don't have a lot of time to get control of this disease, and I am ready to step up to the challenge. I can't offer the rich expertise that you all have, but I'm a pretty good communicator. This is very concerning to all of us, and we need to pool our knowledge, compare notes, and keep gathering information on what is killing the strawberries of Little Acorn."

"I'm right with you, Char." Beau stepped up next to her. "Together we'll visit as many farms as possible in the next week or so, and then I suggest that we meet again to share our findings. Only perhaps in more agreeable surroundings, like the Finn Family Farm lakeside?"

"Deal?" Charlotte asked, putting her dainty white hand into the ring.

"Deal." They replied, one by one covering her hand with calloused, well-worked farmers' paws, dirty but assuring.

Chapter Two

"That was not how I expected this shopping trip to go," Charlotte said on the drive back to the farm. The car was loaded with supplies, but instead of enjoying a feeling of accomplishment, Charlotte had a sense of dread about the unease that was spreading through the Little Acorn farm community. "I am so sorry that Linc said those hateful things to you."

"It may not be apparent, given my flawless complexion and healthy glow, but I'm thicker skinned than that. Poor Linc feels like he's lost his relevance in the world, and that must be a very lonely place. I'll make sure to visit his farm soon and reassure him that his knowledge in this fight is invaluable."

"How do you always do it?"

"Do what?"

"Always see the bright side. Life just isn't unicorns and rainbows all the time. Sometimes things really stink."

"If we were in a musical, this is where I'd start singing."

With that, Beau launched into a chorus of "Always Look on the Bright Side of Life."

Charlotte joined in and, when they'd exhausted the metaphor, said, "I love you, and I am so happy to have Diane living on the farm now, and her following her dreams."

"It's pretty great—she was born to have her own restaurant. Remember how, when we were kids, she would make us her guinea pigs and serve us a tasting menu?"

"Oh God, yes!" Charlotte reached across the console and grabbed Beau's arm. "What was that thing she made that had us laughing so hard I almost peed my pants?"

"Silly of Sole."

"That's it! She took mashed potatoes and formed them into the shape of a fish, tail and all. She used two capers for the eyes, and she sprinkled parsley on top and added buttermilk for the sauce. Lemon wedges completed the dish."

"I thought that it tasted pretty good," Beau remembered.

"It might have if the potatoes had been warmed. Don't you remember we took our forks and ended up in a food-flinging fight instead?" Charlotte's giggles were growing.

"That's right. Then Diane presented us with a bill on a silver plate and left the kitchen." Beau reminisced for a moment before asking Charlotte, "So what's your take on this contractor guy building her restaurant—Danny Costa is it?"

Charlotte nodded. "He seems capable, and his crew genuinely respects him."

"You know that's not what I'm asking about. I've seen the way she turns the shade of a flamingo when he walks into the room."

"I'm not supposed to say anything, but she's pretty much admitted to being infatuated by Danny."

"Why do I not feel excited for my dear sis?"

"Maybe because he's a stranger to you and comes from a life that you've never experienced. I understand that Danny's family has lived in Santa Barbara County for generations. Along with that come many unbreakable traditions. Some are plain to see, like respecting the land and living along with nature, rather than battling it. Diane told me that Danny still lives in the old mission that his great-great-grandfather bought and converted part of it into a large family home. The remaining space is still used as a mission for the local community."

"She's been to his house?"

"I don't know, but Diane's a grown woman and we need to let her explore this relationship in her own way. Besides, Danny comes from a long line of Costa men who ride annually with what they call the Rancheros Visitadores. It's a riding club that Danny says started in 1939 to commemorate the old rancheros' homeward journey from rodeos and ranching. It's a weeklong event and often a platform for raising money for charity. Danny is passionate about this tradition, which seems to have endeared Diane to him even more."

"Therefore confirming once again that you can't judge a book by its cover," Beau said, eying Danny as they pulled up to the construction site. He stopped work to greet them.

"You all have a productive trip? Alice told me you'd gone to the Garden Center, and she was starting to get worried you'd been gone so long." Diane came out of the framed structure to join him.

As she studied him, Charlotte reconfirmed her initial impression that Danny was a little rough around the edges compared to

Diane's prior boyfriends. He was good-looking, but in a disheveled, bad-boy way.

He's kind of a mash up between Owen Wilson and Dennis Hopper, she thought.

Charlotte had noticed, when she'd observed him working in the past, that he got quiet when he felt angry, clearly holding his tongue and his temper in check. Perhaps that explained why his crew, though respecting his leadership, also seemed to show a bit of fear around him as well. Charlotte decided not to share these impressions with Beau just yet—they might be nothing—but she was determined to keep a close eye on Danny, to protect Diane.

"It took more time because of what we came upon in the parking lot." Beau stopped there probably assuming that Charlotte would want to tell the entire story.

"Uh-oh," Diane said, coming toward Beau and Charlotte. "Are you okay?"

Diane was turning more and more into a country girl the longer she lived on the Finn Family Farm. Her shoulder-length auburn hair, which she'd always kept in a tight bun at the back of her head, in an effort to seem utterly professional, was now allowed to fall free. Her large, brown doe eyes, previously left unadorned, now benefitted from some lash-accentuating mascara, giving her a valuable, expressive tool for getting or communicating what she wanted.

"We're fine, although chivalrous Beau took one for the team protecting me and ended up on his keister," Charlotte began. She had Diane's and Danny's full attention, as well as that of the crew, who had stopped working to listen in.

"A large group of farmers was having an impromptu meeting by their trucks, and when we approached, we could hear them talking about some sort of crop blight that they haven't been able to wipe out."

"You should have seen Charlotte step right in the circle and demand to know what they were talking about." Beau beamed at her.

"What did you do? I know how incensed you can get when you're not kept in the loop." Diane shook her head and looked Charlotte directly in the eyes.

"Nothing. But I am a member of this farming community, and if something is harming our strawberries, then I deserve to know about it!"

"What's going on with the strawberries?" Danny asked. "Yours seem to be fine."

Charlotte recounted the damage the other farmers were seeing and the steps they'd taken to stop the destruction.

"So how did Beau end up on his butt?" Diane asked when Charlotte had finished.

"It was really a big misunderstanding—kind of an old-school versus high-tech approach to farming. This older cowboy, a fellow named Linc, got a bit indignant when he heard that the wealthy owner of Barclay Farms had access to and was using computers and digital equipment to try and control the blight. Then Linc threw out an accusation of sabotage, and voices got raised. Beau quickly pulled me out of the ring of fire and tried to douse tempers. As a thanks, he received a few harsh words and a strong shove from Linc." Diane took in an audible breath upon hearing this.

Noticing her concern, Danny jumped in. "That's not right. I don't care how long you've lived or how much you've seen. I'm going to find this guy Linc's place and pay him a visit."

"No need. I've already got that covered," Beau said, quick to respond. "In fact, I've got a few days of research work ahead of me that I can do from here, and Char and I plan to visit as many of the neighboring farms as we can and gather information from the stricken farmers. Linc is already on my list, and tomorrow we plan to drop in on this Ford Barclay and his head farmer, Martin Ross, to see their operation. Charlotte, I suggest that we make this a surprise drop-by event so we get to see what they're actually up to, as opposed to what they want us to see."

"Sounds like a plan. What's your impression of Ford Barclay?" Charlotte asked, hoping for some insight.

"Never heard of him or his farm. Is it nearby?" Danny replied.

"Martin said that it was about three miles from here, so yes, it is close. I'm surprised—you seem to know everyone from these rolling hills. If he's as rich as Martin says, then his place must be hard to miss." Charlotte tried not to look skeptical as she said this to Danny, who just shrugged his shoulders before getting back to work.

Diane, Beau, and Charlotte huddled for a minute, simply happy to be safely together again.

"Your nose"—Diane pointed to Charlotte—"and your butt", she said, pointing to Beau, "are my responsibility, and I intend to keep a close watch on them."

"Yes, Diane." Charlotte and Beau saluted her.

"I'd better go and fill Samuel in. He'll probably want to resume some night surveillance around the farm just in case there's a kernel of truth in Linc's sabotage theory. Come on, Horse—we've got another mystery to solve."

Horse followed Charlotte, who noticed that there was now a distinct skip to his hoofed steps.

Charlotte found Samuel at his workbench in the barn, building something with scraps of wood. She quickly recapped her morning and what she'd learned, while watching Samuel's deft hands saw and plane components for a rough framework that he'd already completed and placed to the side of the table.

"It's an owl brooding box," Samuel explained as the pieces started to make more sense to Charlotte. "Since your mandate—which I am in total support of, by the way—that we transition the farm to being entirely organic, we'll need to call on natural resources for implementing pest control."

"Owls are a problem?" Charlotte asked, and Horse looked at Samuel, perhaps wondering the same thing. Mrs. Robinson flew up onto the workbench to get a better seat.

"Quite the contrary. My plan is to build a handful or so of boxes to attract barn owls to take up residence. You see, while not terribly big, the barn owls have a voracious appetite for rodents. Rats, mice, gophers, and shrews can not only decimate a field, but they can spread disease like salmonella as well."

Samuel noticed Charlotte shudder at the thought.

"But I'm going to spread the boxes out around the fields, with wood shavings inside for nesting. Barn owls breed year-round in Southern California, and a typical clutch yields up to seven eggs. I've already spotted some owls around at night, which is when they typically do their hunting."

"Wow, that sounds great—I can't wait to see them. Horse and Mrs. Robinson, you're going to have some new friends to hang with if you can stay up late enough. Or maybe they'll wake you up."

"Not likely. Owls are silent in flight, which helps make them such stealth predators. But Horse will smell them with that snout of his." Samuel gave the pig a scratch on his pink head.

On the way back to the farmhouse, they ran into Beau, who said that he'd been looking for them.

"Listen, Char, I'm a bit nervous that Danny might do something foolish about Linc. I understand that he can have quite a temper, and I don't want any trouble for the old cowboy. I want to go see Linc now—not let things brew—and apologize to him in the hopes of smoothing things over."

"Apologize to him? He's the one who needs to say 'sorry' for knocking you to the ground."

"He'll never see it that way, and I want to nip this in the bud. For everyone concerned, especially Diane."

Charlotte looked up at him, surprised, but then understood his train of thought. If Danny did something he might regret, then Beau's sister would be impacted as well.

"I'll get my car keys. Let's try and sneak out without anyone seeing so we don't have to explain ourselves. We can brag about becoming fast friends with Linc when we return from a successful mission."

"I'm one step ahead of you," Beau said, dangling her keys between his thumb and index finger.

"Horse, you guard the fort and maybe help Samuel with the nursery."

Beau looked at Charlotte blankly.

"I'll explain on the way."

*   *   *

The Pierce Farm, or what was left of it, was about twenty minutes out of Little Acorn, situated in an area that had seen better days. The nearest town was called El Fuego, which translated to "The Fire," ironic, Charlotte thought, as this area often fell victim to late summer incendiary flare-ups.

The area around Pierce Farm was in sharp contrast to the lush, rolling hills surrounding the Finn Family Farm, and they passed homes and land that had either been abandoned or fallen into severe disrepair.

"No wonder Linc is cranky. This place is downright depressing," Beau said, sticking his head out the passenger-side window. "See? You never know what people are really going through, so why not give them the benefit of the doubt?"

"I hope Linc'll see it that way. I'd hate for that beautiful Roman nose of yours to be broken."

There was no signage indicating that they had arrived at the place, but Charlotte spotted Linc's rusty truck and pulled over. They called out for Linc but got no response.

"Maybe we should split up to save time. It'll be dark in about an hour or so," Charlotte suggested. "I'll take the strawberry fields while you check out the building structures. And be careful: that barn looks like it could fall over at the slightest breeze. Look at the way it's leaning."

"Roger that, and I'll announce my presence and purpose before entering, just in case Linc likes to carry around a break-action rifle in the crook of his arm."

Charlotte nodded to Beau, and they headed in opposite directions.

Charlotte was surprised to see how remarkably healthy Linc's strawberry crops appeared to be. She'd expected the worst given the state of the rest of his farm. At closer inspection, she still saw no signs of damage to the plants or any indication of disease.

What the—

Charlotte walked all along one row of beds looking up, under, and all around for any special equipment, cans of sprays or chemicals—anything that would indicate that Linc was fighting this blight, as he'd claimed to the other farmers.

This should tell me something, but what is it?

He thoughts were interrupted when she heard Beau scream for her several times. The sound was coming from the barn, and when she reached him, he was standing outside the big door, looking quite pale and distraught.

"Are you okay? Did Linc do something to you?"

He stopped her with a shake of his head and pointed into the barn.

Charlotte walked in, and it took a moment for her eyes to adjust from bright sunlight to semi-darkness. When her vision was refocused, she saw the source of Beau's panicked call for help. Hanging from a rafter, limp and most likely dead, was Linc Pierce. It was apparently suicide.

"I've already called Chief Goodacre—she's on her way," Beau told Charlotte in a weak voice as he stood waiting outside.

Although in the past Chief Theresa Goodacre had been more friend than foe to Charlotte and her friends, she was still a cop who took an oath to uphold the law. There were a number of people who had witnessed Beau and Linc's scuffle this morning at the Garden Center, and given Little Acorn's rumor mill, most everybody else had heard about it by now. This discovery would certainly cast a suspicious eye Beau's way, no matter how clearly Linc's death appeared to be by his own hand.

Charlotte realized that she had precious few minutes to look around the barn for any evidence that would either point to Beau or exonerate him, before the police arrived.

"I hope that you didn't touch anything in here, did you?"

"No, nothing—I swear."

"Don't lie to me—now is the time to tell the truth."

"Nothing, I promise." Beau placed his hand over his heart to prove it.

"Okay, stay out there and let me know when you see the Chief's car coming."

Beau nodded but was clearly nervous.

Charlotte did a survey of the barn and started with Linc's workbench. It was covered in several months' worth of dust, but to one side she noticed four metal canisters that were perfectly clean. Which meant that they were probably brought into the barn very recently. They looked like old-fashioned milk jugs or extra-large thermoses. She desperately wanted to open one of them and smell its contents, but wisely resisted.

Strange.

Moving farther along the wall of the barn, Charlotte spotted a well-worn club chair along with a footrest. Across from it was a small TV resting atop a barrel. Just as Charlotte got close to the chair, a field mouse scurried off with what looked like a piece of bread in its mouth. Charlotte peered over the far arm of the chair, where the mouse had come from, and found a half-eaten sandwich sitting on a piece of paper towel on the floor beside the chair. The mouse had absconded with the top piece of bread.

Who eats before they kill themselves?

Charlotte was about to continue her search for evidence, when she heard sirens approaching. Beau whispered her name, and she quietly stepped toward the outside of the barn, not wanting the Chief to think that she'd been anywhere near the scene. As she walked past Linc's hanging body, her sneaker sent something skidding along the barn floor. It looked a bit like a metal banjo finger pick, the kind that Uncle Tobias had used when he played. Only there was an extended hook on one end.

This might be important down the road.

As she moved to pick it up, she heard the Chief's voice and hurried outside instead.

Chief Theresa Goodacre was around Charlotte's age, and despite commanding the respect of the position she held, even in uniform there were telltale signs that she was also in touch with her feminine side. She had highlighted blonde hair that, though worn back for work, was cut into what Charlotte and Diane would call the "Rachel." Her nails were always manicured and painted in the colors of the season. For spring this year, she was sporting something akin to a pistachio. She wore a gold band on a dainty chain around her neck, but no one dared asked what the story was behind it.

"I'm going to let the coroner and his team process the scene first before I go in. Please assure me that they're not going to find evidence of you two being anywhere around the barn."

"No, Chief," Beau and Charlotte said almost simultaneously.

"Based on past experience, I'd be more inclined to believe you, Beau, than Charlotte, since I've caught her hands in the proverbial cookie jar before. But I understand that Beau and the deceased got into a brawl at the Garden Center this morning."

"Wow, even for Little Acorn, the gossip train is traveling at warp speed," Charlotte said, disgusted.

"And it's clear that the story has been blown way out of proportion by every retelling of it," Beau added. "It wasn't a brawl, and it wasn't even an argument. Ask anyone who was there."

"Oh, I intend to. Now who discovered the body, and what were you doing here in the first place?" The Chief looked from Charlotte to Beau, gazing directly into their eyes.

"I did," said Beau. "And we were here to apologize to Linc and smooth things over."

"What did you have to apologize for if it wasn't a fight? Did you take a swing at him?"

"No! He shoved me." Beau's face had gone vermillion. It didn't help when Charlotte gave him an "I told you so" look.

"Let's find a place where we can sit and talk. This is going to take a while. You too, Charlotte," the Chief said. "The last thing I need is you snooping around."

When they were settled, Chief Goodacre took out her notebook and instructed Beau to start with the moment he woke up today. She pressed for details as he began to describe his day, but mostly let him speak freely. There was a rapport established between Beau and the Chief from when they'd first met, and Charlotte hoped that their relationship would factor into her judgment of his actions today.

It was when Beau got to Linc's comment about "not taking orders from a pretty boy" that the Chief stopped writing and asked him to repeat what Linc had said. She also watched for Charlotte to concur.

*   *   *

It was dusk by the time Charlotte and Beau arrived back at the farm, exhausted and shaken.

Not a good day.

When they'd left, the Chief and her deputies were taking over the scene and doing a grid pattern search for evidence. Chief Goodacre gave Beau the ominous "don't leave town until it's officially ruled a suicide" speech and sent them on their way.

Now, in her antique sleigh bed, Charlotte told Horse about all the events of the day, including that she believed that Linc's death was not a suicide. Charlotte presumed that Mrs. Robinson was out on the nightshift, leading other ladybugs into battle with the destructive aphids. Charlotte recalled the strange metal piece that had skidded across the floor and wondered if the cops had found it too. And the fact that Linc had been munching on a sandwich just before his demise.

Hard to explain.

"Oh, and what on earth is killing the strawberries in Little Acorn, Horse?"

Chapter Three

An hour later Charlotte was still not able to sleep and decided to be productive, get out of bed, and do some research on what might be causing the strawberries' demise. As was often the case when she gathered information online, Charlotte was soon sidetracked and was delving into the history of pesticides and fumigants that farmers had employed over the years in Santa Barbara County. Horse, always up for a game no matter what the hour, trotted sleepily over to Charlotte's desk and hopped up on the footrest she'd put out for him.

"I know that you'd prefer to be looking at photos of you and your friends playing around the grounds, but this is really important, Horse."

His expression went from jubilation to intense curiosity. Charlotte could never help but smile and feel her heart swell each time she looked at the pig's long, soft lashes and pink, apple-shaped cheeks.

"Would you look at that? Growers have been fighting the dangerous pathogens in the soil of their fields here since the reckless 1950s." Charlotte pointed to an article that she was reading on her monitor. Next to the text, Charlotte studied a photo of a field being prepared for planting. In the foreground were three people dressed in protective white suits and wearing full facemask respirators and goggles. They were spraying the soil with hoses, just behind warning signs that had been stuck in the ground telling people to "keep out, dangerous pesticides being used."

They clearly knew that they were dealing with harmful, potent materials.

Charlotte went back to the story and learned that The University of California had been experimenting with chemical fumigants in 1950, and ten years later nearly every strawberry field was being treated with a substance called methyl bromide. She read on:

This breakthrough doubled the amount of berries produced per acre on California farms. It took another ten years to discover that methyl bromide gas from the crops was contributing to the depletion of the ozone layer and presented a serious cancer risk. When this pesticide was finally banned from strawberry fruit production in 2016, the growers were forced to turn to innovations like organic farming and breeding for disease resistance. Nothing since has proved foolproof.

"Could this be why Linc's strawberries were so plentiful, Horse? I saw those canisters in his barn. Was he the cheat, and was he treating his produce with a banned substance? Maybe Boyd Hoover suspected so."

Horse looked to Charlotte like he was about to respond, but then they heard a noise outside her bedroom suite door.

"What are you still doing up?" Diane popped her head into the room.

"I couldn't sleep. It ended up being a tough day. How was your date with Danny?"

"Oh no, tell me about it, Sis." Diane curled up on the sofa in front of the fireplace and turned her concerned, big amber eyes to Charlotte. It was impossible to ignore Diane when she did that, and she will give you her undivided attention until you respond.

Charlotte proceeded with the grim task of filling Diane in on Linc's death and how the Little Acorn rumor mill was blowing Beau's interactions with Linc totally out of proportion.

"If the Chief and the coroner rule that Linc's death was not a suicide, but a homicide, I'm worried about what Beau will be put through, no matter how much the Chief may like him on a personal basis." Charlotte decided on the spot not to share the "pretty boy" aspect of the altercation with Diane; things like that could really set her off when it came to her brother. She'd been on the receiving end of Diane's wrath when they were kids, and vowed never to repeat it. Charlotte hung her head down, weary. Horse nuzzled her arm.

"I'm sorry that you've had to deal with all this. Things had been going so well, and the future was looking very promising. I'm sure that this will be judged to be a suicide, and we'll all be able to get back to our wonderful progress. However it goes, we will rise above it—we always do." Diane gave Charlotte a warm hug.

"You never answered me: How was dinner with Danny? You were already gone when Beau and I got back from Linc Pierce's farm. This is getting kind of real, isn't it?'

Diane shrugged her shoulders.

"I met Danny at the restaurant, that new Italian place. Danny left his crew a bit early—he said he had some errands to run and wanted to go to his place to change before dinner. He must have gotten into a time crunch, because he arrived in the same clothes he'd had on at the site."

Charlotte immediately registered that factoid and stored it away in her mind. She waited for Diane to continue.

"So, the date started out fine, but when I began asking him questions about this strawberry blight spreading across our farms, Danny got moody and retreated into himself."

"Are you saying that he started ignoring you?"

"I know, right? People wait months to get a glimpse of this fabulous face." Diane giggled and gave Charlotte several chin-up views. "All the same, the dinner suddenly turned sullen."

"Oh no, what do you think set him off? Was there any word or phrase that you said that triggered this change in behavior?" Charlotte asked Diane, the wheels turning in her mind.

"Not that I can recall. I was rehashing what you told us happened at the Garden Center this morning. I didn't know about Linc then, so it wouldn't have been that. He's done this before— once we ran into an older farmer in town, who claimed to know Danny and called out his name. He said that he'd ridden with Danny's grandfather in the Rancheros Visitadores. Danny told him that he was crazy and said he'd never seen the man before in his life. Danny was downright rude to him when he persisted. I've only known Danny for about six weeks, and there's so much he hasn't told me about his past. Most of the time he's just an easygoing, fun guy. But like all of us, I'm sure there have been some things that happened before I met him that have left a scar."

"Are you sure that you want to spend the time and emotion finding out? You may not like what you learn." Charlotte ran the back of her hand over Diane's cheek.

"I don't know yet. But his crew and friends are steadfastly loyal to him. And he's got that blond hair and crooked smile. And soft lips . . ."

"How do you know his lips are soft, Diane?" Charlotte asked in false anger.

"How do you think I know?" Diane paused for a moment. "Because I see how often during the day he applies lip balm, that's how."

They both laughed.

"Just proceed with your beautiful eyes wide open. Oh, who am I kidding? Beau and I were always the ones wearing our hearts on our sleeves, always saying what was on our minds. You were the one who watched the action from the sidelines. Until you saw something that you knew wasn't right. Then you pounced like Ripley in the *Alien* movies."

Diane thought about that analogy and smiled. Then she stood up, kissed Horse on the head and Charlotte on the cheek, and headed to the door.

"Healing takes time, but I'm sure that Danny will get there."

"What is it with you and Beau and the bright side of life? Did your mom feed you special cereal when you were kids? Were you both breastfed or bottle-fed?"

Diane laughed and shook her head. "Get some rest, my friend."

Suddenly Charlotte felt the beckoning of her warm bed, and moments later she and Horse were fast asleep.

At some point during the night, Charlotte stirred, feeling a chill in the air. The fire had burned down and was no longer providing heat to the stone-walled room, but she also felt a distinct flow of air. She reached around for Horse on the bed, and when she felt nothing, she relented and switched on the bedside lamp, drawing her fully out of sleep mode. There was no Horse to be found, and one of the French doors sat open.

I've got to teach the little guy how to close doors behind him.

He'd figured out how to open them by observing humans, but this skill was becoming a liability. Charlotte quickly threw on some sweats, a warm jacket, and sneakers. Grabbing a strong flashlight that she'd learned to keep in the nightstand, she headed out into the inky dead of night.

After about ten minutes of searching, Charlotte located her pink friend sitting on his haunches in one of the far strawberry fields. His eyes were glued to the sky. As she got closer, Charlotte saw that Mrs. Robinson was also looking up to the sky while nestled in atop Horse's left ear.

"What are you looking at, Horse? Did something spook you? Are you hurt anywhere?"

She lowered herself down next to him and gave him a cursory check. He appeared to be fine, and a moment later he looked back up to the sky and gave a soft grunt. Charlotte followed the direction that his nose was pointed and was left breathless by what she saw.

An extraordinary bird with a heart-shaped face soared silently above the field. Its wingspan of around four feet was covered in soft, fringe-edged feathers. Charlotte's heart fluttered as she saw Horse's face glow with wonder as he watched the bird hover and then dive for its prey. With a rodent caught in its hooked upper beak, the beautiful barn owl flew back up, then landed and entered one of Samuel's brooding boxes that rested up on a pole. Both Charlotte and Horse's jaws went slack. Mrs. Robinson now sat on Horse's shoulder, also transfixed.

Charlotte was about to stand when a second heart-shape-faced owl appeared. This one was slightly larger, with a spotted body. It too made a silent flight, swooped down into the field, and then reemerged with prey in its beak.

"I'm naming them Fred and Ginger for their elegance on the sky's dance floor," Charlotte told Horse.

The show over, Charlotte stood and motioned to Horse.

"Now it really *is* time for bed."

Charlotte heard a rustling of leaves and looked to see if the owls were back, but they seemed to be tucked in for the night. She got an eerie feeling and shivered. Charlotte looked around for the source of the noise and spotted an odd shadow beside one of the apple trees in the orchard. It made her curious because the shadow seemed to end in midair rather than running all the way to the ground.

Huh? So . . . it can't be a sapling . . .

Charlotte knew she shouldn't, but she kept moving closer to the phantom vision. She remembered her flashlight, turned it on, and pointed it in the direction of the trees. When she finally understood what she was looking at, she let out a series of uncontrolled, plaintive screams. Before her, swinging from a branch of the apple tree, was a scarecrow with a rope around its neck. On the pocket of the scarecrow's shirt a white label had been placed with the words "Pretty Boy."

Charlotte collapsed to the ground, sobbing, while Horse stood over her as protection. A couple of minutes later, she heard the whirr of an electric golf cart coming toward her. Joe had heard her cries for help and had alerted Samuel along the way.

"This is probably just some silly prank by teenagers. I'll take it down and drive you back up to the house. What were you doing out at this hour anyway?" Joe asked, helping Charlotte to her feet.

"Don't go near that effigy, and absolutely don't touch it! Tell everyone, and in the morning, I'll have to call Chief Goodacre." Charlotte pulled Joe back into the golf cart.

"Did you hit your head or something, Charlotte? You're not making sense."

"Unfortunately, I'm very lucid. We need to get back up to the farmhouse and gather everyone in the living room. It's time that you all know what's going on."

Twenty minutes later, the sleepy-eyed gang now knew almost as much as Charlotte about Linc, Beau, and the strawberry blight. She'd learned from the last mystery to keep to herself anything that wasn't a fact, until proven, which meant that her suspicions about Linc's death needed to be kept under wraps. Samuel and Joe set out in the cart to do a patrol of the fields and look for any additional evidence of tonight's intruder.

Diane and Charlotte sat with Beau, drinking tea and trying to convince him not to worry about this latest development.

I've got to go back to the apple tree as soon as there's light, and look for clues. Then I'll call the Chief. Heck, another set of eyes can't hurt, can it?

A few minutes later, Joe and Samuel returned, looking somber.

"What now?" Charlotte asked impatiently.

"Everything seems just as it usually is," Joe quickly assured the group.

"But we're now members of a club I'm sure that we never wanted to join." Samuel took off his hat and ran a hand through his hair. "The farm's strawberry plants are sick and dying."

Chapter Four

Not long after sunrise, and working on very little sleep, Charlotte took Horse outside, and they headed in the direction of the orchard. Along the way, they couldn't help passing by the owls brooding house that had been so active only a few hours ago. Horse looked up, checking for any signs of life, but the abode remained serene.

"Owls are nocturnal, Horse. They're the opposite from us. Their day is our night, so right now they are fast asleep."

Which sounds pretty tempting to me . . .

Horse seemed to understand because he turned his attention to snout-rooting around the area. Charlotte did the same with her eyes.

A moment later Horse let out a squeal and looked toward Charlotte to indicate that he was onto something.

"Good boy, Horse—what did you find?"

Horse shoved two white items along the dirt under the owl house and motioned for Charlotte to take a closer look.

"What have you got?" Charlotte picked up one of the pieces. "It's much heavier than I expected. Looks to be a broken off part of something. I can't think of a machine that Samuel would run in this area."

Charlotte picked up the second piece, and Horse looked over her shoulder as she turned it over and back in her hand.

"The edges are sharp and this one, clearly a fragment of something else, is feather shaped. Looks like it's been broken off at one end. I can't put my finger on what material this is. I thought it might be steel, coated in white paint, but now that doesn't seem right. I don't hear the sound that I'd expect when I tap it with my fingernail. It is certainly not plastic," she told Horse, and picked up the second piece with her other hand. "This is made of the same material, whatever that is, but it's a flat, oblong shape. There are holes die-cut into the plate, so this must attach to something bigger.

"Let's bring these to Samuel and pick his brain, Horse."

She and her pig friend moved on to the location of the apple tree with the hanging effigy.

"Look for anything out of place, Horse, just as you did by the owls."

As Horse set to work foraging, Charlotte took a minute to examine the effigy in the light of day. Minus the "Pretty Boy" label stuck to the shirt pocket, it looked like a run-of-the-mill scarecrow. It was of the variety that Charlotte had seen at petting zoos around Little Acorn. This one was well worn because, Charlotte guessed, of being outside for many years. The scarecrow was made with two tree branches tied in the shape of a cross. Overalls, with holes and patches around the knees, created the shape of the body, and the flannel shirt, shredded in some places, made up the torso. The head was comprised of a burlap sack covering an oblong shape underneath. Charlotte resisted looking under the sack to see what it was; knowing that her very next move had to be a call to Chief Goodacre. What was odd was the white label stuck to the effigy's shirt pocket. It was clean and only slightly damp from the morning's dew. But because it had been hanging under the protective foliage of the apple tree, it had suffered little damage overnight. Charlotte was almost certain that it had been made yesterday.

Has this scarecrow been here all along? I don't remember seeing it. And having it hang from a tree is too eerily similar to Linc's demise to be a coincidence.

Horse interrupted her thoughts by depositing another, smaller piece of that white machine part at her feet.

"Hmm, that's a long way to travel, from the owl house to the orchard. Could an owl have brought it here? Aren't owls also deterred by scarecrows?"

Charlotte pulled out her cell phone.

"We'd better start the wheels in motion on this. Beau's going to have to deal with the scrutiny sooner or later. I'm sure that people will devise a scenario where Beau saw this effigy and went to Linc's farm to have it out with him. I don't even want to think about the rest of it. My best approach is to point the finger at as many plausible other suspects as possible."

"Hello, it's Charlotte Finn. Is the Chief available?"

* * *

"I've never seen it before. What about you Samuel?" Joe asked. The Chief, her deputy, and Charlotte had formed a circle around the scarecrow.

Samuel shook his head. "But I often find items around the grounds that are new to me. You've got to remember that the Finns have inhabited and worked this land for decades."

Chief Goodacre donned protective gloves and swung the scarecrow around.

"This shirt is very old, but it's made of wool, which must be why it's still hanging together. Barely," the Chief observed. She peeled down the back of the collar to look at the label.

"Pendleton—no wonder it has lasted. An American classic."

"And too rich for my blood," Samuel said.

"Or for most of the farmers around here," Joe added. "Our clothes mostly come from Sears or the Tractor Supply Company."

"That's a good one, over in Moorpark? I've shopped there." Samuel nodded to Joe.

"Okay, fellas, before we start comparing inseams and glove sizes, how about we focus on the evidence before us. There have got to be some clues here to point us in the direction of whoever brought this here. Step back, everyone," the Chief instructed.

Charlotte felt a strong pang of guilt and was glad that she had hidden in the barn the white pieces she'd found earlier. She went over the "list of suspects" argument she'd quickly formulated in her mind.

"Let's get some uniforms up here to help with the search," the Chief said to her deputy.

"It is no accident that I found this hanging on the same night we discovered that my strawberry fields were now infected, Chief. Maybe poor Linc's suggestion that this blight might be the work of sabotage by another farmer isn't so farfetched?" Charlotte stepped up to the Chief while the others stepped back.

"And good morning to you too, Charlotte," the Chief replied. "That thought crossed my mind, as did the question of why this scarecrow was found hanging from a tree rather than stuck into the ground. The whole idea, I'd heard, was to trick the birds into thinking that they were seeing a farmer."

"That's correct, Chief," Samuel said, and continued, "but we haven't used this kind of animal deterrent for maybe twenty years or more. It's been replaced with chemical sprays, which I can assure you are not used on the Finn Family Farm, or more organic methods like ultrasonic or laser light repellents and decoys. We employ the latter."

"Thank you for the lesson. Where are Beau and Diane this morning, Charlotte?" the Chief asked.

"Working around the farm, I'm sure, Chief. You must know that we all heard Boyd Hoover at the Garden Center accuse Linc of sending some of his men to the Hoover Farm to spy and take samples. Maybe one of them has gone rogue?"

"Possible. Do you know where Beau was when you found this effigy?"

"He was in bed, asleep, like everyone else at that time of night."

"Except you, Charlotte. You were out in the fields."

"I told you why—"

"Would you lead me to Beau, please? I'd like to talk to him. Ah, here comes your search team, Deputy," the Chief said, eying the approaching police.

*　*　*

A little later, while Beau was deciding what to wear for his afternoon excursion with Charlotte, she decided to pay a visit the Finn Family Farm Shop.

Beau had become uncharacteristically quiet after speaking with the Chief, perhaps less from being seen as a suspect and more because he'd thought that the Chief was his friend. Charlotte tried to explain that nothing had changed, that the Chief was just doing her job, but Charlotte could see that Beau wasn't buying it.

The Farm Shop was in a converted small barn situated by the lake and had been doing a brisk business since it opened six months ago. It sold jams and jellies, sauces, desserts, and condiments, all prepared by Joe's wife, the ultra-talented home cook, Alice. She also managed the enterprise, for which she earned an extra commission on sales.

Charlotte and Alice had started their relationship on the wrong foot because of a misunderstanding, and for a long time Alice had lived in fear that she and her husband would have to pick up and start a new life elsewhere. Charlotte's Uncle Tobias had given them the small house below the fields, for lodging, and they had turned it into a warm home. Having decided not to have children, they viewed the farm and the creatures on it as their family.

Alice was always coming up with innovative ways to make the farm more interactive for visitors, and today she was working out plans to assign a small plot of land to Miss Fern's third-grade class.

"We've talked about the kids growing the Little Acorn indigenous white strawberry, as well as nurturing some bare root plants through the growth cycle."

"What fun for them—and I'm sure for you," Charlotte said, looking at her plans. "Say, have you heard people talking about this strawberry blight that we all seem to be enduring? Any more insight from your end of the grapevine?"

Charlotte knew that, although Alice didn't spend too much time out and about off the farm, she loved to talk and catch up with friends by phone. With the convenience of the speaker phone feature, she could make a peach pie from scratch while getting the scoop on everything, from what had been overheard at Sally's Hair & Nails, to how the Phelan kids, now becoming teenagers, were behaving. Spoiler alert: the son was single-mindedly into sports, and the daughter shared that passion but focused instead on the boys who played those sports.

"Really nothing more than what you and Beau were told. But I think that having someone like Beau act as a liaison with the inflicted farms is a perfect assignment for him, and I will help you both in any way that I can."

If only everyone else would see it that way, Alice.

"Much appreciated. In fact, Beau and I are headed out now to the Barclay Farm. It'll be our first farm interview, so tell me about the Barclays."

Charlotte watched Alice's odd, silent reaction. Charlotte had gotten to know Alice's pauses, and they were usually due to a motherly voice in her head saying, "If you don't have anything nice to say . . ." Or, worse, because Alice sensed danger.

"What is it? You may speak freely to me."

"No, nothing—the Barclay Farm is a great place to start. The owner, Ford Barclay, is very wealthy—family money, I'm told, from a pharmaceutical enterprise they founded. If anyone, he would have the best resources to fight this scourge."

Charlotte used her tactic of letting silence fill the air, and sure enough, Alice reluctantly continued.

"I mean the farm can be quite imposing, I'm told. I've never visited, but of course the townsfolk of Little Acorn attribute such extravagance to ill-gotten gains."

"Such as?" Charlotte pressed.

"That's all I know. I've got to get back to work," Alice started to rearrange a shelf of strawberry preserves and didn't look Charlotte in the eye.

"I'll give you a full report when we return. As always, thanks for your help."

On the way back to the farmhouse, Charlotte ran into Diane chatting with another woman outside the restaurant construction site. An old wooden and metal wagon sat by her side and was filled with what appeared to be wine bottle cases.

"There you are, Charlotte. Let me introduce you two." Diane was all smiles. "This is Katharine Hoover, she owns a vineyard located not far from us. Katharine, this beautiful redhead is Charlotte Finn, our master marketer and fearless leader."

Katharine accepted Charlotte's extended hand and gave her a very firm handshake.

Must be from years of pulling grapes, or whatever they call it.

"Welcome to the Finn Family Farm. Any friend of Diane's is a friend of mine."

"I'm flattered," said Katharine. "Diane is a lovely person, but we met only a few days ago in town at Harbb's Wine and Cheese Emporium. I'd be honored to be called her friend, and I hope that working together will lead to that. We started chatting and she told me about the restaurant she was building, and in turn

I told her that I'd just started building my winery full time. It's a passion that I've had for a long time, and it turns out that I'm quite good at it. I've been searching for the right place for me in farming, and I finally found it. And—what luck—now I'm introduced to you. With your perseverance and bravery, you've become a success and, I must confess, a role model for me."

"That's crazy," Charlotte said, laughing. "Mostly I just stick my head into whatever is going on and hope that it doesn't get chopped off."

Tall and blonde, Charlotte could see right away that Katharine held herself with a personal confidence that told whomever she met that she was no pushover. Charlotte liked that. She was not overweight, but she was built strong and had the kind of body a woman might grow into from riding horses all her life. And kicking butt. She seemed to favor an androgynous style of dressing, at least that day, but still gave off a feminine allure, much like Katharine Hepburn.

Her namesake perhaps?

"Katharine and I have been tossing around the idea of offering her wine flights for special evening events once we open. And I thought that the three of us girls could help each other rise above our respective male-dominated sandboxes. I'm going to figure out an evening to make us dinner, and we can swap war stories." Diane hooked her elbows with both Charlotte's and Katharine's to seal the deal.

"I can't wait, and Charlotte you must tell me all your secrets for success," Katharine said.

* * *

Just before noon Charlotte and Beau headed out in her trusty Buick Roadmaster station wagon, and twenty minutes later, they turned off the road and onto a long, winding drive that disappeared from view at the top of the hill. Charlotte appreciated the smooth ride of the paved road, a pleasant departure from the bumpy, rocky dirt paths that led to most farms in the area. It got Charlotte wondering just how wealthy this Ford Barclay could be.

Beau had settled on what he called his "home from prep school" look, even though he'd never attended one. He had on colorful madras pants, a white button-down shirt, and a slim-fitting blue blazer with red piping. Charlotte gently suggested that he leave his Venetian stripe rowing cap in the car.

The long driveway was lined on both sides with what Charlotte was pretty sure were the notable coast live oak trees that she'd read about. The coast live oak had been named Santa Barbara City's official native tree. The majestic limbs of these trees had been pruned to give the appearance that they were reaching across the road to hold hands with the trees on the opposite side. Beau stuck his head out the window and raised his arm, hoping to be able to make contact with their dark green leaves and acorns.

When they reached the crest of the hill, Charlotte had her answer as to Barclay's wealth. On the other side of an ornate wrought iron double gate adorned with flourishes that formed the letter "B" was a breathtaking compound as far as the eye could see. From her vantage point at the top of the hill, Charlotte saw sprawled below them an expanse that looked like a cover spread right out of *Architectural Digest*. The main house had Spanish accents, like white stucco sides, and stone walkways and driveways. But the edifice itself was otherworldly. Two structures with steeply pitched gable roofs were attached on one side, and the facades appeared to be made of the type of glass with a reflective finish for privacy. People inside could see out normally, but people on the outside look into a one-way mirror.

Off to the side, Charlotte could see an indoor/outdoor produce shop that rivaled any fancy market in Beverly Hills. To the far side, Charlotte took in the barns and other farm structures, neat and minimalist. The estate looked more like an elite spa resort than a farm. The resplendent main house was crowned with half-pipe clay tile roofs. Separate bungalows surrounded the infinity pool that was a work of art in itself, zero-edged. From the view that Charlotte had up above, she could see that the bottom had built-in tiers of varying depths. The spa was nestled in the far center and sat exactly at the water level of the pool.

And behind all this opulence were the pristine produce fields that looked almost painted on, they were so neat and precise.

Charlotte and Beau stood with mouths agape in front of the Buick.

"I think we're in Oz," Charlotte muttered.

"I think I'll need a wardrobe change before meeting the proprietor of this masterpiece," Beau said, and Charlotte knew he wasn't joking. She looked at her own attire and concluded the same. As they were returning to the car, a man on horseback rode up beside them.

"It is something, isn't it?" he asked, admiring the stunning view below.

The owner of the voice—and, Charlotte suspected, the estate below—was a middle-aged man who looked tanned and in excellent physical shape, seated high in his saddle. This man had definitely benefitted from good familial genes. His high cheekbones and almond-shaped eyes gave him a distinct look of sophistication. Charlotte got tongue-tied, an exceedingly rare affliction for her.

"I'm Ford Barclay and this is my farm." He swept his hand and arm from left to right, but Charlotte had already assumed that he meant all of it.

"I wanted to make sure that when people dropped by for a look-see that there are places built especially for them to enjoy. If they've brought the kiddos, then there's a zoo and fun rides for them to take. If filling the pantry is more their desire, then the market has everything that you could want. And we sell those items at cost to make them affordable to families small and large. But where are my manners? Please come down and join me for fresh lemonade on the patio—Ms. Finn, isn't it?

All she could do was nod mutely when, out of nowhere and through no apparent action by Ford Barclay, the great metal gates gracefully swung open. Barclay gave his steed a gentle heel to the ribs, and he proceeded down the inside hill. With his back to them, he motioned with his hand for them to follow.

"Now that's how you make an entrance," Beau marveled.

"And an exit. I suppose we should get in the car and follow him down."

They did just that.

*　*　*

They parked near the patio that Ford had pointed to and found that an icy cold pitcher of lemonade and four tall glasses had been set out on a mission-style table surrounded by leather-and-rattan Mexican barrel chairs.

"How's my hair?" Beau asked Charlotte.

Before she could reply, Martin Ross approached.

"So nice to see you again. You too, Beau. I'm sorry about all that arguing the other day. This disease, if that's what it is, has everyone on edge."

Charlotte watched Martin take a chair and pour lemonade into the tumblers. This time she was quite sure that he was flirting with her. He looked to be close in age to her. He had brown hair styled in a fashionable haircut, long on top, close-cropped on the sides, and his beard was neatly trimmed. He was not as muscular as Ford, but Charlotte quietly admired Martin's kind face. Before Charlotte's mind could freely wander in that direction, it was eclipsed by a far bigger presence.

"If you really want to enjoy the tangy juice from my lemon trees, then you must pair it with Chef Josie's citrus goat cheese spread and sweet onion jam," Ford Barclay said, and placed a platter of those items and varieties of breads and crackers on the table. Martin appeared to Charlotte to shrink in his chair.

"Yum—this is my kind of 'living off the land'," Beau mused.

Charlotte, not in the mood for Ford's boasting, which bordered on arrogance, immediately got down to business. "Hidden behind this minimalist-looking Spanish estate, I am noticing some very sophisticated technology, Ford. When I worked in advertising, I had a client that made solar-powered products. I've noticed energy systems here—what looks to be an intricate surveillance and security system and several large satellite dishes that I spotted from the top of the hill. It seems that you travel comfortably between being a gentleman farmer and a technophile."

"You are very astute, Charlotte—I'm impressed."

"So, you men must have been doing some intricate testing on your diseased strawberries," Beau said, taking a cue from Charlotte. "Martin told us that so far nothing has proved viable in treating this?"

"Martin may not be privy to every experiment that I've been running. I have some tests that are looking positive, and we're moving to phase three right now." Ford tried to hide his annoyance with Martin for airing their foiled attempts.

"I'd love to see what you've got in tests, Ford, and see your impaired strawberries for comparison to ours," Charlotte said, standing.

"I'm in the middle of running a sequence right now, so I'm afraid that won't be possible." Ford didn't budge from his chair. "Another time perhaps. My chef's wild-caught halibut is legendary—perhaps dinner and a tour soon?"

"We promised the farmers transparency in our research interviews. Are you saying that you won't cooperate?" Charlotte could feel her face getting hot.

"Of course not. Martin, would you please give Charlotte and Beau a copy of the report on our findings to date?"

Martin left the patio and went inside.

"Didn't you just say that Martin doesn't know everything that you're doing, Ford?" Beau asked after Martin was out of earshot.

"I'll be updating the report shortly when these new tests are completed."

"How soon will that be?" Beau persisted.

Seeing that this was going nowhere, Charlotte asked Ford, "How well did you know Linc Pierce?"

"Linc Pierce?" Ford shrugged his shoulders. "I'm too busy running this large operation to meet many people. Who is he?"

"Unfortunately, he was found dead two days ago." Charlotte didn't sugarcoat it.

Martin returned and handed Beau a thick manila envelope.

"You know a fellow named Linc?" Ford asked.

"Pierce," Charlotte reminded Ford.

"Linc Pierce? Nope, don't think so," Martin replied.

"What do you mean? You and Linc were very vocal with each other at the Garden Center." Beau looked him square in the eyes.

"The old man? I never knew his name," Martin quickly answered.

Maybe too quickly.

"They're saying that poor Linc is dead, Martin," Ford informed him.

Just as Charlotte was about to pursue this line of questioning, her cell phone vibrated. Charlotte looked at the screen and told the group, "I've got to take this, and we've occupied enough of your time, gentlemen. The lemonade was superb." Charlotte turned her back on them and marched to her car.

When, minutes later, Beau opened the passenger-side car door, he heard that Charlotte already had the engine running. Almost before Beau got situated, Charlotte took off back up the hill toward the gates of the Ford Barclay Farm. Once she was a fair distance away from the property, she pulled over to the side of the road.

"What's gotten into you? I know Ford Barclay can be a bit of a pompous ass but—"

"That was Chief Goodacre, who called from the coroner's office. Linc Pierce did not die by suicide. The coroner concluded that human hands made the markings on Linc's neck, and the blood, or lack thereof, indicated that he was dead before the noose was placed around his neck.

"Linc Pierce was murdered, Beau, and the Chief says that you are officially on lockdown."

Chapter Five

"Ah, two of my favorite people," Beau said, seeing Diane and Horse sitting on the front steps of the farmhouse when Charlotte pulled up. "Hello, dear ones."

"You don't have to do this, Beau."

"Do what?"

"Pretend as if everything is fine. It isn't, and you need to be open about being a suspect so that we can support you and work with you to get this cleared as soon as possible."

"You're right, my lovely sister—wait until I tell you where we've been and what magnificence we've seen." Beau couldn't help himself.

"You look kind of down, sweetie. What's the matter?" Charlotte had looked in her eyes and noticed that her BFF had drifted off into a distant place in her mind. It was her coping mechanism.

"What? Nothing, I'm fine!"

"Diane?" Charlotte scolded. "Horse will tell me."

"Danny and I had an argument, and he stormed off." Diane's words were barely audible.

"Did I hear you correctly? Did Danny lose his temper again? Where is he?" Beau was up on his feet, ready to go.

"Beau, you're not going anywhere. Let's hear Diane out. And considering your situation, I insist that you steer clear of anyone in Little Acorn except for immediate family."

"What situation, Charlotte?" Diane asked, wide-eyed and grateful to have someone else to take the attention away from her.

"No, you first, Diane. Anyway, it's just a silly misunderstanding that is being sorted out as we speak." Beau sat back down next to his sister and stroked her hair.

"After only a half a day's work, Danny up and left. The crew and I did our best to carry on. To tell you the truth, I can't even remember what specifically we'd been arguing about. You might ask Alice; she unfortunately witnessed the blow-up."

"Oh, honey," Charlotte soothed, and took her place on Diane's other side, next to Horse. It didn't go unnoticed that he lifted his head and broke into a big smile being around the people he loved the most.

"Danny's been in a foul mood ever since he heard you talk about the possible sabotage of our young strawberry plants, Charlotte."

"Why would that concern him? He makes his living with hammers and nails and bricks and mortar." Beau reached for Diane's hand and petted it.

"This is—what?—the third or fourth time that Danny has blown up in front of you, Diane? And for what reason? It may be time to rethink things," Charlotte gently told her.

"The last thing that I remember saying to him was that I felt so sorry for Linc and how important it is to care for other people who might be suffering in secret."

Charlotte and Beau quickly look at each other.

"Diane let's go in and see if Alice has any sun tea sitting on the window ledge. Beau and I have some things to tell you."

*   *   *

Dinner that night was en famille at the kitchen table and was a somber affair. The winds had picked up over and around the hillside, putting everyone a bit on edge. Alice did her best to make us happy with individual homemade chicken potpies while Joe delivered some good news about a big sale of tomatoes. Everyone had now heard about Linc being murdered, the second such death to be committed in Little Acorn in as many years. This was unheard of, and Charlotte felt the weight and burden of possibly being the catalyst for these crimes since they'd only happened after she'd moved back to the farm. In the first case, the very next day.

"Beau, you were going to tell me about your visit to the opulent Barclay Farm. Tell us all, please," Diane urged.

Charlotte saw Samuel put down his fork as one corner of his upper lip rose into a sneer.

"Charlotte called it Oz, but I prefer to describe it as a mashup of *Willy Wonka, Peter Pan*, and the famous old Christmas window displays that Lord and Taylor used to create each year."

It was hard not to share in Beau's glee, and everyone laughed except for Samuel.

"There is a zoo, and the goats have little mountains and catwalks to climb. I've got to convince Ford to agree to host one of my event extravaganzas. This is something new, even for a jaded L.A. crowd."

As Beau continued on his tour of the wonderful features of Barclay Farm, Charlotte instead took a mental review of today's events. Now that the Chief and probably the rest of the town had heard about the scarecrow effigy found hanging in her orchard, there were theories swirling about its meaning. Definitely the "Pretty Boy" was a reference to what Linc had called Beau, but that didn't necessarily mean that Linc put it there. Everyone who was in the Garden Center had heard Linc call Beau that, and moments later the Little Acorn rumor mill had taken it live.

Then, as she heard Diane ask Beau a question, Charlotte's attention turned toward her friend. She remembered how happy and excited Diane had seemed introducing her new acquaintance, vintner Katharine, to her. Diane seemed to think that a team of three strong women in complementary businesses could go really far here.

What a change when Charlotte next saw Diane after returning from Barclay Farm. Danny clearly had issues, and Charlotte was going to have to keep him on a very short leash.

Could he have killed Linc? Does the timing work out?

Then there was the surreal Barclay Farm and Ford and his agriculturalist, Martin. She'd picked up the tension between those two alpha men. And with all that money, why hadn't Ford built his farm empire in a more extravagant location, like the Rhone region or Tuscany? The thought reminded her of the brief conversation she'd had with Alice earlier that day in the Farm Shop. Charlotte tuned back in and heard Beau winding down his travelogue.

"Alice, you seemed to have heard some things, probably only rumors, about the origin of Ford Barclay's vast wealth?"

Hearing Charlotte's question, Samuel abruptly stood from the table.

"Real farming can't be bought, damn it. You have to get your hands in the soil to be able to understand nature. People shouldn't try to run a farm with computers. Trying to mix artificial intelligence with the earth and elements God gave us upsets the natural balance. The way the planet spins. This is why we have all these deaths and crop blights. These people are trying to control things that need to be understood, not obliterated. It's a rule that goes as far back as the beginning of time."

"That's pretty much what Linc said to the other farmers like Martin," Beau said, but perhaps shouldn't have.

"I'm going to check the owl houses." Samuel made a quick and deliberate exit.

Horse, sensing an opportunity, hopped up on Samuel's chair and eyed his unfinished potpie. He barely saw Beau's hand come across and slide it to his place.

"Are the Santa Ana winds blowing tonight? Is that why everyone has a hairpin trigger? We're on a farm; this is not how it's supposed to be, with everyone angry." Diane shook her head.

"Can someone tell me the origin of these winds and why they put people on edge?" Charlotte asked.

Alice laid down her fork and began: "It's said that the name comes from a Native American word for *wind*, which Spanish missionaries, detecting an evil presence, translated as "Santanás," or what we call today the 'Devil Winds.' They're deceiving; you wake up to a cloudless blue sky and assume that this is just another day in paradise. But there's an eerie stillness in the atmosphere and a positive ion-driven aggravation erupting all around you. Then the fires start, little scattered pockets that encounter each other in travel and join forces, ultimately turning the sky into a blanket of orange and gray. It's a weather phenomenon to be respected."

"I generally stay in bed until the Santa Ana winds have gone," Beau explained.

"The offshore winds will be strong tonight but gone by morning, Charlotte. Hopefully, that will help us return to a more harmonious mood."

"Thank you, Joe—I look forward to it. Alice, I was asking about the Barclay fortune before Samuel left. What can you and Joe tell me about it?"

Charlotte watched Joe give Alice a wide-eyed glare.

"Nothing, really. I shouldn't even have brought it up. They're just silly, small-town rumors, that's all."

"You know that I can ask around for this information, but I trust you and would like to hear your perspective."

Alice nodded.

"The Barclay family is in the business of pharmaceuticals, going back centuries. There have been some questionable medications they've put on the market over the years, but I don't know the details. Only that they did more harm than good," Alice explained.

"Could this be a Big Pharma conspiracy theory, Alice?" Diane asked, and when she saw Alice's blank stare, she continued, "you know—that the pharmaceutical companies are really working against the public good for financial gains?"

"We haven't heard anything so deep or sinister as that," Joe said, jumping in. "What got our attention was word that the Barclay family business was reputed to have done extensive research into crop disease treatments over the last two decades. That's what fueled the rumors."

"Meaning that Ford Barclay could direct that expertise for damaging the other local farmers' crops or, worse, use those farms for his own fumigant experiments? That sounds pretty sinister to me," Beau summed up.

"Ford Barclay claims to have nothing to do with any businesses in the family company. He maintains that when he turned twenty-one, he took his portion of the trust fund and headed west to California to build his farm. Nothing's ever come up to contradict that, so we're back, as Alice told you, with Little Acorn rumors," Joe said. "And for every one going around that is based in fact, there are a hundred more that are not."

"Boy howdy, ain't that the truth?" Beau said.

"Ford and Martin told us that their strawberries were also hit with this mysterious disease, and they gave us a briefing on the tests that they've been conducting. Please share this with Samuel, but you may need to wear protective clothing when you give it to him." Charlotte slid the manila envelope across the table to Joe.

"I took a brief look at the documents earlier. What I could understand seemed pretty thorough," Beau added.

"How badly were their strawberries impacted?" Diane said, jumping in.

"You know, Diane, we never did get a chance to see Ford's fields, he had some excuse about being in the middle of running tests, which seemed pretty thin to me," Charlotte said, thinking back to their trip that morning.

The rest of the table nodded in agreement.

*   *   *

As was becoming customary, Charlotte woke in the middle of the night to find the spot in the bed beside her empty. Horse had snuck out again, and she found him in the strawberry field, watching the owls hunt. Mrs. Robinson had hitched a ride on Horse's shoulder again and had tilted her ladybug head to observe the action. Charlotte understood their fascination; the owls' soundless, graceful acrobatics were mesmerizing. Suddenly Horse pricked up his ears, listened intently, and froze. Charlotte focused her hearing as well, but all she could make out was a very faint, shrill buzzing like you might hear if a mosquito or a gnat were circling your head.

"What is it, Horse? Is someone coming?"

Charlotte followed his eyes, which were roaming the sky, but not to watch the owls, as they had both returned to their brooding house.

"Samuel told me that pigs have an excellent sense of hearing, better than humans like me do, and especially with high-pitched frequencies. Maybe you can show me what has caught your attention, Horse?"

Charlotte watched him for several minutes, but after a bit it was clear that whatever Horse had been listening to had stopped. It took a bit of coaxing, but eventually they were back and tucked into bed.

*   *   *

Sipping her tea the next morning, Charlotte watched a dust cloud wind up the drive toward the farmhouse. It was Chief Goodacre in her police van. Before asking, Charlotte went to the kitchen and fixed the Chief a cup of coffee just the way she liked it, almost white with milk and a few drops of agave nectar.

"Morning Chief," Charlotte greeted her at the door, "here's your coffee."

"I can't ever complain about the hospitality at the Finn Family Farm—thank you, Charlotte."

"My pleasure. Who are you here to see, Chief? Everyone's up."

"You, actually, and of course you, Horse." His corkscrew tail whirled. "And Mrs. Robinson, looking lovely."

"Oh, okay. Want to sit on that bench under the Acacia tree?" Charlotte offered.

"Perfect. So how are you doing Charlotte? You've got a lot on your plate right now."

"You mean the strawberry blight?"

"That, and there's major construction and a new business startup happening on your property. There's that odd and disturbing effigy you found hanging in your orchard. And let's not forget that you and Beau found Linc Pierce hanging from a rafter in his barn, which turned out to have been a staged suicide in an attempt to disguise a murder. Isn't that enough for you?"

She nodded. "But most important to me is hoping that you find enough evidence quickly to take Beau off the suspect list. You know that sweet man could never be capable of violence of any kind."

"That's one of the reasons I came here to talk to you. Please, if you would, retrace your steps for that day from the moment you two stepped onto Pierce's property. And to the best of your ability, provide a time sequence for those events. How long until you two split up, and how long after that was it until you heard Beau scream?"

Charlotte tried to calmly deliver her narrative despite feeling a cold sweat rise in her body.

The Chief's found something at the crime scene in Linc's barn, but what? And who does it incriminate? Could she have proof that I was in the barn before she arrived?

When Charlotte had finished her "edited" description of that visit, the Chief asked, "While you were at the Pierce Farm and by his crops, did you see or suspect that there was anyone else out in the fields? Besides Beau?"

Charlotte thought for a moment, not about the question, but about what was behind the Chief's question. She finally shook her head "no."

The two went silent and Charlotte mulled over the conversation. The Chief was likely doing the same.

"Chief Goodacre, I'm so glad that you're here," Diane said, marching up to the bench. "I'm worried about Danny. He hasn't shown up for work at the construction site after walking off early yesterday, and he's not answering his cell phone. This isn't like him. I'm starting to really worry.

"Did you ask the crew—do they know anything?" the Chief inquired while also sending a text.

"They have no clue."

"I'm sure that he's got a plausible reason for being gone, honey," Charlotte consoled. "We'll all get the word out and should know something soon," the Chief said, nodding in agreement.

"Hi, all—I have some good news," Samuel said as he approached.

"Wow, you sit here long enough and everyone on the farm will pay you a visit. Send in the baby geese next, Samuel. I love them," the Chief joked, and Samuel looked confused.

"What's the good news? Charlotte asked. "We could all use a heaping spoonful of that right about now."

"Joe and I have been walking the strawberry fields since dawn, and we haven't found signs of any new crop damage. Hopefully, that will continue—or cease, depending on the way you look at it." He gave Charlotte a lopsided grin that she found appealing.

"Let's hope that the great Goddess Demeter has returned to her post to preside over the earth's rich bounty," said Beau, carrying a vine-made cornucopia piled high with tomatoes and other fruits from the fields that he'd just harvested.

Chapter Six

Just after lunch, Beau, showered and changed after his morning harvest, then announced to Charlotte and Diane that he was heading out to visit a list of five farms with ailing strawberry crops.

"Be kind and be careful," Diane warned her brother.

"Aren't I always?"

"No!" both Diane and Charlotte replied.

"Well, the kind part, yes. These meetings are about teamwork and collaboration, but of course you know that," Charlotte said, following Beau outside to his car. "There are a lot of things at play here that I don't have enough information to understand," she continued. "I know that you'll use your best judgment." Charlotte doesn't add that she hopes that will be enough, given that the Chief has practically tried and sentenced him.

"Isn't that Danny's truck?"

"Sure, looks like it. You'd better go back inside and have my dear sister tell you what's up."

"On it!"

* * *

"Beau seems in good spirits despite all the scrutiny," Charlotte told Diane, who was pouring over a notebook in the kitchen.

"He's very good at the 'stiff upper lip' thing, as he calls it. But naturally he's hurt and a little bit scared. I'm hoping that going around to the farms today will be a nice distraction."

"Me too, as long as he strikes the right chord of friendly cooperation from the start of each visit. I think that I spared him the one potentially scheming and nasty farmer, Boyd Hoover. He's the one who accused Linc of sending his men to the Hoover Farm to spy on his crops. He's impatient and seems to lack empathy so I also wouldn't be surprised if Boyd Hoover's the one who blew Beau and Linc's altercation way out of proportion. Maybe to keep the spotlight of suspicion away from himself." Charlotte watched as Diane took items out of the pantry and lined them up on the kitchen island.

"Who would have thought that this little farm town would be such a hotbed of subterfuge and deceit?"

"I saw Danny's truck outside," Charlotte said, hoping that Diane took her comment as a non sequitur rather than what had actually come to her mind upon hearing the word *deceit*.

"Yes! He pulled up a few minutes ago and is in fine spirits. He apologized for worrying the crew and me. He apparently fell off this horse during a practice ride for the Rancheros Visitadores meet and was hospitalized with a concussion. His cell phone was stomped on by his horse, and the concerned doctor kept him overnight for observation and limited his activity and interactions."

How convenient.

"That must be a relief for you; I know it is for me. Are you taking inventory of our supplies? What is all this?"

By now Diane had filled the kitchen island with cans, grains, spices, cutting boards, and a set of impressive and imposing butcher's knives.

"I'm going to spend the entire day experimenting with recipes for my restaurant menu, and I plan to use Horse as my taste tester." He gave her his best angelic look of admiration.

"I couldn't be happier that all this is coming together. Your dream has come true! Are you nervous at all?" Charlotte asked Diane.

"Nervous? A little—or that might just be excitement. One thing that I know for sure is that the feelings of fear and dread that used to plague me every time I went to work at the restaurant are gone. Inside this feels so right and what I was meant to do." Charlotte could see Diane's eyes grow moist. "Horse, are you ready to become a food critic?"

"You may want to enlist Alice as well. I'm not confident that Horse has such a discerning palate."

"Something to consider," Diane said, and smiled.

* * *

When Charlotte reached the barn, she found Samuel working outside in the paddock at a gardening table with tiers for pots, seeds, and tools. He was making some sort of liquid concoction.

"What's all this?"

"It is an organic, nonchemical pesticide that I use on the strawberries. Up until last week, it did the trick. But with this disease hitting us, I've decided to test some different mixtures, Charlotte."

"Interesting. What are you pouring from that big can?"

"This is one hundred percent cold-pressed neem oil. Ever heard of it?"

Charlotte shook her head but moved in closer to examine its consistency and take a whiff. "Ew! I smell garlic and something else."

Samuel nodded. "Sulfur. The oil is extracted from the seeds of the neem tree native to India. To use it on plants, it has to be mixed with other liquids in order to emulsify."

"Can't you just buy this, say, at the Garden Center?" Charlotte inquired.

"Yes, you can—already mixed and ready for application. But I like to order the neem oil in bulk online from India and prepare my own pest control recipe. It's much less expensive, and I can test different batches of liquid. I'm adding a mild liquid soap and water and incorporating it with the oil to make a natural pesticide. I keep a log of the amounts of each I use and record weekly results."

"Wow, I'm impressed. You're mixing ingredients outside, and Diane is doing something similar in the kitchen. I love it."

Watching Samuel work, Charlotte was reminded of Linc's workbench and the canisters she'd seen on his otherwise dusty and unused table. She wondered if they contained something that also smelled like garlic and sulfur.

I wonder if they're still in Linc's barn?

"How effective is this neem oil solution?" The wheels in Charlotte's mind were turning.

"Very, given the mixture is made up of the right proportions. Neem oil is ideal for controlling white flies, mealy bugs, leafhoppers, bagworms, beetles, aphids, mites, and many other species.

It is safe for ladybugs because they don't eat the leaves of plants where it is sprayed, and best of all, it's harmless to humans and animals."

"So why wouldn't every farmer use it?"

"I wish I knew. This takes a little more effort, but not that much. It's mostly the older ones who don't. I guess they've been conditioned over the years to think that nothing beats chemicals."

"Are you going to use that now?"

"Yes, starting with the plants around the diseased strawberries."

"I'd like to see the damaged crop so I have something to compare it to as I visit other farms."

"Sure, follow me."

They headed out and when Horse saw that they were walking in the direction of the owl house, he raced out to them and scampered ahead, presumably in the hope of seeing those beautiful birds in daylight.

The damage to the strawberries was worse than Charlotte had imagined. An entire row of young strawberry plants was now hanging limp. The plants had yellowed, then browned, and were withering.

"If I didn't know better, I'd guess that the fruit suffered from some type of fertilizer burn. But I promise you that I only use organic matter to stimulate plant growth, such as compost, plant byproducts, animal manure, and other biological materials. I hope we've seen the last of it, but since I don't know what's causing this blight, I really feel helpless."

Charlotte let her knees go weak and sank to the ground. Samuel joined her there, and they sat in silence for a moment.

Seeing them sitting still, Horse took the opportunity to go investigate the brooding box.

"We've got to figure out what's going on here. It's my livelihood—heck, it's all our livelihoods, and we can't forget that there's a murderer out there."

Charlotte succumbed to a moment of emotion and shed a tear. Samuel gently put his arm around her shoulder and leaned into her.

She took a second to recover and then asked, "What do you know about Boyd Hoover, Samuel. I'm about to visit his farm."

Self-consciously, Samuel removed his arm from her. "He's from up North," he began. "Castroville, where he was a young artichoke grower working on his family's farm. They're all very competitive people. The story goes that he wanted to branch out on his own, not be part of a bigger clan. So he came down here to grow strawberries and prove that he could start and manage a successful farm. He's willful and headstrong, and he raised his daughter to be the same way."

"He sounds charming. I'm excited."

Samuel chuckled. "Be careful. He has the single-minded goal of becoming the biggest produce farm in the county. And he'll step on anybody who tries to stop him. It's Boyd Hoover's way or the highway."

"I can't stand bullies. That's one part of my past in advertising that I don't miss."

"You miss other parts?" Samuel asked as Horse burst onto the scene and nearly trampled them.

"Horse! What is it?" Charlotte asked as he pressed his snout against the side of her butt to try and get her to stand up.

"I guess he wants us to follow him." Charlotte giggled as she stood up.

"He has an interesting way of asking, but we'd better hurry up—this pig has no patience." Samuel rose and the two of them broke into a trot as Horse let the way. When they arrived at the strawberry field with the brooding box, Horse stopped and began hopping up and down with excitement.

"Is there a ladder nearby? I want to see what Horse is fussing about."

"I'll get it, but you must be very careful not to disturb them."

"I won't."

As soon as Samuel placed the ladder against the pole, Charlotte climbed up, taking two rungs at a time. Samuel had to use both hands to hold it steady for her.

Somehow Horse knew to stay quiet. After a few minutes, Charlotte climbed back down, this time slowly and softly.

"Both owls are in there, and the female is sitting on eggs," Charlotte whispered. "We're going to be grandparents!"

*   *   *

Hoover Farms was made up of a sprawling estate dotted with two Spanish hacienda–style homes, behind which Charlotte could see fields and fields of strawberries and off to the west side, a smaller grouping of what appeared to be grapevines.

Charlotte drove down the hill slowly and calmly, mindful of Boyd's distrust of strangers and trespassers. There was a small parking area, room for perhaps five cars, in front of the Hoover Farm Shop. Next to it was an information office. Charlotte got out of the Buick and decided to check in there and ask to meet with Boyd. On her way, she heard raised voices clearly engaged in an argument. About twenty feet away, Charlotte spotted, from behind, someone on horseback berating a farm hand who appeared contrite. The only words that she could decipher were "I get priority." Charlotte realized that there was something familiar about her.

When the farmworker left, and the horse and rider turned around, Charlotte got her answer.

Of course.

"Charlotte Finn, how nice to see you! If I'd known you were coming, I'd have prepared a wine tasting. Even on short notice I'm sure that my people could come up with something that you'd like."

"Katharine Hoover—I didn't make the connection until just now. You are Boyd's daughter, aren't you?"

Katharine dismounted, embraced Charlotte, and gave her a warm smile. "Come—I'll show you around my vineyard."

"Actually, I'm here to see Boyd and get a look at the damaged strawberry crops. We're doing a farm survey to compare information and, as a group, to try and find a solution to this awful blight."

It looked like Katharine was trying to hide her disappointment.

"I couldn't help overhearing your discussion with that farmer. Is there anything that I can help you with? In my previous career, I was mostly around men who mistook me for a pushover. I can share some of my techniques in setting them straight if you wish. We women have to stick together."

"Thanks. This is a daily occurrence as I am always fighting with the strawberry-growing cash cow for resources and investment spending. My father keeps telling me that as soon as the vineyard turns profitable, the money will flow. But how can I do that without start-up help? Sometimes I think that my father loves his strawberries more than he loves me!"

"I completely understand. I'll try and put in a good word with your dad."

Katharine shrugged. "Suzie, in the office, can page him. Dinner soon!"

Katharine quickly mounted her horse and retreated in the direction of her vineyard.

"Hi—Suzie is it?" Charlotte asked, entering the office, which she now saw also opened into the Farm Shop from the inside.

"Yes, how can I help you?"

The young girl asked this with an odd look of intimidation on her face, as if anything that Charlotte said would strike fear in her.

"I'm here to meet with Boyd Hoover. If you could just point me in the right direction, I'm sure that I can find him myself. My name is Charlotte Finn."

Charlotte watched Suzie send a text from her cell phone. Moments later she turned to Charlotte and said, "He'll be up in about ten minutes. Feel free to look around the shop, or you can wait outside at the picnic table under the bottle brush tree."

"But I need to see his ailing strawberry crops—this impacts the entire farming community."

"I'm sorry, Miss Finn, but Mr. Hoover has a policy of never allowing visitors past this area. We had some trespassers last year, and if it weren't for Miss Hoover and her security team, things could have gotten very ugly."

"Miss Hoover as in Katharine?" Charlotte asked, confused.

"Yes."

"But I thought that she was a vintner, running the winery." Charlotte examined some wine bottles on display in the shop.

"Now she is, but she managed security for the farm for a number of years before that. At least that's what I've been told. My mom got me this job—it's part-time. I'm a senior in high school. I'm saving up for a prom dress." Suzie smiled shyly.

"Miss Hoover also took courses in martial arts, and I've heard she got quite good at it. She's also one of those computer wizards—you know what I mean? So, she had all the cameras and alarms and stuff installed."

Suzie was certainly a font of information once she relaxed a little, Charlotte thought.

"How is the winery doing?" Charlotte asked, thinking about Diane and the business venture that she was about to enter into with Katharine.

"I only know what I hear. I think at this point most of the business is selling her grapes, frozen, to local purveyors, who then go and sell them in bulk on the internet. Whoever buys them then makes the wine, I guess."

"I heard her arguing with a farmworker when I arrived. Does that happen often?"

Charlotte had moved to a cork bulletin board on the wall, where people could post ads for goods and services. Prominently in the center was a color card for a school for 7 Star Praying Mantis Kung Fu. Charlotte had never heard of this, but the photo of two men fighting made it clear that you'd learn some serious self-defense methods.

This prompted Charlotte to ask, "Suzie, was Boyd angry when he found out that trespassers had gotten into his fields?"

"Are you kidding? He was livid, and we all walked on eggshells for weeks after."

"Did he blame Katharine at all?"

Suzie nodded and was about to speak when she clammed up and went to work on her computer at the counter.

Charlotte turned to see a tall, barrel-chested man with a proud face stomp toward the office. His mop of blond hair was being mostly kept in control by his black and yellow Hoover Farms cap, the same one she remembered from the Garden Center parking lot.

"Howdy, Charlotte, what can I do you for," he asked, noticing Suzie. "Let's step outside to the picnic table, where we can sit and enjoy the breeze."

Boyd didn't wait for a response from Charlotte and marched out.

Charlotte was suspicious but also intrigued by the guy. You could sense a temper bubbling just below the surface, but his face and demeanor were so animated that it was easy to guess what was coming from him. She was also fascinated by his bushy, bushy eyebrows that danced up and down constantly like marionettes from a Punch and Judy show.

Sitting across from each other Boyd waited for Charlotte to speak.

A page out of my book.

"Since we all met at the Garden Center, Beau and I have been conducting surveys of farms afflicted with this strawberry disease," she began.

"That wasn't much of a meeting, and I don't mean to be rude, but what does Pretty Boy know about farming?" Boyd didn't mince his words.

The attack on Beau instantly turned Charlotte's "honey" approach to the conversation into "vinegar."

"Interesting that you put it that way. We found an effigy of a man hanging by the neck from an apple tree in my orchard a few days ago."

"So?" His brows had stopped moving.

"There was a note stuck on the shirt pocket. Do you know what it said?"

"How the hell would I?"

"It said 'Pretty Boy,' the same phrase that you just used, Boyd. Oh, and guess what? My strawberry crops right in that area have also succumbed to this blight."

"Are you accusing me of something? 'Cause I'm sure the guys would back me up that Linc was the one to coin that nickname for your friend."

"I'm glad that you brought up poor Linc. I have news. His death was not by suicide—he was murdered, Boyd."

"You don't come onto my property and start naming me for some horrible crimes. Who the hell do you think you are?" He stood up so quickly that his stomach got stuck between the bench and picnic table, nearly knocking the whole thing over, along with Charlotte. "You've overstayed your welcome, Miss—I need you to leave. Wait, I never welcomed you to my farm. You just barged in," Boyd screamed.

Charlotte saw Suzie step out of the office, cell phone in hand. From another direction she saw Katharine running up the hill.

76

"You've given away a lot with your reaction today, Boyd. I most certainly didn't accuse you of anything. Don't worry—I'm leaving."

Charlotte tried to walk calmly to her car, which was difficult given Boyd's irrational tirade. What she really wanted to do was run.

*   *   *

When Charlotte arrived back at the farm, she was still shaken by the encounter with Boyd Hoover. There was no sign yet of Beau, and she hoped that he was having better visits with the farmers. She decided to focus her mind on other things and headed down to the restaurant site to check on its progress.

Things had moved fast in the last week. The framing was done, as was the exterior of the building, including the window installation. Diane had always had a distinct vision of what her own restaurant would look like, and Charlotte was incredibly happy to see that it was coming to life.

The outside finish was made of all kinds of reclaimed wood, creating a visual mosaic of colors and knots and rings. One entire wall was made up of paned glass that could roll all the way up like a giant garage door. Charlotte had heard that Beau was designing the sign for the restaurant, and she could only imagine how spectacular that was going to be. Diane wanted nature to flow in and out of the space.

"Hi, Danny. This place looks like it's been here for a hundred years, and I mean that in a good way."

"Thanks, Charlotte. Too bad we need all this wiring in here, or my job would be a lot easier." He was supervising a team of electricians, who were following plans and running electrical connectivity throughout. Charlotte couldn't help seeing his black eye and the wince his face made when he put weight on his right leg.

"Are you sure you should be back at work so soon? Diane told me about your accident."

Danny waved his hand through the air. "I'm fine."

"I know that you're job isn't easy, but you are doing fantastic work. You seem to be ahead of schedule. Do you have a completion date in mind?"

"Diane is being cool and not pressuring me. She says that she wants to do a 'soft open' to get out the kinks before making a bigger debut. But I'm hoping to have everything completed by the last week in April."

"That's not far off. Have you got another job lined up? Or a vacation planned?"

Danny chuckled and pulled out a couple of wooden crates for them to sit on.

"No, nothing like that. The first Saturday in May is the Rancheros Visitadores ride, and I haven't missed one since I figured out how to stay atop a horse as a kid."

"That's right; I vaguely remember it from last year. Can you fill me in on the details?"

"Sure. It's both a historical tradition and a charitable event. My great grandfather was the first in our family to ride. There've been at least a handful of Costa family members that go on it every year."

"Will you be okay to ride after your accident?" Charlotte asked.

"You all will want to see us off when we start at the Santa Ynez Mission. The padres bless the horses; we have a ceremony on horseback that we've been rehearsing; and we announce the recipients for this year's charitable donation. It's a great day."

Danny was beaming thinking about the event, but Charlotte was stuck on the fact that he'd ignored her question about falling off his horse.

"Boss? We want to go over these plans with you," shouted one of the electricians.

"Back to work— it was nice talking with you, Charlotte."

Charlotte wouldn't get to ask Danny her question again, so she went on a search for Horse instead.

She entered the paddock and found Samuel taking a little break and kicking around a soccer ball with the farm's amazing chestnut horse named Pele, as in the famous soccer star.

"Hi, Samuel, Pele. Who's winning?"

"Which one of us has four legs?" Samuel grinned.

"Silly of me to ask. And where's Horse?"

Samuel dipped his head toward the shady side of the barn, where a pink mound was softly rising and falling. Horse was on his back, sound asleep, a smile still formed across his face.

"Diane gave him too much food to taste, I'm afraid. I wonder if I can convince him that he's already had dinner and won't be eating again until morning."

"Good luck with that." Samuel laughed.

Charlotte's cell phone rang, and she quickly answered it, expecting Beau to be on the other end."

"Are you on your way back? How'd it go?"

"Back from where? Did we have a date that I missed, Charlotte?"

Charlotte checked the caller ID on her phone.

"Sorry, Ford, I was expecting to get a call from Beau. He's been out all day inspecting farmers' strawberry crops."

Charlotte noticed that Samuel was pretending unsuccessfully not to be listening in.

"I'd be interested to hear what he's learned. Perhaps you can fill me in over dinner at my farm tomorrow night? In addition to a meal you won't soon forget, I promised you a more in-depth tour of my farm and the systems we're using."

Samuel was now not even trying to hide that he was eavesdropping.

"Dinner tomorrow night at Barclay Farms sounds wonderful, Ford. I'd love to!" Charlotte gushed for Samuel's benefit.

"Shall I send a car to pick you up at six?"

"That's not necessary—I'll drive myself. Bye." Charlotte disconnected the call and smiled. That was when she saw that Samuel had stormed off into the field.

Chapter Seven

O ver breakfast with Beau the following morning, Charlotte and he compared notes on their farm visits. Charlotte had told him about her meeting with Boyd Hoover as delicately as possible, leaving out the "pretty boy" dialogue, but Beau still seemed unsettled by Boyd's temper.

"What is it all of a sudden with these people? It's like a strong wind came in and swept all the civility off the mountain."

"Were the farmers rude to you too?"

"No, but I wouldn't say that they set out tea and biscuits either," he replied before taking a bite out of a slice of Alice's freshly made banana bread.

"I can see that you're making up for lost time," Charlotte said, laughing.

They'd decided to have their breakfast on the front porch of the farmhouse since it was such a beautiful, crisp morning. Horse ambled up to them with his ladybug friend, Mrs. Robinson, perched on his shoulder. He was still licking his lip for crumbs from his own breakfast.

"Hello, you two, what are your big plans for the day?" Charlotte asked them.

"I got up early to battle aphids so I'm going to take a mid-morning repose on this lush pink pillow," Beau said in a high-pitched voice meant to be Mrs. Robinson's.

Charlotte was still laughing when Joe and Alice pulled up in a golf cart. In the back storage area were stacks of boxes.

"Alice, this bread is sent from heaven—thank you," Beau said in between chomps.

"I'm so glad you like it. If you've finished your breakfast, then maybe you'd like to hop on. We've got something exciting to show you."

"Sure. I hope it's *good* exciting."

"Oh, it is," Joe assured her.

Horse wasn't about to miss out and hopped on just as the cart started moving.

"Hey! I'm napping here," Beau said in his Mrs. Robinson voice.

They stopped by the area that had been cleared for the geese. Alice walked to the small shelter they had built and began dropping a trail of barley. Sure enough, first one and then a string of goslings emerged and pecked their way along Alice's trail.

Joe and Charlotte followed along slowly in the cart, and when, out of the corner of her eye, she saw Horse get down on his back legs, ready to jump, she pulled him back.

"Oh no, you don't. That barley is for the birds."

Horse's mouth curled downward, making him look sad, especially after he watched Alice toss a particularly large handful of seeds on the ground.

When they reached a large area of strawberry crops, Joe stopped the cart and got out. He grabbed a fistful of barley from

Alice's bucket and scattered it into the field. The goslings waddled in after it. Charlotte looked to Alice for an explanation.

She giggled and said, "Geese love slugs. And slugs love strawberries. We put them together and let nature take its course."

As if on cue, Charlotte watched one of the birds open its beak and swallow a slimy creature. After watching the feasting for a few minutes, Joe said, "Hop back into the cart. We've got another stop to make."

"Will the goslings be able to find their way back on their own?" Charlotte asked.

"Their navigation skills are exceptional," Alice said, nodding. "It is believed that they use the sun for orientation. And at night they use the stars. How cool is that?"

"Very, very cool," Charlotte said as they stopped at another field of strawberries. "Do we have more geese around here, Joe?"

"Nope, this time we're going to employ a different kind of pest control."

"Hopping different," Alice said, and laughed.

Joe went to the back of the cart, grabbed one of the boxes and placed it on the ground. As soon as he lifted the lid, a couple of frogs flew up into the air and out toward the fruit. Horse's eyes got as wide as saucers. As soon as he would get near enough to inspect a frog, it would leap up and land several feet away.

Everyone laughed as they watched poor Horse try to figure out what these green things were and how he could make friends with one. Mrs. Robinson, seeing that getting her beauty sleep was impossible, flew off for calmer pastures.

"These indigenous frogs are a farmer's best friends, Charlotte. In addition to feeding on slugs, these guys help us control pests such as cutworms, beetles, grubs, and all kinds of menaces. I read somewhere that a frog can eat as many as one hundred insects in a day," Joe explained.

"Then bon appétit, froggies. I never knew that all this went on."

"That's one of the key lessons you learn in farming."

She turned toward the voice and saw that Samuel had ridden up to them on Pele.

"Every pest has a natural enemy. You give the two the opportunity, and they'll sort it out organically," Samuel continued. "I feel sorry for those ignorant farmers who are trying to control something that Mother Nature already has a solution for."

He tipped his hat to her and rode off.

* * *

The rest of the day Charlotte and Horse spent the time exploring the farm, something that she seldom got the opportunity to do, what with often having to tend to a disaster of some kind.

They started at the lake, water being a natural lure because of its serenity and life-giving properties. Horse couldn't resist a wade in and a roll in the wet soil at the water's edge. It looked so inviting that Charlotte dipped her toes in as well and watched tadpoles scurry away from her steps. *Life is good.*

Next, they headed downhill toward Alice and Joe's cottage. They stopped partway down to a flattened area that was designated for experimental planting systems. Here Samuel and Joe were testing a vertical, hydroponic system for growing strawberries. Samuel had tried to explain it to her in theory, but this was the first time that she'd had a look in person. She discovered Joe at the end of one row, adjusting a drip irrigation system.

"This whole thing fascinates me. Do you mind giving me a little tour?"

"Of course," he said grinning with pride. "This method is practiced in the East and in urban areas where space is at a premium. It's also called 'tower farming,' Charlotte. You can see that each stake has four containers sitting one above the other, starting at about three feet above the ground. This system uses over eighty percent less water and no soil, so it requires much less pest control. If this proves successful, vertical farming would generate a much higher revenue stream per acre than we currently have."

Horse was utterly confused by these structures that resembled owl houses but were homes to strawberries instead.

"That sounds fantastic. What's holding us back, and why the testing?"

"A couple of things—but mainly the upfront investment in the hydroponic irrigation system. We'd have to purchase pumps and tanks and build the water infrastructure over the fields. Not a cheap endeavor. Which is why it is prudent to start small and scale up once we start to see financial returns. The best part is that if we continue to experience such terrible droughts, we'll be ahead of the learning curve. It's the right way to be headed, growing with just water and nutrients. Ultimately we'll see fast growth of healthier plants, all while using less of nature's precious resources."

"I love that this is making use of the natural tools around us rather than the high-tech, artificial shortcuts that Ford Barclay employs."

"Never mess with Mother Nature," Joe said with a big smile.

* * *

On her way out at dusk, Charlotte paused in front of Uncle Tobias's eight-foot framed mirror that leaned against one wall of the bedroom suite. She hadn't thought twice about this dinner being anything more than an exchange of ideas with a fellow farmer, but suddenly she cared about looking her best. She was wearing a square-neck, sleeveless sheath dress that buttoned all the way down the front. It was a creamy beige color, and she'd paired it with darker brown, cork-soled wedges. At the last moment, she kicked off the casual sandals and flung open closet doors until she found her red stilettos.

I mean it's a night out . . .

Naturally, whom did she run into when she was leaving the farmhouse?

Samuel.

"So, you're keeping your date with that imposter farmer, are you?" he asked while looking at her up and down.

"It's not a date—just two farm owners comparing methods, Samuel."

He'd stopped at her red high heels. "I see. Be sure to tell him about the 'natural enemies.'"

Was that meant to be a threat aimed at Ford Barclay?

* * *

Barclay Farms looked even more magical as the sun went down. The outdoor lighting had been carefully designed to showcase the beautiful architecture of the main houses and majestic palm trees. A colorfully tiled fountain with a base the size of a large tractor wheel was spraying water out of a tiered sculpture of a pineapple lit from below. As Charlotte parked her car where she had before, she saw Ford emerge onto the patio wearing pleated soft gray pants and a bright white dress shirt.

I wouldn't be surprised if he's had his initials embroidered on the breast pocket.

As Ford Barclay walked toward her, he wore a warm smile, and Charlotte began to relax. *So what, if he's a bit older—a lot older,* she thought. *He's intelligent and polite and could be influential in helping me grow my farm.*

"Simply stunning," Ford said, taking her hand and leading her to a chair by the firepit on the patio. "I thought that we'd start with a Paso Robles rosé along with chilled artichoke and an array of dips that my chef, Josie, has made. She has a skilled hand with delicate flavors. Cheers." He raised his glass and Charlotte did the same. "Barclay Farms" was etched into the glass.

"Martin filled me in on what occurred in the Garden Center parking lot. I'm impressed by how you hold your own among all these opinionated macho tillers of the soil."

"It's only a man's world if you let it, my great-uncle Tobias would always tell me. I've certainly run into some big obstacles since I took over the family farm, and at times have wished that I could be just about anywhere else. But I've also always believed that I can be equal or better than any male counterpart. It just takes hard work."

Ford clapped his hands. "I admire your spirit. Bravo!"

Is he patronizing me?

"It is so much more than that, Ford. And let me remind you that we both owe our livings to the same boss, *Mother* Nature."

Ford was saved from digging himself into a deeper hole when Josie informed them that dinner was served.

*   *   *

Charlotte's breath caught as they walked through a glass facade, and three large panels turned ninety degrees. The towering interior opened up all the way to the pitched ceiling, giving Charlotte the sense that she had just entered a revered cathedral—but the space was clean and modern rather than ornate. The light oak wood floor continued up the walls, broken only by more glass in the form of balconies leading to other rooms. From the back of the long room, it looked as though Charlotte was standing in a luxury squash court with elevated spectator access. Charlotte stifled a giggle, imagining Horse belly-skating across the slick, highly polished flooring.

The furnishings were equally minimalist and cold looking to Charlotte. Sofas in tones of gray in flat suede did not invite someone to sink down and cozy up with a good book. The fireplace was built flush with the oak walls, also in another shade of gray travertine tile. Charlotte looked at Ford, who'd been watching her expressions, and smiled.

"Did you design all this yourself?"

"Do you like it?" he responded with another question.

"It's breathtaking," Charlotte replied, avoiding the actual "like" or "dislike" aspect of his question.

"Then yes, I did. All the way down to the rivets in the garage. We should get seated in the dining room before Josie scolds me for letting the food get cold."

Ford led Charlotte up the wooden oak stairs, minus a hand railing, up to the second story. It had been awhile since Charlotte had walked in heels, and she clung close to the safety of the wall in her climb. The spaces on this floor were all partially open and defined by glass partitions and more travertine. Charlotte thought back to the al fresco group dinners at the farm and longed for that kind of warmth and organic dining experience.

"Please allow me to guide you into your chair," Ford said, pulling out a gray suede barrel chair for her.

Two place settings had been laid at one end of the marble-top dining table that seated ten. When Charlotte reached for her linen napkin and touched the surface, she discovered that the marble was ice-cold.

I am the opposite of all of this.

"To the beginning of a wonderful friendship," Ford said, raising his champagne glass.

Charlotte picked up her flute and said, "To the farmers who tend the land and feed America."

Ford froze for a moment, clearly not happy with Charlotte's unromantic toast response.

* * *

"I would have thought that being a city girl, you'd be more receptive to embracing the use of technology on a farm. This is the one area where I disagree with you." Ford let the young waiter working for Josie clear his plate as he refilled both their glasses with a delicious local pinot noir.

"That's fine too. I'm not closed to using artificial intelligence, but only after I have a firm grip on what nature can do."

Dinner had been elaborate, and although everything was locally sourced, it had been quite a while since Charlotte had sat down to such a lavish meal. They'd had oysters and local mussels, followed by a little gem salad with tomato relish and locally grown, toasted pistachios. For the main course, Josie had outdone herself, serving crisp duck breast with sweet potato gnocchi and sweet and spicy heirloom cauliflower.

"You have quite a sophisticated palate. The last time I had food like this I was entertaining the CEO of my old ad agency's biggest client in Chicago. Did you live in Europe for a time?" Charlotte was hoping to disguise her ploy to get him to talk about his past.

"I like Europe and visit as often as is possible, but no, I have lived in the US my entire life. My family heritage is English, but given their cooking, that certainly couldn't have been the origin of my discerning appetite."

They both chuckled.

"In either case this was absolutely delicious. Please thank Josie for me and gently let her know that I cannot manage another bite. May we start our tour now before food drowsiness really sets in?"

Ford chuckled at the phrase and nodded. "Sure. Please excuse me—I'll meet you outside momentarily. Feel free to use the facilities; they're just past that glass wall to the right."

"Perfect, thank you."

Charlotte walked through to the next area and saw the bathroom that Ford had talked about. She also saw a room beyond with the door ajar. Flickering blue and white lights made the room look animated. She couldn't resist taking a closer look. Charlotte did a quick check over both her shoulders for anyone coming and, satisfied, pulled the door a little wider and entered the room. Inside was a wall full of computers and monitors keeping surveillance over every corner of Barclay Farms. Activity on one set of screens caught her eye. The camera had focused on an area in a tomato field where she spotted a group of frogs hopping about.

Aww.

Suddenly Charlotte saw a laser light hit one of the amphibians, and she gasped. Before she could see the result of the strike, the screens went black.

"You should wait for Ford to give you the tour, to explain all these methods to you," came a voice that she recognized as belonging to Martin.

"You scared me. And what happened to that frog? Is he dead?"

"Like I said, I believe that Mr. Barclay is waiting for you outside. He can answer all your questions." Martin stepped aside, making it clear that he wanted Charlotte to leave the room.

Charlotte didn't budge.

"I'm not leaving until you answer my question. What have you done to that frog?"

"I wouldn't keep him waiting," Martin replied, ignoring her question. "You're about to experience the main event in the Ford Barclay courtship ritual."

"I don't know what you're talking about. This is a business meeting between the actual farm owners and nothing more."

Charlotte saw from Martin's physical reaction to her comment that she'd hurt him, and instantly regretted it.

"I didn't mean that your wisdom is not important. In fact, I've already seen that you are the genius behind the success of Barclay Farms."

"Like I said, you'd better go outside and meet him. Ford Barclay doesn't like to be disobeyed. He's on his best behavior tonight, but mark my words, he has a wicked temper."

Martin turned his back to her and fired up the bank of monitors.

Shaken and more than a little frightened, Charlotte walked with purpose to the front door. She'd decided that any tour of the Barclay Farm would need to happen in daylight with at least Beau by her side.

What she saw next took her breath away.

Ford Barclay had changed into riding pants and boots and was seated atop the same horse that Charlotte had seen him riding when they first met. His white dress shirt practically glowed in the dark.

"Your ride awaits, Ms. Finn," Ford said extending his arm down to her.

"I'll walk alongside if that's okay with you," Charlotte replied, but she couldn't help smiling at the romantic gesture.

"It most definitely is not okay. How can you resist such an offer? Please?"

She thought about the warning that Martin had just given her. Ford reached his hand down again, and this time she accepted it. He pulled her up with ease and set her to ride side-saddle in front of him. He had to wrap his arms around her to hold onto the reins.

"Off we go," he said softly in her ear.

Charlotte felt her face flush and was grateful that he could not see her blush. Even if she accepted their age difference, (she thought of her late uncle and his young true love), she wasn't comfortable with all his money and power.

Or was it how he used it?

As they trotted to the middle of the fields, Charlotte admired the midnight-blue inky sky. The stars were not being timid tonight and gave off smiling twinkles to prove it. Clusters of constellations shone together, proudly telling their story. The shooting star arrived right on cue.

"We'll dismount here and start the show," Ford said, and lowered her off the horse just as gently as he'd raised her onto the saddle.

Ford dismounted and spoke into a handheld radio that Charlotte had not noticed he was carrying. "In position, Martin—let's begin," he said into the device.

The mention of Martin's name gave Charlotte a sudden chill. She could not erase the attack that she'd seen them make on those poor frogs.

Suddenly Charlotte heard a buzzing sound and looked all around for its source. Overhead she saw a fleet of drones flying low and spraying the fields. They looked like mechanical black crows.

"Robotics is the future in crop dusting. We can spray herbicides, fertilizer, and fungicides cost-effectively over acres of land," Ford explained. "On tonight's run the drones are spraying liquid nitrogen for maximum growth and yield. With this method they can be much more targeted, and we can more carefully control the supply. Too much nitrogen can lead to excessive leaf growth and runner production. Many growers who haven't switched over to robotics use drip irrigation to dispense liquid nitrogen, and that has many limitations and drawbacks."

"Are the drones complicated and difficult to learn how to fly?" Charlotte asked. "I mean they are performing pretty intricate maneuvers."

"In business you hire people to shore up your own weaknesses." Ford smiled. "And that's why I have Martin. While I can do this, Martin is a pro with technology. That affords me the time to focus on the big picture."

Once again, he is reinforcing the idea that Martin is just a second fiddle.

Ford chuckled. "Martin has even discovered how to target the pesky frogs that have begun to invade my fields. He kills them with a quick laser zap. I might have to ask my chef to learn how to make frog's legs one of these evenings. I hear that the dish is a delicacy in France and China."

Charlotte took a breath and squinted her eyes at him. "Where to be begin with everything that you've just said?"

"No need to respond. I know from your beautiful eyes that you agree with me."

As quickly as they'd flown in, the drones moved away from them, emitting a high -pitched whine.

"First of all, thank you for the incredible business lesson. I didn't realize how much I missed all the trite, misogynistic business babble from my days working in Chicago. You see, Ford, in advertising we are hired to replace that empty language with ideas that matter and that people understand."

"I like 'feisty Charlotte.'" Ford grinned and moved closer to her. Charlotte grasped that she was out there alone and took a step back but couldn't control her growing temper.

"Secondly, if you and your wizard agriculturalist, Martin, were worth your salt, you'd have learned that the indigenous frog population here is in fact like the canary in the coal mine. Frogs eat insects and pests that can carry dangerous diseases. And most importantly, they are called an indicator species, which means that they are the first to know if an area of farmland is polluted or diseased. Curious though that you have so many since you claim that your strawberries, which I still haven't seen, are afflicted with this blight."

"You want to see my strawberries?" Ford shockingly and awkwardly moved in for a kiss.

"What are you doing? Get off me—now!" Charlotte said, and pushed him back.

"Come on. You've been flirting with me all night. And those red heels." Ford grinned; he still wasn't listening to her. He moved to her again, and they scuffled. Finally, Charlotte stuck a red stiletto into his ankle and was able to break away.

"You like these shoes so much? They're yours." She hurled them at him and then broke out in a barefoot run toward her car.

She heard him behind her, mounting his horse, and realized that she only had a few precious minutes to make it. In no time he was beside her on horseback.

"You've misunderstood the entire situation, Charlotte, as you have my farming methods. Now stop running and let me explain. You'll shred your feet in these fields." Ford said this not in a caring way, but with the fierce temper of a man who was used to getting his way. Martin's warning had not been in vain.

The ground was wet from the drone spray, and Charlotte slipped and skidded face-first into a row of grape vines. The plants were being supported and trained by metal posts and vineyard wire. She scooted in a little further, knowing that Ford and his horse would not be able to trot into the area to see where she'd gone. After about ten minutes of silence, Charlotte quietly slid out from under the vines and made a stealth beeline to her car.

Charlotte was confused, embarrassed, and angry at the same time. He'd accused her of flirting. Had she? Then there was Martin, creeping around: Was he threatening her? Ford certainly didn't treat him very nicely.

And what would Ford have done if I hadn't been able to escape? Forced himself on me?

One thing Charlotte was sure about was that if Ford Barclay set his mind toward getting something, he'd be ferocious about going after it. If Linc had been going around Little Acorn saying that another farmer might be sabotaging the strawberry crops, Charlotte could see how that would have gotten under Ford's skin. Add to that Linc's distain for pouring wealth and technology into farming, instead of common sense, and you'd definitely have fuel for the fire.

Is Ford Barclay capable of murder? After tonight it's a possibility . . .

Chapter Eight

"You look a bit worse for wear this morning Charlotte. Late night with Ford Barclay? I can't wait to hear every last detail."

Charlotte gave Diane a half grin and busied herself with the newspaper, not yet ready to speak. They were sitting on the front patio.

"I see. I'll wait for you to speak when you're ready. In the meantime, I'll just admire the gorgeous view around us, the lake, an emerald green that ripples every time a barn swallow dives for a bug. Or the glistening sweat on Samuel's bare chest as he chops wood over there."

"Where?" Charlotte looked up.

"Hah! Got you. I know that you've been fighting an attraction to him. Why not just go with it?"

Instead of responding, Charlotte returned to the newspaper and turned the page.

A moment later she said, "He was actually a nice-looking man when he wasn't snarling."

"Samuel?"

"No, Linc Pierce." Charlotte folded the paper and held it up to show Diane Linc's photo in the article.

"That's the guy!" Diane sat up in her seat.

"Right, it's a picture of Linc."

"No, I mean yes if you say so, but that's also the guy who was in town when I was with Danny. Remember? He kept trying to make conversation with Danny about riding with his grandfather in the Rancheros Visitadores. Danny got angry without provocation and told Linc he was crazy and needed to go away."

Charlotte's stomach sank. Danny had been missing from the job when she and Beau found Linc dead in his barn. His reason when he finally returned was that he'd fallen off his horse and had been in the hospital for observation. She made a note to check into that.

Charlotte dropped the newspaper on a side table, and Diane picked it up and began reading. As best friends know each other well, Charlotte was sure that Diane was now wondering the same thing about Danny. They remained silent in their thoughts for a few minutes.

"I know how this looks," Diane said, laying the paper back down on the side table. "I keep making excuses in my mind, but it is becoming pretty clear that Danny had some deep-seated anger with Linc."

"Yes, and he was conveniently away from the farm when Linc was killed. But I could just as easily assign blame to that hothead Boyd Hoover. And others. You need to be cautious but rational, Diane, and wait out Chief Goodacre to solve the case. Maybe I can subtly nudge her into looking at certain facts that may speed up the process."

Charlotte grinned and then groaned as Horse jumped onto her lap. He was getting bigger every day.

"Change of subject," Diane finally said. "Start at the beginning. I want to hear all about your date with the fabulous Ford Barclay."

"I keep telling you it wasn't a date; it was a dinner among farmers."

"And at the end of the evening, was it still that?" Diane raised her eyebrows in anticipation.

"No, it was not."

"Aha! Do tell."

"It was a nightmare, and Ford Barclay left me so shaken that I spent the night outside with Horse, watching Fred and Ginger soar over the strawberry fields. I just couldn't fall asleep, never mind how hard I tried."

"Charlotte, honey, what happened?"

Charlotte broke her promise to keep last night to herself, and gave Diane every detail. She had to admit that her shoulders felt lighter once she'd finished.

"How frightening. It just goes to show you that the true character of a person is on the inside, no matter how well they dress or how big a house they own. He needs to be held accountable. Do you think that you should report this?"

"To whom? The Chief? I don't think so, plus I have no proof that it even happened."

Unless Martin was watching the whole thing play out, which is even creepier.

"Then let's all go out to his farm, and I'll give him a piece of my mind. He'll have to listen—there's safety in numbers." Diane stood, ready to go.

"He's not worth it. Men like that don't change. And who knows what kind of security measures Ford and Martin have in place. I saw a control room that they have in the house. It looked like they could run a village with the equipment they've got. I don't trust Martin. Both of them give me the creeps."

They heard the water from the pump nearby turn on and then quickly off.

"Beau? Is that you?" Diane stood to get a better look.

"No, it's Samuel," Charlotte said. "How much did you hear, Samuel?"

He had placed his T-shirt, now wet, over his shoulders, to cool off.

"I won't lie—all of it, Charlotte. I didn't know anyone else was out here, and I went to the pump to rinse off. I heard you start to speak and was about to reveal myself when you said that last night was a nightmare. I guess I just froze."

"It was not a conversation that you were meant to hear, and I hope you will respect my wishes and keep it to yourself."

Samuel looked her in the eyes, and Charlotte saw his go glassy with anger or, worse, pity.

"Of course." Samuel turned and quickly headed back to the barn.

"Well, that was strange," Diane said.

"I just hope to God that he doesn't get it into his head to confront Ford Barclay. I know how much Samuel hates bullies."

* * *

A little later Charlotte encountered Horse returning from breakfast in the paddock.

At least someone is having a normal morning.

"Hello, my pink friend. Shall we go see how Diane's restaurant is coming along?"

He instantly turned in the direction of the construction site and hopped along happily.

What a life.

Charlotte was hoping to chat with Danny again and, as nonchalantly as possible, try and get more details about what caused his horse to buck and send him to the hospital. *If that story is even true.*

The restaurant (it is now correct to call it that rather than the *site*) was full of activity inside and out. Additional people had delivered essentials like windows and appliances and were working on installing them. Utility company technicians were also on the scene, doing their job. Everyone was wearing a hard hat, so Charlotte watched from the doorway.

"Danny, hi!" Charlotte called out to him.

He waved to her. "I'll be right out."

Charlotte watched Danny give out directions to some of his crew. His black eye had turned yellow, and today his limp was not as pronounced. A change in color of a bruise around someone's eye usually means that it's going away. Yet he had said that he'd been hospitalized for a concussion. If that was true, then his head should still hurt, and the black eye would appear *after* the head injury.

"Hi, Charlotte—nice to see you," Danny said, and stepped outside. "Can you believe all these people? I tried to stagger deliveries, but I guess that Little Acorn works on its own time zone." He removed his hat and walked over to a picnic table by the lake.

"How's the head?" Charlotte asked, looking concerned.

"Fine," he quickly answered, and then put his hand to his eye as if he suddenly remembered the injury.

"If everything keeps running smoothly, Diane will be able to get in there and start cooking by tomorrow or the next day." Danny seemed to be trying to change the subject, but Charlotte persisted.

"I'm glad that you're recovering so quickly—that must have been some accident for them to keep you in the hospital. What happened?"

"Something spooked my horse, that's all. Why all the questions?"

"And there was no one else around to help you? Has your horse thrown you before?"

"No, of course not. I've been riding since almost before I could walk. And I'll be back in the saddle way before the Rancheros Visitadores ride in May."

"I'm relieved to hear that, and your doctor must be very pleased with your recovery. How does someone join the Rancheros? Is it like trying to get into Harvard or Vassar?" Charlotte asked, watching his reaction to every word that she'd just said.

"For many years, the club was made up of the richest, most powerful men in America. Walt Disney used to ride with them. Ronald Reagan."

"The club is men only?"

"Absolutely, and historically the weeklong ride left a path of debauchery in its wake. These days and since I've been a member, it's much more of a fundraising event for worthy causes like breast cancer research. And I'm sure you can see that I didn't get to join because of my enormous wealth. You have to be invited to become a member of this exclusive club, and if you don't have money, then you'd better have lineage," Danny explained. "And it helps if you love horses and the great outdoors. In other words, if you're a cowboy."

"Like Linc Pierce? Was he a Ranchero?" Charlotte asked.

Danny gave her a dry chuckle. "Our little Q and A session is now over. I need to get back to work. And I suggest that you focus more on your farm and less on me. Last I heard, someone or something is still killing the strawberry crops."

*　　*　　*

"You're back! Open the note, open the note!" Diane said, coming out of the kitchen, followed closely by Alice.

Their excitement was caused by the gorgeous flower arrangement in a large vase on the table in the foyer of the farmhouse.

"I had to send Beau to the market for things that we don't need just to keep him from seeing who sent these to you. He thinks that you have a secret admirer."

Charlotte grabbed the sealed note and headed to her room. "I'm pretty sure that I know who sent these, Diane, and I can assure you that there isn't an ounce of romance about it."

Once she had privacy, Charlotte opened the envelope and immediately recognized the embossed *B* on the letterhead. As she'd suspected, the flowers were from Ford.

Feeling guilty for her reaction, Charlotte texted Diane:
You can come in.

A few moments later there was a soft tap on her door, and Diane entered.

"They're from him, aren't they?"

"Yes, I was just about to read the note, but then I got cold feet. I just want to forget the entire evening. Will you read it to me?" Charlotte handed her the note.

Diane cleared he throat and began.

Dear Charlotte,

I fully recognize that even if I had the skills of the most gifted poet, no words of apology would suffice. My behavior was beyond any excuse or explanation, and I am profusely ashamed. I would not question your decision if you do not wish to see me ever again.

"He's chosen some good words, but who can tell if he's sincere about his apology," Diane commented before she continued reading.

I would like to offer the services of my agriculturalist, Martin, however. As I so ineptly tried to explain, his technical skills, along with his knowledge of farming, make him a valuable asset within the realm of his abilities. It is the least I can do, and I'd like to send him to your farm, at your convenience, to inspect your diseased strawberry crop and provide solutions. Here is his number:

"See? He couldn't do it. Ford Barclay is incapable of being contrite."

"Because he offered to send his guy over to help us with our strawberry problem?"

Charlotte shook her head. "No, because he had to tell me one more time that he was right, and I was wrong. We spent the evening arguing over the place of computers and technology in farming. We are polar opposites when it comes to that subject."

Diane nodded and thought about what Charlotte had said.

"And can you imagine how Samuel and even Joe would react if Martin came over here to show them a thing or two? You're right: Ford is a snake, just in designer clothing."

Charlotte picked up her cell phone and started dialing.

"Who are you calling?" Diane asked.

"Martin Ross."

"But you just said—"

"I'll bring Samuel in on the ruse, but we are going to get Martin to spill the beans on his boss and overlord."

"That's my girl!"

* * *

"Look who I found," Charlotte said, entering the kitchen that night.

"Katharine, welcome. You must stay for dinner. I'm serving a tasting menu of the new recipes I've developed. We're out on the patio." Diane moved to usher Katharine outside.

"How nice! I really just came by to drop off a case of my Syrah. I think that you'll like it."

"A girl's got to eat," Charlotte said, grabbing a piece of cheese off a platter and popping it into her mouth.

"That's for the feta and watermelon Greek salad!" Diane said, slapping her hand. "Now outside—both of you."

A lovely table had been set using linens and colors that Diane planned to have in her restaurant. Soft French blues mixed with whites and yellow to make it feel like it was always springtime, Diane had explained.

"You must know Chief Goodacre, Katharine," Diane said, motioning to the guest already seated at the table.

"Please, I'm off duty and it's just us girls, so call me Theresa."

Charlotte registered the stunned look on Katharine's face.

"Another wonderful surprise," Katharine said. "Diane I really do have pressing jobs at the winery to take care of tonight. Perhaps another time?"

"Nonsense, you're here and you can take an hour out for dinner," Charlotte insisted and pulled out a chair for Katharine.

"Good—that's settled. I'll be right out with your chilled gazpacho." Diane actually skipped back into the kitchen.

"I promise only to bring this subject up once, and then we can move on to brighter things, Theresa, but I have to ask if you have any updates on Linc Pierce's murder."

Diane had returned with the soup, and she sat down to hear Theresa's response to Charlotte's question.

"I know this is going to sound trite, ladies, but it's the truth. We collected a fair amount of evidence in Linc's barn, and we are following all the leads."

Diane groaned.

"What sort of evidence, Chief—I mean Theresa," Katharine asked. "Maybe I could help. I've been around barns and farm supplies all my life."

Charlotte tried another angle. "And though I'm new to farming, I'm very observant. You must have photos of what you took away, may we see them?"

"Charlotte, you should know from the last time that I can't share that information with the public while the case is still ongoing. All in due time, and I promise you that we will find this killer."

Charlotte watched Horse attempt to tiptoe quietly on little pig's feet toward Katharine's purse, which she had set on the floor beside her chair. He was intrigued by something, and Charlotte decided to let it play out a little longer, to see what had captured his attention.

"I understand completely," Katharine said. "It's so unimaginable that someone living among us could have done such a horrible deed. I wonder, has any of the evidence caused you to throw out a wider net? We do have farmworkers coming and going almost on a daily basis."

"We are pursuing all leads. Diane, I know that this is a tasting dinner, but I just must have another spoonful or two of your delicious gazpacho."

"Coming right up, and I'll bring out the next course too. It's one of Horse's favorites."

On hearing his name, Horse stopped in mid-sneak. Only after Diane returned with the food, and the conversation picked up, did he continue to move closer to Katharine's purse.

"Diane you must be so proud. This meal is incredible, and I've had nothing that measures up to it in the entire county." Katharine dug into her plate of quarter-size corn fritters topped with fresh crab and avocado.

Charlotte watched Horse zero in on his target, charge up his hind legs, and get ready to pounce into Katharine's bag. She was momentarily torn about whether or not to stop him.

"Charlotte, I'd love to hear what you and Beau learned from your visits to our Little Acorn farms." Theresa looked at her.

Just then Theresa's radio squawked loudly and came to life. Horse dove for the purse, and Katharine screamed and stood up from her chair, knocking it over. Horse thought the wiser of staying at the scene.

"I apologize—I thought that I'd turned my radio all the way down, but the opposite is true. Rookie mistake," Theresa said.

"And I have no idea what Horse was doing down there, but I can assure you that he will never be allowed around the dinner table again." Diane looked at Charlotte with wide eyes, and Charlotte calmly brushed a strand of red curls off her face. Diane smiled, seeing that Charlotte had subtly crossed her fingers.

"You were asking about our farm report. Let me go get our notes."

As Charlotte went to the foyer Diane turned to Katharine.

"I'm sorry that this was so startling. We're used to it with all the farm animals marching around. I expect that a winery is a much calmer environment," Charlotte heard her say.

Didn't Katharine just say that she'd been around farms her entire life? How could she be so frightened by a sweet little pig?

"You must realize that my winery sits beside my father's farm." Katharine laughed, and Theresa joined in. He owns the property my grapevines grow on, and he reminds me of it every chance he gets."

"Here you are, Theresa. We've made copies of our notes and had planned to give them to everyone."

"Wonderful, thanks." Theresa skimmed through the pages and stopped at the second to last one. "Speak of the devil—a little joke, Katharine. Here's the section on Boyd Hoover's farm."

"Anything stick out to you, Theresa?" Diane asked while filling plates with salad.

"Nothing he said—it's more what he didn't divulge. Please understand, Katharine, that this has nothing to do with you. Your father has been extremely uncooperative in this investigation and in working to solve the disease that has invaded our crops."

"I am not my father. You don't have to pussyfoot around me. Believe me, I have firsthand knowledge of his cantankerous side, and I don't condone it or excuse it. But I wanted you to know that he worked himself up from nothing in order to gain independence from his family. Along the way he had a lot of bad breaks and failures, many due to disloyal friends and farmworkers who mistook him for a pushover. That's what has turned him into a sometimes angry man who thinks that everyone is out to cheat him."

"Understood, and you are correct: that doesn't excuse his behavior." Theresa patted her hand.

"I'll talk to him and make sure my father gives you all access to the fields. He has his faults, but in his heart, he loves the land and will do anything to keep it producing."

"That's settled then." Diane stood up. "I have a wonderful, *light* dessert I'd like to serve."

"Not for me—I still have some things to finish tonight and an early morning appointment. But you are a winner, Diane. Everything was exceptional, and your place will be a huge success. Kudos to you too, Charlotte, and don't be too hard on the pig. He was just trying to get attention. Chief, goodnight."

Katharine picked up her purse, which Charlotte noticed had been zipped shut after Horse's attempt to raid it.

Theresa helped Diane carry plates into the kitchen, and Charlotte watched Horse slowly and deliberately approach. His head was hung low, making his ears flop forward and cover his eyes.

"It's okay, Horse. I know that you weren't trying to cause trouble. You smelled something in her bag, didn't you?"

He lifted his head, and Charlotte swore she saw him nod.

"A smell you were familiar with, right?"

Charlotte heard the deep growl of Katharine's car starting up and then the sounds of tires crunching gravel.

"Diane, you know how much I hate sweets," Charlotte said as she watched Diane carry out plates and a tray of mini pies and custards.

"So true," Diane said, and picked up the plate that she'd just deposited in front of Charlotte.

"Don't you dare!" Charlotte quickly grabbed it back, laughing.

Theresa, never shy, helped herself to one of everything.

"Despite what Katharine says, I find Boyd's chronic evasiveness curious for someone who claims to be so proud of the farm he's built."

"Do you think that there is more going on at Hoover Farms than meets the eye, Theresa?" Charlotte asked between bites of a large, chocolate-dipped strawberry.

"All I can tell you is that my deputies have been called out there on more than one occasion to break up fights between Boyd and his staff. Some involving shotguns. Then a few days later, those involved are no longer working there."

"So is Boyd Hoover a suspect?" Diane asked.

"Are we starting this all over again? I thought that I explained my position."

"You did—just curious." Diane gave her a half grin.

"I'm sure that Theresa and her officers are following a list of suspects," Charlotte continued. It could be Boyd, yes, or Martin Ross or Ford Barclay or both of them together, one or some of the farm owners in the valley that Linc snubbed or did something even worse to in the past." The entire time that Charlotte was running through her list, she and Diane were watching Theresa's expression for possible confirmation or denial. Charlotte had also taken care to leave Danny Costa off the suspect roster.

"Diane, you have one confirmed regular customer for your restaurant, and I'll spread the word." Theresa stood and turned the volume back up. And Charlotte, I enjoyed listening to your fishing expedition, but I wasn't biting. You'll have to find out who killed Linc Pierce at the same time everyone else does."

* * *

Later that night Charlotte had second thoughts about not sharing her suspicions about Danny with the Chief, especially after learning that he'd had run-ins with Linc. She was being protective of Diane, she supposed, but what if Danny was the murderer? A lot of evidence pointed his way.

Charlotte hopped out of bed, grabbed her laptop, and got quickly back under the covers. Horse, hoping for some fun, snuggled next to her and watched the screen come to life. She typed in some search parameters and waited for the results to pop up.

"Wow, Horse, Danny wasn't kidding. There are records of his family going back to the late 1800s. They must have joined the Rancheros Visitadores right when it started."

Horse pointed his snout to the screen and took in a deep sniff.

"You can't smell that?" Charlotte laughed. "you'll have to take my word for it." She read on.

"The Costa family were ranchers at first but moved on to produce about the turn of the century, it says. They grew corn, broccoli, and other vegetables. Look, Horse, here are some pictures of their old crates. I love the artwork that they used on the stamp; it looks like a view of the ocean from their farm on the mountain top."

Charlotte jumped ahead with her search to around the time she guessed that Danny came onto the scene. She searched records from 1990 onward and saw that around then Costa Farms had switched primarily to growing strawberries and had more than tripled their annual output.

"Oh no!" Charlotte said suddenly. Horse looked at her with a concerned face.

"It seems that when Danny was five, a number of family members close to him died of cancer. His great-grandfather, his great-aunt, a couple of cousins, and his grandmother. Nothing like that ever happened to the Costas before or after."

Finally, Charlotte came across court papers about a lawsuit that the Costa family had filed against a company named Agripharm.

Interesting name and spelling.

Charlotte opened another tab in her browser and brought up a previous search that she'd done about the use and history of pesticides used by the local farms.

I'll bet they couldn't resist the promise of producing bigger and better strawberries and fell into the trap of using the now-banned chemical-intensive fumigants with heavy methyl bromide solutions. And it looks like the lawsuit was thrown out for lack of evidence, she thought.

"That explains so much about Danny. He was way too young to be asked to shoulder such pain and sorrow. Eventually his grief must have turned to anger, but he has no one to blame for the deaths in his family," Charlotte said to Horse, who was on the precipice of dozing off.

Or did he finally discover who had sold the deadly fumigant to his family for all those years?

Chapter Nine

Charlotte was too keyed up with this new information about Danny and thought that it would be good to share it with Diane if she were still up. *It doesn't make him any less of a suspect in Linc's death, but it does explain the anger that is bubbling just below Danny's surface.*

Charlotte didn't want to just barge in, so she listened outside Diane's door to check if she was on the phone or sleeping. She heard Diane's voice talking softly and assumed the former. Charlotte was about to give the door a tap, when she heard a man's voice.

Embarrassed, Charlotte quickly and quietly disappeared back down the stairs. She wasn't sure what to think. On the one hand, as she'd said to Beau, Diane was a grown woman and entitled to make her own choices and have her privacy. On the other hand, Diane may be entering into a romance with a man who was set on avenging the deaths in his family.

Charlotte crawled back into bed, bleary-eyed, and reached over to hug Horse. His spot was now empty. She looked over to the French doors in the bedroom, and they remained shut.

*Where are you, Horse? Don't tell me you followed me upstairs
and now you can't get back down.*

Horse was an agile pig, but he was growing and getting
heavier, and the old wooden staircase was steep. Charlotte got up
and this time donned one of her great-uncle's oversized flannel
shirts before venturing out of her room. She had no idea whom
she might run into.

The grand foyer was almost pitch black, with only a sliver
of moonlight creeping through from under the front door.
Charlotte tilted her head in the direction of the second floor and
listened. She could no longer hear any voices. She resisted turning on the lights because she didn't want to be branded a snoop
or an overreactor to every little noise.

Charlotte stood still, listening. After about a minute, the
silence was broken by what sounded like heavy breathing coming from the living room. She looked around for something—
anything—that she could use to protect herself in case this was
an intruder.

Charlotte tried to orient herself in the foyer, remembering
that she'd stocked a side table with flashlights after the blackout
on her first night on the farm. She found a wall and began moving along it with her arms extended in front of her. She heard the
breathing again, and it was closer. One more step and Charlotte
felt the entryway to the living room.

One set of drapes for the French doors had been drawn back,
letting in more ambient light from both the moon and the solar-
powered footpath illumination. Charlotte could just make out
a dark figure peering out the glass and fogging it up on and off
with its breathing.

Finally, she heard a low grunt of displeasure and knew that the dark figure was Horse.

"What are you doing, Horse?" Charlotte asked in a whisper. "These late-night expeditions have got to stop, or you'll be sleeping in the barn."

He grunted again, and Charlotte followed his eyes out and down to the fields, where she found the subject of Horse's curiosity. Something was flying over the strawberry field. It was too large and the wrong shape to be an owl, and it had the ability to stop in midair and hover.

A drone! And I know who owns lots of drones. Ford Barclay.

Charlotte now had a valid reason and flipped on a lamp in the living room. She heard footsteps outside and then the closing of a car door. As the engine started up, Charlotte ran to the front door and threw it open. If she'd had another fifteen seconds, she'd have seen who was driving instead of just watching the dark back end of a vehicle without lights disappear down the drive.

*   *   *

The next morning Charlotte rose, dazed and confused. Had she seen and heard the things that she was now remembering? Had Danny spent the night with Diane? Was the person she heard snooping around the strawberry fields the one sabotaging their crops? It couldn't have been Danny if he were otherwise engaged.

Then there was the drone sighting.

Did I dream that?

Charlotte let Horse out, and he raced down to the field where the drone had been seen.

I guess it wasn't a dream. I'm back to Ford and Martin. Could he be that petty just because I snubbed his romantic advances? And what the heck is Boyd Hoover hiding?

Charlotte found a kettle of warm water on the stove in the kitchen and made herself a cup of English breakfast tea. Diane and Alice were working side by side, creating an array of lunch dishes. It felt to Charlotte as if they were speaking their own language.

"Do you have any julienned carrots you can spare?"

"How long should the figs braise in port wine?"

It's nice to see how Alice has come alive under Diane's guidance in cooking, Charlotte thought. At first, she was protective of her domain, never having been challenged before in the kitchen. But Diane was bringing out skills in Alice that she never knew she had, and there were few things more joyous to Charlotte than watching a person grow.

In a way, Charlotte was glad to see Alice because it meant that she couldn't talk to Diane about last night. And maybe this was a reminder that this was none of her business.

"Morning, chefs. Everyone have a good night?"

"Inspiring." Diane smiled. "Look how productive we've already been."

"That looks yummy," Charlotte said, reaching for a sundried tomato.

"Charlotte Finn! No sampling allowed. I banish you from our kitchen," Diane proclaimed, and punctuated her words with the wave of a wooden spoon.

"Alright, I know when I'm not wanted."

Charlotte turned toward the doorway and ran smack into Martin Ross.

"What are you doing here?" she said, flustered.

"We have an appointment. I did knock several times, but no one answered, and the door was ajar."

"We probably drowned you out with appliances," Alice said, smiling at Martin.

"Yes, of course, thank you for coming. Let's head down to the barn, where Samuel is waiting. They left the farmhouse and ambled down the hill.

"It sure is beautiful up here, and seeing the lake filled again, it's like paradise."

"No, you're the one who lives in paradise. That farm is jaw-dropping," Charlotte replied.

"It looks that way because Ford wanted it to and made it so. This here . . . there are no boundaries, no big walls—this farm is the way it is because nature wanted it to be." Charlotte noticed Martin struggle to find the words he seemed to be filling with emotion.

"I'm surprised you say that, being the techno wizard that you are."

"You can be both, Charlotte. I'm an agriculturalist first. If I didn't love the land, then I might as well be in a rabbit-warren cubicle in Silicon Valley." Martin grinned at his description.

"That's right," Charlotte continued. "Controlling the world with a joystick and a keyboard while drinking a big, gulp-sized energy drink."

They both laughed at the thought as Horse came racing toward Charlotte.

"Hello, you sweet man," Charlotte greeted him. Samuel looked up to Charlotte and smiled before realizing that she'd been talking to Horse.

Awkward.

"Samuel, you and Martin have met before, haven't you?" Charlotte quickly said to cover for the mistake.

"A couple of times," Samuel said, and shook his hand without making eye contact.

"Good to see you Samuel. You still working on restoring that old Ford pickup? Nineteen sixty-six, isn't it? I'd be happy to help if I get some time off."

Samuel looked surprised by the gesture, and Charlotte was equally taken aback. She'd had no idea that he had a project that he was working on for fun.

Why shouldn't he?

"The strawberry fields are this way," Samuel replied coolly.

"Samuel!" Charlotte reprimanded, and then instantly regretted it.

Horse followed along and looked back and forth from Samuel to Martin, as if he were trying to figure out the dynamic between the two of them.

"I don't see any bait traps or plants like garlic that repel rodents. What are you doing about them? Could they be the culprits destroying your strawberries?" Martin asked.

Before Samuel could respond, Charlotte saw Ginger swoop down and dive-bomb Martin's head. She looked at Horse and could swear that he was laughing.

"That's our rat control. Very effective," Samuel replied, deadpan.

"They have never done that before. I am so sorry. See, Fred and Ginger are expecting, so they are understandably protective of their brooding box," Charlotte explained. "But during the day, that's very odd."

Charlotte's mind immediately started processing what had just happened as Samuel showed Martin the damaged strawberry crops. *Had the owls encountered Martin before today? Maybe he'd chased them off the Barclay Farm before coming here? That's a giant leap even for you, Charlotte.*

Ultimately Charlotte decided that the owls sensed some danger when they all walked past their brooding box. It could have been triggered by any one of them. *Still . . .*

When Samuel and Martin returned from their inspection, Charlotte could hear that their conversation had gotten argumentative.

Charlotte watched Horse stop in his tracks and look up at the owl house. This time Fred was peering out and down, ready to swoop.

Oh no.

Seeing the concern on Charlotte's face, Horse launched into a chorus of grunts while running around the post holding the owl house. The circle grew in diameter as the men neared, forcing them to give the pig and his antics a wide berth. When Charlotte looked back up, the owl had retreated.

"This isn't a farm; this is a zoo without cages," Martin shouted to Samuel as he began walking at a fast clip away from Horse.

Samuel gave Charlotte a look, and they both snickered.

"Look, if you change your mind someday and want to install some computer-controlled traps, let me know, and I'll help you set them up, Samuel," Martin said. Charlotte thought it was a sort of peace offering for his snide comment about the farm.

"No thanks. Instead of trying to cheat nature, I prefer to respect it. You see anything in our strawberries you can share?

At least what might be causing this disease? If not, I've got work to do."

"As a matter of fact, I did. It looks like your crop was exposed to too much nitrogen, which basically caused the berries to freeze. Although I've never seen this kind of thing happen overnight. I'd expect lots of residue from a heavy spray. Can you think of anything with high levels like that that might have been applied to the crop?"

Samuel hung his head down in thought.

"No, I can't. I would never use any fertilizer that wasn't one hundred percent natural, and that's where the nitrogen would come into play with farms that don't." Samuel looked at Charlotte, who gave him a slight nod. "How does this compare to the problems you're having with your strawberries on Barclay Farm?"

"Well, we've been a bit lucky because of our motion sensor fields," Martin explained. "How are your tomato crops doing?"

"Tell us about these sensors, please?" Charlotte moved closer to him, hoping to stop Martin from changing the subject again.

"Ford installed microwave-based sensors all over his fields. The technology sends out microwave pulses and then calculates the reflection of any moving object. Once it's tripped, the system sends an alert to our control room—the one you saw Charlotte—and we determine if there is a threat or not."

"And this runs all night long?" Charlotte asked. "It can't be good for the animals to be constantly exposed to microwaves. There could be long-term damage done."

"It has greatly reduced our critter problems." Martin half grinned.

"You imbecile! Don't you have any clue what role these creatures play in ensuring the success of your farm?" Samuel shouted at Martin.

"I'm not the one with dead and dying strawberries." Martin stood up tall to him.

Charlotte could see that the situation was close to a boiling point.

"Samuel?" Charlotte got his attention. "Maybe we should show Martin those pieces of metal that we've been finding in that specific field?"

"I don't see how—"

Charlotte gave Samuel a look that stopped him from continuing. "This way, Martin."

Once inside the barn, Samuel walked to the side where the tackle for Pele was stored and took a burlap bag down off a peg on the wall. He walked over to a workbench and laid the metal pieces out on the tabletop.

"See? They appear to be pieces that have broken off from a larger metal object. You have any idea what?" Charlotte asked as she watched him pick up a fragment and turn it over in his hand.

"This isn't metal—it's carbon. And this piece is made of thermoplastic. Both are parts of a quadcopter or hexa-copter." Martin continued to examine the items.

Charlotte and Samuel stared at him, waiting for some sort of translation.

"In other words, these are parts of a drone," Martin clarified. "This is most likely part of the frame of the device and is made from something called carbon fiber–reinforced composite. The material has the lowest density and highest strength, to keep the drone light but tough as nails. These other pieces look to be from a broken rotor. These blades often break and need to be replaced, so you'd typically go with ones made of thermoplastic. It's cheaper."

"You fly drones like this one?" Samuel bluntly asked.

"Similar, but if you know Ford Barclay, he has to put his own stamp on everything. Including the design, size, and color of a drone. This one is definitely not part of his fleet."

"Wouldn't we have heard if someone was flying drones over our fields?" Charlotte asked, intrigued.

"Not necessarily. They're built to run with limited noise. Especially if they are being used for stealth operations."

Martin didn't say that as a joke, and Charlotte got a chill.

"Okay then. Thanks," Samuel said, and walked out of the barn.

"I'll walk you back up," Charlotte said. As they started up the hill, she asked, "Are there many people in Little Acorn that operate drones? For agricultural use? It sounds like this would be quite expensive to pursue as a hobby."

"Like everything, cost and quality run the spectrum. But if you cut corners on the investment for commercial use, you're pretty much throwing your money away. Farmers aren't using drones to watch their neighbors in the shower; they're using them for irrigation, fertilizer distribution, pest control, and all-around efficiency," Martin replied looking her directly in the eyes.

Once again, she got a chill. *In the shower? This guy is making a habit of giving me the creeps.*

As they approached the Finn Family Farm's big circular driveway, Charlotte thought back to something Ford Barclay had said about Martin not knowing about everything that he did or experimented with. He could have an arsenal of drones that Martin's never seen, and the pieces she'd found could be a casualty.

Once on the drive, Charlotte waved to Danny, who was getting some tools from his truck. Martin had stopped dead in his tracks.

"You know you can't come near me, Danny Costa," Martin shouted at him.

"My only problem with you, Martin, is that you work for a monster. He's the one who killed my family. I don't know what business you have with this guy, but by association I have to see you as an accomplice," Danny shouted. He spat into the dirt and then headed down to the restaurant.

Suddenly Charlotte felt Samuel rush up behind her, presumably after having heard all the yelling.

"What was that all about, Martin?" she asked him.

"Nothing to do with me. You'll have to ask Danny Costa what he's talking about."

"I intend to, especially since he accused Ford Barclay of killing his family!" Charlotte leaned back against Samuel's chest, frustrated and frightened.

This feels better.

"Look, I'm sorry for the dust-up, but it really has nothing to do with me," Martin said, and got into his shiny, sleek black car. Charlotte and Samuel watched him drive off, nearly running into a car coming up to the farm.

"That's a helluva car for a farmer to drive," Samuel said.

"Danny said that he'd never heard of Barclay Farms or Ford and Martin," Charlotte turned and told Samuel. He nodded and paused in thought for a moment.

"You know that I don't stick my nose in other folk's business, and I expect the same courtesy in return."

"Of course."

"But there are some things about Danny you ought to know that will help explain what you just witnessed. And hopefully stop you from going off on a wild horse ride before you have a firm hold of the reins."

"Just what is that supposed to mean?"

"Whoa, woman, don't get your Irish up," Samuel said as he stepped back from her and put his hands up in a "surrender" pose. "I'm just asking you to listen to all the facts first."

"Of course, I will, Samuel. Why wouldn't I?"

Samuel started to respond but then thought better of it.

"Well?" Charlotte prodded, her hands on her hips.

"Let's walk out to the dock so we can look at the lake while I tell you the story."

She nodded and followed him. When Charlotte inherited the farm, the lake had been neglected for years, and instead of the beautiful body of water she remembered swimming in as a child visiting her uncle, it was nearly empty and had a broken-down dock and an accumulation of dead leaves and branches rotting on the bottom. Charlotte insisted on restoring it to its original glory and got help from the local fire department because it was a valuable water resource during wildfire season. Toward completion, the entire town had come out to help and celebrate its rebirth.

The new lake had also become host to a wide variety of Grebe aquatic diving birds that liked to gracefully slip underwater, one right after the other like synchronized swimmers, then reemerge, sometimes twenty feet away. Ducks and geese had adopted the lake as their favorite watering hole; and contributing to Horse's pure joy, along with everyone else's, a great blue heron had graced them with his presence. Looking like a cross between a prehistoric pterodactyl with a majestic long neck and delicate giraffe-like legs, this heron gave off a Zen-like aura every time it stood statue still atop a tree, stalking its prey. Because of its color and backswept head plumes, Charlotte had named him "Elvis."

"I don't know how much you've heard or read about the use of dangerous pesticides around here in the past," Samuel began, "but some squirrely politicians and chemical companies dodged restrictions that the rest of the country had to obey, in order to grow monster crops of strawberries."

They had sat down at the end of the dock, both with their legs dangling over the water. It was getting close to midday, and the sun was burning the last of the morning mist from the surface of the lake. It was magical. Horse and Mrs. Robinson nuzzled between them, making it one big, happy family.

"I've read about it, Samuel. Pretty unconscionable what was allowed to continue given the deaths and damage to the ozone layer. Makes me sick to my stomach."

"Understandable, so hopefully you won't think too harshly of Danny for his actions.

Charlotte knew what the pesticides had done to his family, but nothing else. She wondered where Diane was right now.

Samuel paused to watch a snowy egret, its wings spread, run with the grace of a ballet dancer in toe shoes atop the water in the shallow edge of the lake. Its feet stirred up sediment that startled its prey into motion. Horse was on his feet in admiration.

"In a way Danny wasn't lying when he said that he didn't know Ford Barclay, or Martin for that matter. He was obeying a court order that stipulated that he stay clear away from them and essentially pretend that they don't exist."

"But why?"

"That's what I'm coming to—a little patience."

Instead, Charlotte pouted.

"Danny got it into his head as a teenager that the Barclay family whose business is pharmaceuticals, had branched off into agriculture and was supplying the poisonous fumigants that the local farmers were using. At that point Danny had lost three family members to cancer that was believed to have been caused by this methyl bromide."

"Is that true?"

"It was never proven, but Danny and other folks continued to suffer losses."

Charlotte thought back to her research and recalled that the Costa family had filed a lawsuit against a company named Agripharm. *Worth delving into again.*

"At fifteen, Danny was caught trespassing on Barclay's property. This was before Ford had gotten so rich and installed all that fancy security equipment. Word had it that evidence showed that Danny was coming close to lighting a match that would set the whole place ablaze."

"Oh wow. He was fifteen?" Charlotte put her hand to her mouth.

"Yes, but keep in mind that for at least the past three years he had watched his beloved aunts, uncles, and grandparents suffer and die. That's too much for an adult, let alone a boy."

"Poor Danny. So, what happened?"

"He spent a couple of nights in jail, but because he was a juvenile, his record was sealed, a prison sentence was waived, and he got a permanent restraining order to stay away from Ford Barclay and anyone associated with him. Does that help explain things?"

"More than you know."

Chapter Ten

Charlotte and Samuel sat silently on the dock. She allowed Danny's story sink in and tried to evaluate where this information might fit in with the murder of Linc Pierce.

"There's also what Martin told us about Barclay Farms to throw into the mix," Charlotte said after a moment.

"You mean using microwave sensors to keep his fields secure?"

Charlotte nodded. "Great job worming that out of him."

"I would have gotten a lot more if you hadn't been there."

"Good thing that I was. We need to keep them thinking that they are not suspects," Charlotte said, standing up.

"Maybe they are and maybe they're not. But I'm going to talk to Joe about the legalities of using those sensors around people and animals. It makes my blood boil."

"And I guess it really doesn't matter who supplied this killer fumigant to Little Acorn. It was being used all over the state and distributed by some very large manufacturers. Swirling around in this cast of characters is a motive and a murderer."

Samuel nodded and stood as well.

"But as far as we know, Linc had no involvement with any pesticides—maybe back then, but certainly not in the last fifteen years or more. You just have to look at his decomposing farm to know that."

Samuel's statement triggered a thought in Charlotte's mind. She remembered two things: the liquid that she'd seen on the workbench in Linc's farm and the state of his lone strawberry crop. Which could only be described as vibrant and prosperous.

"When was the last time you visited Linc's farm?"

"It's been a while, haven't had any cause to go there. It might even have been right after your uncle passed. I wanted to tell some of the guys who knew him from way back, in person."

So Linc had had plenty of time to get his hands on some of that pesticide or make it himself. That would explain the condition of his now blossoming strawberries. Time to pay a visit to Chief Goodacre . . .

As Charlotte quickened her steps back to the farm, another dark car caught her eye as it wound its way up to the farmhouse.

"Just the person I wanted to see!" Katharine Hoover shouted out her window as she parked in the shade under an acacia tree.

"Katharine, nice to see you. Let me introduce you to Samuel Brown, the real farmer in this oasis."

"We know each other," Samuel mumbled, and then turned and headed down to the barn.

Katharine seemed not to notice or care. Charlotte decided not to probe further as it was clear Katharine had something on her mind. But it didn't stop Charlotte from wondering if the two of them had been romantically involved in the past. *Why is this bothering me?*

"I can't believe how warm it is already—it isn't even noon," Charlotte said, opening the car door for Katharine. "Let's go sit at one of the outside tables by the restaurant. I'm sure that Diane would love to see you as well."

"Sounds perfect. I just wanted to update you on my latest conversation with my dad," Katharine said, watching Charlotte walking beside her. "You seem so at ease here, it's hard for me to imagine that you were ever away from this farm, let alone working a fast-paced job in a big city."

Horse once again attempted a stealth root inside Katharine's bag, triggering a less than stealth admonishment from Charlotte.

"I'm right with you—sometimes I have to pinch myself. But I don't regret a thing. I learned, often the hard way, what I was capable of in Chicago—I don't mean literally with my career, but overall, as a person going through life. I think that's why I've been able to face the enormous challenges on this farm head-on and deal with them, in no small part because of the help from Diane and Beau. And of course Samuel."

Charlotte checked for a reaction from Katharine at the mention of Samuel's name but got nothing.

"I've attempted to speak to my father, who you know can have a temper that runs just a degree below boiling point. Chief Goodacre has been by twice to try and talk to him. He's refused to do so without a warrant, and the sight of her just adds fuel to the fire. He is convinced, Charlotte, that you have implicated him in the murder of Linc Pierce."

"What? I've done no such thing!" *Does Boyd have a guilty conscience?*

"I know that, but at the moment there's no trying to reason with him. He wasn't always like this, Charlotte. He had a happy childhood growing up in Castroville. His family grows artichokes, and the business has expanded into quite the enterprise. But my father is the youngest and was constantly under the thumbs of his two bigger, older brothers. They are twins and could gang up on him and easily bring him to tears. My grandfather was grooming them to take over the farm, leaving my dad with not much of a future. So just after they got married, he and my mother moved down here. She lasted about a year and a half but missed her family and friends terribly, and one day just left us high and dry. On top of that, strawberry farming was difficult for dad. He had no idea what he was doing, and people took advantage of him. He turned into a bitter man at a young age, Charlotte."

"I'm sorry to hear that. A man's pride can be as fragile as a house of cards during a windstorm." Charlotte tried to weigh whether this backstory made Boyd any less of a suspect in her mind.

"Unlike us women who can stand up to anything. I'm not making excuses for him—he's stubborn as a mule and can be positively nasty when he's in a mood. My father and I have had some legendary fights and even brought out the Chief and her deputies a few times. But dad is not a murderer."

Charlotte studied Katharine's face with a look of compassion that disguised her attempt to look for any signs that Katharine wasn't being entirely honest with her.

"Give him a little more time. He'll settle down—he always does. Then I'll have you over and give you a tour of my vineyards.

You'll be impressed. And I'll make sure we run into my father, and I promise that he'll be on his best behavior." Katharine patted Charlotte's hand.

How can she be so sure? Does she have some kind of hold on her dad?

"Why wasn't I invited to this party?" Diane asked, walking up to them.

"You were—that's why we're here waiting for you to finish in the restaurant," Katharine explained.

"And what am I? Chopped strawberries?" Beau asked as he followed close behind Diane.

"This was to be a girls' gathering, but I guess we can make an exception," Charlotte said, looking at the others for approval.

"Whew. I was starting to think that I'd need a wardrobe change to be invited to join this exclusive band of Sisters of the Soil."

"Katharine this is my brother Beau; Beau meet Katharine Hoover."

"The pleasure is all mine," Beau said, taking her hand in both of his.

Katharine giggled. "Are you visiting Diane, or do you live here as well?"

"Up until about an hour ago, I would have had to say the latter, but Chief Goodacre has finally been convinced that my conversation with Linc Pierce was just that and not some big, threatening altercation as some of the farmers would have you believe. Wait—did Diane say that your last name is Hoover?"

"Yes, Katharine is Boyd Hoover's daughter, but we have no proof that he is responsible for grossly exaggerating what happened with Linc," Charlotte said to Beau.

"I can vouch for his behavior—"

"Of course, I humbly apologize." Beau was genuinely contrite; he hated the idea of hurting someone's feelings.

"I hadn't finished. I was about to say that this is exactly the kind of passive aggressive behavior that I've come to expect from my father. Having been bullied by his brothers growing up, he has turned into one himself," Katharine explained to the surprised group.

"It was probably several of the men who were there, Katharine, but in either case, we certainly don't hold it against you," Charlotte said. "So, Beau, does this mean that you are free to roam as you please?"

"I'm a ramblin' man, Charlotte. I'll be returning to the homestead for a spell, but I'll be back for my belle sister's grand opening." Beau kicked some dirt in an "aw shucks" gesture.

"I've got to get back to the winery—I'm expecting a delivery shortly," Katharine announced, and they all headed back up to the farmhouse.

They said their goodbyes in front of the house, and as Diane turned to go inside, Charlotte held her back.

Without bringing up last night and the male voice she'd heard from behind the closed door of Diane's bedroom, Charlotte shared the story Samuel had just told her about Danny's run in with the law and Barclay Farms when he was still a teenager.

"I am shocked. Are you sure it's true?"

"I could list many things about Samuel that annoy me, but I am hundred percent sure that he does not or would not lie to me. In fact, he's often too blunt."

"But clearly Danny does. Why would he keep his past troubles a secret from me unless he has something more to hide?" Diane plopped down on the front steps.

"Technically Danny hasn't lied. He's just chosen not to share what must have been one of the most desperate times of his young life. Why has he kept it from you? Are you two at that stage in your relationship? Are you ready to share some unpleasant secrets of your own?"

"What? No! Just out of curiosity, which secret were you thinking of? You know all mine." Diane raised her eyebrow, waiting for a response.

"I'm not saying that Danny is guilt free or honest as the day is long, Diane. That's why I passed along what I'd been told. Keep your guard up, but I wouldn't approach him about this right now. You're too close to finishing the restaurant."

"Agreed, and you do the same. Promise?"

"Promise." *Unless I sense some real danger . . .*

* * *

Charlotte decided that a face-to-face meeting was the best approach. The Chief had obviously made some kind of progress on the case, or she wouldn't have released the restrictions on Beau. She also wanted to confirm what her deputies had found in Linc Pierce's barn.

The small-town atmosphere was as usual in full swing as Charlotte parked in front of the police station. The extra-wide main street through town was built that way to accommodate farm truck passage and so that both sides of the road had ample head-in parking. Only on special occasions, such as the Fourth of July parade, were latecomers forced to leave their cars in the outdoor lot two streets over.

You encountered basically two kinds of people on any given day in Little Acorn—those going about their business with purpose and those whose purpose was prying into your business. In other words, the vibrant rumor mill. It could take the form of neighboring shopkeepers appearing to get some air in their doorways while keeping watchful eyes on the foot traffic, or a collection of the area's elder farmers emeritus who maintained that they'd earned their right to sit in the Adirondack chairs provided by the town on the sidewalks and share what they knew or what they'd "heard."

Lastly there were the "floaters," who could be any age and gender. These people were the carrier pigeons of local gossip, quick to move up and down the thoroughfare, spreading the word. They never stayed in one place too long, which explained why some rumors got greatly distorted as they were passed along from recipient to recipient.

"Hello, Charlotte," Chief Goodacre said, running into her while exiting the station.

"Just the person I wanted to see. Can you spare a few minutes to compare notes on the Linc Pierce case?" Charlotte asked, putting on the charm.

"Not here, I can't. I'm on my way to meet up with Linc's great-granddaughter at his farm. Her name is Margaret, and she's not a farmer, so she has started the process of putting it up for sale. You're welcome to tag along. We can stop for lunch on the way back."

Perfect, and the best segue for discussing what was found at the crime scene.

* * *

136

This being Charlotte's second trip to the Pierce farm and because she wasn't doing the driving, she was able to really take in the surroundings. The transition was subtle, but Charlotte recognized that the farms and the land they sat on were growing less vibrant, less well maintained, and in some cases downright moribund.

"The more we drive into this area, the more it looks like the people living here just up and left from one day to the next. Like they gave up. How long has it been this way, Chief?"

"That's a good way of describing it, as depressing as it sounds. I would say that many of the farms you're looking at never fully recovered from the 1980s crisis. Production was way up, but that led to a steep fall in the price of produce. The farmers were carrying heavy debt from land and equipment bought in better days, and interest rates had gone through the roof. They were banking on being able to use the pesticides and growth chemicals they had been using, but then the loopholes were closed, and they were banned."

"Not a moment too soon, from what I've read," Charlotte said.

"Amen to that, sister. The old guys had been farming the way their families had for generations. It became an old-dog-new-tricks situation, and many just gave up. Ah, that must be her."

The Chief pulled into the dirt entrance to the Pierce Farm, and Charlotte watched as they approached a thirtyish woman, very inappropriately dressed for the terrain, standing beside a rental car.

The Chief wasn't exaggerating—she looks like she can't wait to get out of here. If only she could run in those shoes.

"You must be Margaret," the Chief said, exiting the police van. I am so sorry for your loss. Your great-grandfather was a fixture around Little Acorn."

Perfect way to express it without saying what kind of "fixture" he was.

"Hello. I'm Charlotte Finn. I own a farm nearby."

"And she and a friend of hers were the ones who found Linc." The Chief studied Margaret's face for a reaction.

"Thank you, I guess. This is all so overwhelming to me," Margaret replied.

"Completely understandable. I know what it's like to be dropped in an entirely foreign environment. A little over a year ago, you would have found me working as an advertising exec in Chicago."

"Don't worry—we'll walk you through everything." The Chief patted Margaret's shoulder.

"You said over the phone that this has been ruled a homicide? I'm in shock. Is there any news on who did this?" Margaret looked to the Chief for answers.

"Some. We started with a very big suspect list that we have been able to narrow down in the last week. As you know, your great grandfather had lived a long life, so we've had quite a large pool of people to look at. And then there is the element of motive. Someone, or some people, tried to disguise his murder as a suicide. That adds a whole other dimension to the case." The Chief laid out the facts with a gentle tone.

Margaret shook her head and sighed. "Look, my great-grandfather could be monumentally ornery, especially as he got older. He believed in conspiracy theories and always said that people were out to get him. Sometimes he made it incredibly difficult to be around him, which is why my brothers and sisters and I have kept our distance.

Sounds just like Boyd Hoover.

"But one thing I know for sure is that he would never take his own life. He loved the land and farming too much. And he wouldn't have passed up a chance to prove himself right that someone wanted him dead. I'm here to get the property ready for sale, bring home any belongings that might matter to the family, and then we can mourn him in our own way."

"Your great-grandfather was a farmer his whole life?" Charlotte asked, sensing an opening for learning about Linc's past.

The Chief was tacitly leading them toward the barn.

"He was a salesman at heart. He started out peddling farm equipment and tools all around the county and eventually transitioned over to fertilizers and pest control. My parents told me that for several years he was making an impressive amount of money," Margaret explained, and shivered in spite of the hot day when they arrived at the entrance to the barn.

Charlotte and the Chief looked at each other after hearing that.

"You would come here to visit when you were little? That's what I did with my great-uncle." Charlotte snuck a glance into the barn, looking for the workbench.

"Not that I can remember. We're all from Bakersfield, up north, and the family has worked in the oil and gas industry for years. We're engineers mostly. My great-grandfather always preferred to earn his living by using his 'gut sense' as he called it. He'd tell us that the best thing about his job was that when you woke up in the morning, you had no idea what the day would bring. Usually, Mother Nature would reveal herself before the dew burned off the vines."

Margaret stopped talking, and Charlotte could see that she was lost in her reminiscences.

"We've gotten everything that we need from the crime scene, so there shouldn't be any encumbrances to you selling the property right away," the Chief told her.

That also gave Charlotte the green light to enter the barn and look around. It wasn't an exaggeration to say the place had been swept clean. There was nothing on the workbench; the old furniture and TV had been removed; and there was nothing hanging from the rafters. Charlotte could hear the Chief and Margaret talking outside, and did a survey of the area while they were distracted. She started by walking the perimeter of the four walls, and with each round moved a little closer in. By the third pass, Charlotte did another check outside and saw that Margaret was signing some papers on the hood of the Chief's car.

I've got another couple of minutes . . .

The sun had moved to the backside window of the barn, casting a spotlight across the floor to just beyond the workbench. Behind the far leg of the bench, something was glowing bright and caught her eye. She remembered the piece of metal that she had kicked on the day they found the body and quickly moved in to retrieve it. Charlotte got on her hands and knees and crawled under the table to retrieve it.

"Just what are you doing?" she heard the Chief holler at her.

Think fast.

"I'm trying to get the cat. You saw it—black with white paws. It ran past us when we got to the barn. I would hate to think that the poor thing ends up locked in here with no food or water."

Charlotte was reaching around with one hand behind her back while looking at the Chief.

Chief Goodacre grabbed her flashlight off her utility belt and shone it in her direction.

"Perfect, that should help," Charlotte said just as her hand closed around a cool, hard object that felt like metal.

"Here kitty, kitty," Charlotte coaxed.

The Chief did a sweep with her flashlight and then brought it back, so the light was directly on Charlotte's face.

"I've been around the rodeo, and I am sure that this is not about any darned cat. I don't know what you're up to, but it better not be messing in my investigation."

"But, Chief, it was so cute."

"Drop it."

"Yes, Chief."

It was clear that you'd have to get up very early to put one over on the Chief, and Charlotte was just relieved that she hadn't demanded to frisk her . . . yet. Charlotte wasn't feeling guilt-free for hiding possible evidence in Linc's death from the Chief, but she wanted to know what it was first. For Beau's sake, as he had just been taken off the suspect list, and for Diane's sake in the event that it pointed directly to Danny. A couple of days were all she'd need, and then she'd turn it over with some excuse on how it came into her possession. She reached into her pocket and used her fingers to try to assess what this small piece of metal was, but got no clues.

When they walked out of the barn, they saw that two cars had pulled into the farm. Margaret made the introductions: one gentleman was the real estate agent, and the other was handling her great-grandfather's estate.

"Finally, a bit of good news," Margaret told them. "It seems that my great-grandfather was more prudent with his money than we ever suspected. He set aside enough to get the property ready to go on the market. And a nice sum left over for his heirs."

"That's a relief. I'm so happy for you, and I wish you the best of luck. If you need anything—advice, a shoulder to cry on—I've written down my number for you." Charlotte handed Margaret a folded scrap of paper and gave her a hug before following the Chief to her car.

I wonder how long that money has been sitting in Linc's account and, more importantly, where it came from.

Chapter Eleven

"I want to take you to my favorite creamery and dairy farm for a bite, Charlotte. I suspect that you've never been there, and I always support our local farmers whenever possible."

"I love it already." Up until now they'd driven mostly in silence, and Charlotte suspected that, like her, the Chief was ruminating about the new information that they had just gotten concerning Linc Pierce and his estate. Charlotte figured that she'd let the Chief lead the conversation over lunch, and if she still didn't get the information she was searching for, she'd find a way to worm it out of her. Or, better yet, she'd just up and ask her.

They pulled off the highway and onto a dirt road that had no signage on the cattle fence. Charlotte looked ahead and saw nothing but more dirt and pastures. She gave the Chief a questioning look.

"We're going in the back way—saves us about thirty minutes. But I promise that you won't be disappointed."

"Is this all part of the dairy farm?" Charlotte asked.

"No, but for some reason no one bothers me when I cut

through in my cruiser. You'll know when we hit the outskirts of the farm." The Chief grinned; she was enjoying keeping Charlotte guessing.

About five minutes in, Charlotte saw a moderate change in the terrain. The road had become paved, although crudely, and the land had turned greener and was populated by oak trees. It appeared that any landscaping was done by a smattering of free-roaming cows and sheep.

"This may look like a poorly maintained pasture with a rag-tag collection of grazing farm animals, but it's actually a carefully planned and designed system for climate-smart agriculture. The farmer boys call it 'silvopasture,'" Chief Goodacre explained.

"Really? How does it work?" Charlotte was intrigued.

"I only understand the broad strokes, but it has to do with creating the right combination of pasture with its natural grasses, trees, and animals to greatly improve soil health for multiple yields. That's how it was explained to me. I think of it more like a potluck supper, where everybody brings something to the table."

"I love that idea!" Charlotte beamed. "It is kind of like what we're doing with fertilization and pest control. All our resources support a common goal. Speaking of which, I was hoping that we could share what we've learned about Linc Pierce's tragic murder?'

Charlotte was treading lightly and hoped that this was an appropriate segue.

"Nice try. I'd love to hear what you've discovered in your latest attempt at sleuthing, but the case is ongoing, and I won't divulge much." The Chief was not to be played, and Charlotte hoped that some crusty bread and ripe cheese might loosen her up.

They had reached the perimeter of the creamery, and Charlotte saw a wrought iron archway over an open gate that read "Blue Fescue Ranch & Creamery."

"And here we are. How about you grab us a table on the patio, and I'll go in and organize a cheese and charcuterie plate?" the Chief said, not waiting for a reply.

Charlotte did as she was told and was immediately captivated by the show going on just about fifty feet away from her in a large, fenced, natural enclosure.

"That's our goat pen and barn," a young woman explained, placing napkins and ice-water glasses on the table. They put in the big red barn enclosure about four years ago and lined it with soft hay, which makes for cozy sleeping."

Charlotte smiled at the girl, who couldn't have been more than seventeen or eighteen.

"I love how they scamper and play with each other. We only have a couple of goats on our farm, and this makes me want a lot more!"

"Wait until you taste the cheese. Happy goats make for delicious milk."

The Chief appeared with a long platter that looked more like an abundant horn of plenty.

"I couldn't say no so I thought that we'd try one of everything."

"Thank goodness you did—this looks amazing!" Charlotte took a moment to "eat with her eyes" first. On one side were all the creamery products and their accompaniments: warm baguette slices with truffle butter, goat cheeses and hard cheeses, fresh and dried fruits, toasted almonds, homemade honey, olives, and a selection of crackers. On the other side were the cured, thin-sliced meats—salami, prosciutto, smoked sausage—along with quartered figs and grain mustard.

"That announcement about Linc's estate was a surprise, wasn't it, Chief? I mean, to look around his farm, you'd have thought that it had been abandoned."

"On the surface, yes," the Chief said in between bites, "but his strawberry crops were in excellent shape. Have you tried these olives?"

Charlotte reached for a couple.

"Maybe Linc was too afraid or stingy to spend any of the money that Margaret told us he made years back selling fertilizer and pesticides." Charlotte watched the Chief's face for a reaction, but all she saw was a closed-eyes look of pure delight as she let some goat cheese melt in her mouth. "And maybe Linc was still experimenting with banned substances like heavy doses of methyl bromide? That would explain the success of his strawberries. Was there any evidence of that found around his property?"

"You're going to need to put on your waders and get yourself a wide-brimmed sunhat because you're going to be fishin' a long time before you'll drag confidential criminal case information out of me."

The Chief let out a hearty laugh but then stopped, presumably after seeing Charlotte slump her shoulders and let out a big, disappointed sigh.

"I understand how this process is supposed to work. You've certainly drummed that into me over the past year. It's just, you have to appreciate what's at stake for me. For us. There's a blight killing all our strawberry crops and thus our livelihood. It's hard to imagine that not being somehow connected to Linc's death.

And if this blight is manmade, which I'm almost sure it must be, then who would stand to benefit the most by being the last strawberry farm standing?"

The Chief took a long moment to wipe her hands with a paper napkin, having satisfied her cheese and charcuterie itch. In fact, she began methodically cleaning each individual finger. Charlotte fought with herself to stay patient and quiet until the Chief was done. She was clearly thinking about what Charlotte had said, and Charlotte didn't want to jeopardize any possibility of quid pro quo.

"Okay, let's play the hypothetical game. But remember this is conjecture, not fact."

"Of course." Charlotte nodded her head slowly to show her respectful compliance.

"Let's start with Boyd Hoover—such a charming fellow. His goal is to win at all costs."

"Win what?"

"Everything—it doesn't matter what. It could be as serious as building a strawberry growing monopoly and driving all the other farms around into bankruptcy. Or it could be guessing how many eggs a hen has laid overnight. He was born without scruples, so sabotage would most certainly be in his toolkit. And since I haven't been able to inspect his own crops yet, his claim about damage might be totally bogus. I just need enough evidence to go to the judge for a warrant."

Charlotte once again felt the metal object in her pocket and wondered if that was the piece the Chief needed. When she pulled her hand back out, she noticed that her thumb and been cut and was bleeding lightly. She quickly daubed it with a napkin, keeping her hand hidden under the table.

"Do Boyd and Linc have a history of animosity?" Charlotte asked.

"Not more than anyone else in terms of hating Boyd. As far as I know."

"What about the opposite? Could they have been conspiring together on some scheme? Maybe Linc got greedy or just didn't want to continue working with such a nasty character. That would give Boyd a reason to kill him."

"Good thinking, but we need proof. For now, Boyd Hoover stays firmly planted on the suspect list."

"Nothing found in the barn seemed out of place, Chief?"

"You're like a dog with a bone, aren't you?"

She gave the Chief a shy smile and shoulder shrug.

The Chief woke up her cell phone and scrolled through her apps. "Here's what we got:

Workbench with an array of rusty, old tools
Rakes, shovels, and hoes—also seen better days
Barrel of fertilizer pellets, (all legal)
An old TV
Worn upholstered chair and footstool
Substance resembling breadcrumbs found on floor by chair
Eight 50-liter canisters of liquid nitrogen

"And that's all she wrote." The Chief rose to return the empty platter to the creamery.

Charlotte let this sink in for a moment. The first thought that came to mind was that the half a sandwich that she'd seen was gone. She figured that the mouse had come back and taken it in the time before the police arrived. She also reasoned that this item served the purpose of indicating that Linc's death wasn't suicide, which they already knew.

Next Charlotte thought about the liquid nitrogen. *Wasn't that what Martin suspects killed my own strawberry plants? This has to tie in somehow . . .*

"Come on, farmer girl, I've got to get back; crime awaits."

Chapter Twelve

It was time for Charlotte to make her own list. When she arrived back at the farm, she felt a strong pull to talk this all over with Samuel. He knew a lot more than he was letting on, not just about farming but also about the people in Little Acorn that he had grown up around.

Diane, Alice, and Danny were completely consumed with putting the finishing touches on the restaurant. Beau had gone back to Los Angeles, and Joe had left early in the morning for a conference about produce farm futures.

Charlotte found Horse lazing on a porch swing and wondered first how he had safely gotten up there, and second, how the suspended seat continued to sway. Horse was lying on his back, dozing to the gentle back and forth rocking.

"Come on, sleepyhead—let's go find Samuel," Charlotte said as she walked right past Horse.

He hopped off the swing with surprising grace and started to follow her down the hill. It was now mid-afternoon, a glorious time on the farm, when everything slows down a little to appreciate the day. Farmers who had been up with the roosters had completed their chores, growing produce that had benefitted from irrigation and TLC, and had soaked up the nutrients from the afternoon sun; and warring insects and rodents had called a truce in their battles.

The barn and paddock were no exception. Pele the horse was out of his stall, enjoying the fresh air, and the goats were huddled in the shade of the barn doors, nonchalantly observing what they considered their domain.

Samuel was nowhere to be found. Charlotte thought about knocking on the door of his cabin but didn't want to disturb him if he, too, was enjoying a much-deserved break.

"Horse, do you know where Samuel is? In his house resting?" Charlotte asked her pig friend, who was giving her his undivided attention. "That's it, isn't it?"

Charlotte could swear that she saw Horse shake his head from side to side. Suddenly he took off at a trot, and Charlotte had to break into a jog to keep up. He took her on a trail from behind Samuel's house and up and down a hill on the northwest end of her property line.

It was untended land with beautiful, old oak trees, wild sage growing everywhere and fragrant brush like bay laurel, sugar bush and California lilac. It immediately reminded Charlotte of the silvopasture that she'd seen earlier in the day with Chief Goodacre.

Suddenly she heard Samuel's voice.

"Hello, Horse. What are you doing away from that feisty redhead you call 'mom'? She's something, isn't she, Horse?"

Charlotte peered from behind a sycamore tree and saw a clearing where a crudely built garage structure stood. Halfway in and halfway out of the building sat a vintage red pickup truck. Even in its dilapidated state, it was a thing of beauty.

Charlotte spotted a generator that supplied electricity to power up several work lights that hung around and under the vehicle. Charlotte saw no sign of Samuel as she moved closer, but she could still hear his voice.

"I've never met another woman like her. Tough yet feminine. Bossy, but in a way that makes you want to do the work for her. Tantalizingly beautiful, although she doesn't know it, or she couldn't care less."

Finally, Charlotte noticed Samuel's farm boots sticking out from under the truck.

"So, this is your secret hideout," she said with a chuckle.

"What the—" Samuel tried to sit up while still under the truck and Charlotte heard the thud of his head hitting metal.

"Are you all right? That didn't sound good."

"I'm fine. Don't you know that you shouldn't sneak up on people like that?"

Slowly Samuel rolled himself out from under the truck, with a homemade creeper seat.

"I heard voices. I didn't think that I was sneaking up on anyone."

Samuel sat up and raised his hand to his forehead.

"No blood, but you're going to have a nice goose egg. It's already turning red. So, I take it that this is the restoration project? It's a beauty. I remember Martin saying that it was a 'sixty-six?"

"Yes, a Ford F-100. It looks like a heap now, but when I get it back to its original state, it will be a supercharged machine with a five-speed transmission and adjustable suspension." He grinned, avoiding eye contact with Charlotte, probably still a little shy from being overheard talking about her.

"I love it. How long have you been working on it, Samuel?"

"Oh, about four years or so."

"Four years? That's crazy. Is it because you don't have enough time for it? And here I am taking you away from the job right now."

"It's time and parts. I can spend months just looking all over the country for the right part."

"That's something I can help you with. I'm rather good at online research, if I do say so myself. Give me a list and I'll get to work on it."

They both watched Horse trot up to the truck and take in a big sniff. And then he did something that made both their jaws drop. He kicked one of the tires. Samuel and Charlotte looked at each other and burst out laughing.

"What can I help you with, Charlotte? You didn't come all the way over here to watch Horse take a test-drive, did you?" Samuel asked with a smile.

"No, but I don't want to take up your time working on the pickup."

"I was just about to stop for the day anyway," Samuel said, walking to the rear of the truck. He opened the tailgate and patted it, indicating that he wanted her to sit down. Samuel hopped up onto the flatbed, opened a cooler, and extracted two glass bottles of Coca-Cola. He popped the tops, offered Charlotte one, and plopped down next to her.

"What's on your mind?" he asked.

"I need to talk to someone about Linc Pierce's murder and the evidence that I have so far on the killer."

"What about Diane? She always has a clear perspective on things."

"Not this time. Diane's in a romantic relationship with someone on my suspect list." Charlotte took a sip of her soda. It was so cold that she could see teardrop-sized bits of ice ski down the side of the bottle.

"I thought that I explained about Danny and the hard childhood he had to live through."

"You did, but there are some facts involving him that still make me suspicious."

"Such as?"

"For one, he's still got a fierce temper that he has trouble controlling. He's filled with emotion, and something someone says or does can push his buttons. He'll get so angry that he'll walk off and disappear for days."

"That he does, but you'll need to have a lot more than that to point to him as the killer."

"I do. On the day that Beau and I found Linc dead in his barn, Danny left the construction site early. He had a dinner date with Diane that evening, and he told her he had some errands to run and wanted to go home to change clothes, so they agreed to meet at the restaurant."

"Sounds reasonable," Samuel said.

"Yes, it does except for a couple of things; earlier that day, when Danny heard about Linc shoving Beau to the ground, we had to stop him from going right over to Linc's farm and talking some sense into him." Charlotte looked into Samuel's eyes for a reaction, but he remained stoic.

"And the other thing?" Samuel asked.

"He arrived late at the restaurant to meet Diane, and she saw that he was still wearing the same clothes from the day."

"Did he say where he'd been all afternoon or what he was doing?"

"No, Samuel, and he became quite irritable, so Diane didn't push it."

Samuel nodded slowly.

"I see why he's on your suspect list, but I can't believe that Danny's motive would have been because Linc got into an argument with Beau. That's no reason to kill a guy."

"I agree, and I think it has something to do with illegal pesticides that Linc may have been experimenting with, but all I have are the canisters of liquid nitrogen that I saw on his workbench in the farm."

"Interesting. Let me think about that for a while. Who else is on your list?"

"Boyd Hoover. He's a nasty piece of work. With Boyd it's not so much what I know, but all the things he refuses to disclose. The only thing that's clear is that Boyd Hoover and Linc Pierce had a history of fighting with each other." Charlotte took the last swig of her Coke. She hadn't had a soda from a bottle in years, and for some reason it tasted better. Samuel smiled and opened a fresh one for her.

"What sorts of things do you need to know?"

"Like what goes on at Hoover Farms. He won't let anyone on his property. He claims that his crops are also suffering from the strawberry blight, but no one's seen any evidence of it. And we know how competitive he is, so I'm sure that if his plants are dying, then he's trying everything possible to combat the disease, legal or not, and he sure wouldn't share that solution with any of the other farmers." Charlotte hopped off the tailgate and paced in frustration.

"I'd steer clear of Boyd Hoover. You know how I feel about bullies. But perhaps we could do a little stealth surveillance, Charlotte?" Samuel raised his eyebrows and looked at her.

"Are you suggesting a spy mission? You are full of surprises today."

"Nothing illegal, but you must remember that I grew up on this land. If there was a spot to fish or swim or a big rock to climb or a tree tall enough to allow full view of an undraped window, then my friends and I found it."

"You sound like a bunch of little perverts. That window didn't happen to belong to a young Katharine Hoover did it?"

"What are you talking about?"

"I saw the way you two avoided each other a couple of days ago. It was the dance of a romantic history if you ask me."

"You've got it all wrong, and for the record I didn't ask you. While we're running through suspects, shall we talk about Ford Barclay? All that money and supposed good taste, and what does he try to do? He goes after you like a dog in heat. You want to know why I'm out here working on my truck? Because I've got to get my mind off wanting to kill him!"

"I've told you over and over again that I can take care of myself."

"And that Martin Ross is a shady guy as well. What if the two of them had come after you?"

"I don't think that Ford is the sharing sort of guy. Look, they can both come off as arrogant asses, and together or apart they could certainly have killed Linc and been embroiled in this strawberry crop disease. But I'm just a distraction. At least with Ford, he can buy almost anything he desires. Except me."

Samuel stepped down from his truck and began picking up the tools he'd been using. It looked as though he was struggling with what to say next to her.

"But," Charlotte continued, and Samuel froze in place, "his family's pharmaceutical firm—the one that makes fertilizer and pest control products—keeps coming up. He adamantly insists that he has nothing to do with his relatives and their enterprise, but I know firsthand that what he says and what he does are two different things. I need to spend some time exploring that connection further."

Samuel didn't respond and continued to put his equipment away in the wooden garage. Although now he dropped the tools with a thud to show his nonverbal objection to Charlotte's words.

"Maybe you could help me with that too? The only things I know about pesticides are what you've taught me."

Samuel rolled the generator into the shelter. Charlotte crossed her arms and watched him.

"And there's one more thing I need your help with."

Samuel released the hand brake on the pickup and pushed it slowly into the garage. Charlotte turned her back to him.

"Goats."

After about a minute, Charlotte heard Samuel say, "What about goats?"

"We need bunches of them, packs of them—colonies. Whatever you call it."

"A herd. What on earth for?"

157

"We're going to turn this whole area into a luscious pasture. Between the trees, the natural vegetation, and the animals, we'll have our own silvopasture, and in a season or so, we'll be able to plant a whole new crop here."

"Where did you hear about silvopastures, girl?" Samuel asked, shaking his head with surprise.

"You have to get up pretty early to pull one over on me." Charlotte grinned, proud of herself. "We'll preserve this area and maybe improve on it for your automotive pastimes. What do you say, Samuel?"

He hunched over a little on himself, something that Charlotte had noticed Samuel did when he turned shy.

"Aw shucks?" He gave her a lopsided grin. An irresistible one.

Before Charlotte could help herself, she grabbed the front of his loose chambray shirt, pulled him down, and planted a kiss on his soft lips. If she had meant for it to be a peck to show benign affection, she'd have stopped after a few seconds, but this was coming up on the minute mark. Finally, she pulled away, and they both looked at each other with expressions of surprise and delight.

Samuel was about to say something, when Charlotte announced, "Come on, Horse—we've got to go goat shopping!" She set off at a run back to the farmhouse, with her little pink friend clipping her heels.

"Like I said, a feisty redhead indeed." Samuel watched her go.

Chapter Thirteen

Charlotte called upon all her self-control to forget about that kiss and focus on solving a murder before Little Acorn growers lost all their strawberries. It was clear that, despite Samuel's helpful input and prodding, what she had was solid theories and watery answers.

Charlotte heard voices and commotion coming from the house kitchen but veered off to her bedroom suite first, to regroup. Horse followed her into the room, and they both plunked down on the sofa facing the fireplace.

Horse seemed overly affectionate and climbed on her lap, nudging her chin with his snout.

"Not you too, Horse—I've had enough smooching for one day." But he made her giggle.

He took in a great big sniff and moved his pig nose down to her lap.

"Ouch!" Charlotte screamed after Horse used a hoof to try to open her pants pocket. "What are you doing? Are you in heat or something?"

Horse had jumped down to the ground after hearing Charlotte scream, and sat staring at her.

"That hurt," she said to him. Charlotte reached into her pocket and felt the sharp metal object from Linc's barn. She'd nearly forgotten about it.

"Is this what you were after, Horse?" Charlotte finally had a chance to examine the piece in the light. Upon seeing her holding it, Horse grunted and spun around with his head held proudly in the air.

"Do you know what this is, my pink friend?" He stopped his dance and looked at her. "No?" The spinning resumed.

Charlotte walked over to the large, antique floor lamp in her suite to have a closer look at this strange, sharp, silver metal object. It fit on her finger and reminded Charlotte of a banjo or guitar pick. Yet, at one point in the ring, there was a curved piece of metal that jutted out. Almost like a fingernail, but it was sharp on the bottom side. That ruled out using it to pluck strings because it would slice through them or at least cause damage and fraying. Charlotte turned the ring in her palm and searched for any markings or engravings. It didn't appear to be of much value. It was lightweight, and the metal was thin steel or aluminum.

I'd better put this in a safe place to preserve any fingerprints just in case . . .

Applause and laughter coming from the farmhouse kitchen distracted Charlotte from hopping online to do some research. Horse had already taken off to join the fun, and Charlotte followed, to retrieve a plastic bag.

"Diane, how many times have I told you that if you are having fun, you're to call me immediately!" Charlotte bellowed at the BFF.

"Wait until you see what she's creating—it's pure magic," Alice cooed.

Alice was now properly dressed as a sous chef, clad in a navy-blue apron with the words "Finn Family Farm-to-Table" embroidered in white across the bib.

"I love the aprons."

"They just arrived. They all look the same except for the one I ordered for Beau. His is in a color called 'Flamingo' with black lettering that spells, 'Finn Family Farm-to-Drafting Table Design Team.'"

"He'll flip when he sees it. I take it the apron will be a surprise?"

Diane nodded. "What have you got there?" Diane asked, watching Charlotte drop the ring knife into a bag and seal it. "It looks positively Medieval."

"That's what I'm trying to figure out," Charlotte said, and held up the bag for Diane and Alice to see.

"That's a ring knife. It's a harvesting tool, although we mostly pick our strawberries by hand. Too much risk of damaging the stems because they go blunt so quickly. Lots of farmers swear by them, though."

"Thanks, Alice," Charlotte said, although her stomach sank when she heard that last sentence. If these little tools were so prevalent, it would be almost impossible to trace this one back to one person. Not to mention that it might have absolutely nothing to do with Linc Pierce's murder.

"Alright, girlfriend, let's see the magic that has Alice walking on air."

The butcher block prep counter was nearly covered with everything from green molded pulp baskets (both filled with strawberries and empty), bottles of milk, sugar, citrus fruits, cutlery, and a collection of stainless bowls and pitchers.

"I'm going to use these for a welcome glass of sangria and a one-spoon appetizer when guests are seated. See these quarter-sized puff pastries? They'll be filled with triple cream cheese and topped with what I am about to make."

It was as if Diane had her own cooking show and was filming an episode.

"Okay, I'm hooked—please proceed, Chef!"

Charlotte watched Diane fit the bowl of a large food processor in place and toss in fresh, hulled strawberries, cream, and condensed milk. She then set the control to "Blend," and while the mixture was getting smooth, Alice added some grated lemon rind through the feed tube. The fruit and the other ingredients had incorporated into a luscious, semi-thick coulis. Diane poured the mixture into a tall squeeze bottle like the kind used for holding condiments at a burger restaurant.

"I want a taste," Charlotte declared, holding out a teaspoon to Diane.

"Of course you do, but you must be patient. Now comes the magic." Diane and Alice giggled to each other.

Alice placed a large hotel pan on the counter, and Diane lifted a canister from below and held it above the pan.

"Should we be wearing some sort of protective gear?" Charlotte asked, stepping away from the table.

In lieu of responding, Diane pressed a button at the spout of the canister and white smoke and clear liquid poured out into the pan. When the bottom of the pan was filled, Diane put the canister aside and proceeded to pour droplets of the strawberry mixture from the squeeze bottle into the clear liquid. They immediately formed into beads.

"What did I just see?" Charlotte nevertheless broke into applause.

"I used liquid nitrogen because its properties enable it to rapidly freeze anything that comes into contact with it. It's stored in a vacuum flask and can be kept for long periods of time and easily transported. The restaurant I worked at in Los Angeles used it for all sorts of things, including freezing fruit for their signature sangria. Fun, isn't it?"

"Diane and Alice, I'm so proud of you! Soon this method will be all the rage in Little Acorn as well."

Charlotte left the kitchen, with thoughts swirling and finally starting to coalesce in her mind. It had been a long day, and Charlotte sent Horse down to get his dinner. (She didn't have to ask twice.) She returned to her suite armed with a small plate of Diane's special appetizers and vowed to get an early night's sleep. She placed the ring knife on her great-uncle's desk beside her laptop. Charlotte sat down and booted up her computer with the idea to do some quick reading on how to start a silvopasture. And maybe shop for some goats.

It didn't take long for Charlotte to get sidetracked and launch into a search of Boyd Hoover and his family history. She'd watched Chief Goodacre run some internet searches and had memorized some of the keywords she'd used. Charlotte typed in his name and then this series of queries: *arrest, assault, abuse, childhood,* and *family.* She hit "Return" and waited for the results to come up.

The first three keywords produced little information. It appeared that Boyd didn't have an adult arrest record, although she'd found some local news reports about bar fights that he'd been involved in. Charlotte wrote down the names of the men listed in those articles, but none rang a bell. She was about to move on, but a second photo in one newspaper clipping caught her eye. She'd missed it the first time because it was below the fold, and she hadn't bothered to scroll down that far. Sure enough, there was Linc Pierce shouting back at a group of angry farmers and clearly standing beside and in support of Boyd Hoover. The article had appeared almost a year ago.

They didn't always hate each other. What would make their relationship change to the point of murder? If it did?

Charlotte moved on to the Hoover family history and was encouraged to see that much more information was available. The artichoke-growing business that they ran in Castroville had garnered awards and lots of attention over the years. They were active participants in the annual Artichoke Festival, as she saw in the photos and videos that had come up. It seemed that this tradition went back sixty years, and one year Marilyn Monroe was even the honorary artichoke queen.

The festival, Charlotte read, attracted visitors not only from all over the state but across the country as well. Charlotte clicked through a gallery of photos showing past bands that had made appearances, a mascot dressed as a walking talking artichoke, games for the kids, and artichokes prepared in every way imaginable, including ice cream cones.

Sounds like something I'd like to attend. And I know Diane would!

When Charlotte arrived at the section showing photos of farm tours, she found the Hoover Artichoke Farm. From the photos, Charlotte could see that it was an impressive operation spanning hundreds of acres. She came across a local newspaper article featuring the farm, dating back fifteen years. The headline read *The Hoover Artichoke Farm Masters*. In the foreground, the photo showed three proud men standing with chests puffed out, and behind them, artichoke plants that were almost as tall, stretching back as far as the horizon line. The older man, most likely the father, wore weathered denim overalls and stood about a head shorter than his sons. But from his posture and his stern look directly into the camera, it was clear that he was the boss and would not tolerate any challenges. Next to him stood two men, somewhere in their late thirties, dressed in jeans and flannel shirts of different plaids. They had matching crew cuts of light brown hair, matching expressions and demeanors. Charlotte knew that they were identical twins. She tried to imagine being bullied by them, like Katharine explained Boyd had been, and shivered. No wonder her father carried a huge chip on his shoulder.

I wonder how Katharine feels about her uncles or if she's even still in contact with them.

Before turning in for the night, Charlotte initiated a couple of searches on Linc Pierce and his family. Horse had returned with a full belly and a contented smile. He hopped up on the sofa across from the fireplace and rested his head on the arm facing Charlotte at her desk.

Life was good.

Short of asking the Chief again and getting a rejection, Charlotte couldn't think of a way to find out what she really wanted to know: where Linc's money had come from. If he'd had it since his early days of selling pesticides and other farm products, he certainly wouldn't have been living in the squalor that he was. And still doing farmwork, the man had been in his eighties. If this money was a new acquisition, then where had it come from? Or if he was doing a service job for someone, what had he been paid to do?

Charlotte took out a pad of paper and made some notes:

- *Linc has a dilapidated farm but a healthy crop of strawberries.*
- *His great-granddaughter Margaret said he was a salesman most of his life, peddling farm equipment and, later, fertilizers and pesticides. He most likely sold the now-banned substances to the local farmers.*
- *Linc has been estranged from his family for many years.*
- *A large supply of liquid nitrogen canisters was found in Linc's barn.*
- *Linc's farm was rundown almost to ruin, yet there was enough money in his estate to cover getting it ready for sale and to give a nice sum to his heirs.*

Charlotte sat back and reread her notes. It seemed clear that Linc knew something and probably did something that had gotten him killed. And it was most likely part of this whole strawberry crop sabotage plot.

Who was bankrolling Linc Pierce?

Charlotte had given his great-granddaughter Margaret her phone number, but she didn't have hers. She couldn't ask the Chief without raising red flags, but perhaps there was a way to look it up. She had to think about that.

Charlotte had still not seen with her own eyes Ford Barclay and Boyd Hoover's strawberry fields, so she could not be certain that their produce had actually suffered from the blight. That needed to be rectified right away.

And then again, if Linc Pierce was back to peddling pesticides, the illegal ones that may have killed his family, Danny Costa may have figured it out after hearing about the altercation in the Garden Center parking lot. He could have gone out to Linc's farm to confirm his suspicions, killed Linc, and still made it back in time for his dinner date with Diane. Which would explain why he hadn't changed his clothes. If this was the correct scenario, she needed to find someone who had seen Danny at Linc's farm on the day he was murdered.

Charlotte cast her eye to the clear bag containing the ring knife.

Had this been Linc's, or was it accidently left behind by his killer.

Charlotte was struck by a memory of her great-uncle Tobias. In her mind, she could hear his voice saying:

"Picking a strawberry that you've grown from seed is a very precious event. You must be as gentle as you would with a newborn baby. Cradle the fruit in your palm while holding the stem of the berry between your thumbnail and index finger. Sever the fruit with pressure from your thumbnail while slightly twisting the stem. Allow the strawberry to gently roll into your palm. You are literally now in possession of the fruit of your labor."

That is how a farmer who loves what he does and loves the land would harvest strawberries. That's how Linc Pierce would have done so as well. Charlotte picked up the bag with the ring knife.

I've got to swallow my pride and give this to Chief Goodacre . . .

Chapter Fourteen

"Good morning, Chief, how are you today?" Charlotte tried to sound cheery and nonchalant over the phone by pitching her voice a notch higher.

"Busy."

Oops! Not a good sign.

"I've got to go into town to pick up a few items, and I thought that I'd pop my head in and say 'hello'."

"I just saw you yesterday, what are you playing at?"

"Nothing, I swear."

I am such a chicken.

"Good, because I've got a busy day and will be out in the field for most of it. Goodbye."

The call ended.

"So much for trying to come clean," Charlotte said to Horse as he trotted out to breakfast in the paddock.

Everyone was so busy on the farm preparing for the soft opening of Diane's restaurant in two days that they didn't even notice as Charlotte wandered the grounds. Even she got lost in her own thoughts as she walked in the warm sunshine. The ambient sounds of alto and soprano bird chirps, the rustle of stems and leaves busy growing and the distant dripping of water irrigation had put Charlotte into a Zen state.

"Hello, boss, what brings you down here? Anything I can help you with?"

Charlotte looked up to see Joe Wong's smiling face.

"Hi, Joe. I almost forgot where I was, it's so beautiful out."

"It always is, Charlotte—heaven on earth. 'For I have the warmth of the sun,'" Joe said looking up and smiling.

"Chinese proverb?" Charlotte asked.

"Beach Boys."

They both laughed.

"What are you up to here?" Charlotte asked, eying a workbench covered with baskets of strawberries, some large plastic freezer bags, and a box with some canisters inside.

"Since Alice is so busy helping Diane launch the restaurant, and loving it by the way, she hasn't had the time to make her jams and jellies for the farm shop. I'm experimenting with flash freezing and storing our freshly picked produce so she can use it any time she wants. It's kind of cool." Joe grinned at his pun.

"Everybody on the farm seems to be playing with this magic liquid nitrogen. Did you order cases of it, Joe?"

"Not at all. Diane had some canisters she could spare when she realized how much of Alice's time she was taking up."

"I wonder where Diane got it from. Maybe one of her former restaurant colleagues sent it to her."

Joe shook his head. "Diane mentioned something about a friend having some extra liquid nitrogen and thinking that she'd have a blast playing with it."

Joe grinned again.

"That's the worst pun I've ever heard, Joe." Charlotte groaned.

"Sorry." Joe pulled a cylinder out of a slot in the corrugated inserts of the box. "Back to work—the key is to freeze the fruit immediately after it is harvested for best flavor and keep it frozen until you use it. If it starts to thaw and isn't eaten, it will turn to mush."

"Interesting. Have fun," Charlotte said, and turned to climb the hill back up to the farmhouse.

When she reached the top, she saw that everyone was still immersed in their jobs to get the restaurant ready for opening. She poked her head inside and spotted Diane hard at work in the open kitchen. Tables and chairs stacked at the side awaited their proper placement, and the natural wood floor was getting a final buffing. Charlotte noticed a pink corkscrew tail in motion, poking out the side of the high kitchen counter.

"Horse," she stage-whispered.

Nothing.

"Horse, come here!"

A pink snout and then Horse's full head replaced the tail.

Charlotte waved him to her. Horse hesitated for a moment, but thinking about the scraps of food he'd miss out on, he ultimately acquiesced.

"Good boy! Want to take a little road trip with me?"

He did a little circle dance, excited at the proposition.

Charlotte nearly ran smack into Samuel, his line of vision blocked by the large bale of wildflowers, vines, and brush that he carried.

"Sorry! Diane texted me and wanted these right away for the bar and tables. She told me to find as much color as possible, so I hope this will do." He held the huge bouquet out to show her.

In his arms Samuel held stalks of purple salvia, sweet white honeysuckle, exotic-looking buttonbush globes, blue and green passion fruit flowers, and lots of woody branches and vines.

"I think you did a fantastic job—Diane will be overjoyed."

"Good," Samuel replied, and then there was an awkward silence between them.

"Samuel," Charlotte began, "about yesterday—"

"Already forgotten," Samuel quickly responded.

"Forgotten? I was talking about asking for your help in doing some recon on Boyd Hoover's farm. After dark, this evening?"

"Oh yes, of course. We'll take my truck, so we blend in with all the other farmers in the area."

"Great. I'll come by when I'm ready, and let's keep this to ourselves."

Samuel nodded.

"What were you talking about?" Charlotte asked him.

"I better get these to Diane before she has my head." Samuel rushed past her and into the restaurant.

"Ready for an adventure, Horse?"

Charlotte didn't have to ask twice.

*　　*　　*

The road and the surrounding farms were just as depressing to drive by as the last time when she'd been with the Chief. A bright, sunny day did nothing to sugarcoat this dilapidated area. Horse sat in the backseat despite repeatedly making stealth attempts to ride shotgun.

"Stay where you are, mister. It's too dangerous for both of us to have you ride up front," Charlotte admonished.

She got a dissatisfied grunt as a reply.

"This may end up being nothing more than a drive in the country, but I can't think of another way to try and talk to Margaret without raising red flags with Chief Goodacre."

Horse had resorted to sticking his snout out the car window and taking in the aroma of his porcine friends along the way.

Charlotte had been concerned about not remembering where to turn off for Linc Pierce's farm, but when she came to a driveway with several utility trucks parked along it, she figured she'd found the right place.

As she drove in, Charlotte heard police sirens and caught a flash of blue and white speed by in the direction that she'd just come.

I wonder what that's about . . .

Unlike the last time she'd visited, Charlotte found the Pierce Farm buzzing with activity. All the debris and garbage had been removed, and the barn had been razed. It looked like the house was getting a good airing out: all the windows and doors were opened. Charlotte shuttered when she thought about how rundown and worse the interior must have been. Margaret was sitting on the front steps, talking on her cell phone and still looking very much like a fish out of water. When it was clear that she had ended her call, Charlotte approached.

"Hi, Margaret—how's it going?"

"Nice to see you, Charlotte, and thanks again for the offer of help the other day."

Margaret had one of those accordion legal file folders on her lap that looked to be already halfway full.

"Looks like you have your hands full; anything I can help with?" Charlotte sat down next to her.

"Oh my, did Linc Pierce have farm animals?" Margaret shrieked, seeing Horse trot happily over to them.

"No, no, he's mine, and he was supposed to wait in the car. Life is very busy at my farm too. We're opening a restaurant in two days. I thought that we'd get out of everyone's hair. This is my pig, Horse."

Margaret slid up one more step to put some distance between herself and Horse, and gave Charlotte a blinked look of confusion.

"We named him that because he eats like one," Charlotte added.

Horse climbed up to Margaret, gave her his cocked-head smile, and Charlotte could literally see the tension leave her body.

"Horse, come sit over here with me."

Horse looked over his shoulder at Charlotte and before complying gave Margaret another smile and a wag of his tail.

"He *is* kind of cute," Margaret conceded. "You drove all the way out here just to see how I was doing, Charlotte? That's kind of you. I have very little understanding of all of this, but I think that I'm in the right hands. I'm hoping to be able to head back up north in a week or sooner."

"Then I must invite you to the opening of our restaurant. It will be loads of fun, and Horse and I can vouch for the fact that the food is excellent. My best friend, Diane, is the chef. I was going to extend the invitation by phone, but I realized I didn't have your number."

"I have yours, but I guess I didn't reciprocate," Margaret said, and she texted Charlotte the information.

"We'll get out of your hair then," Charlotte said, standing up. "But I wanted to ask you why, with the estate that was bequeathed to you, didn't Linc spend some of it on improving his day-to-day life on the farm? I hate to think of him living in squalor. If this is too personal, I understand."

"I wondered the exact same thing. It turns out that the capital he left had been earned in about the last six months." Margaret stood as well.

Horse had climbed the steps to the front porch and had begun a full-on snout root. Charlotte kept one eye on him as she spoke.

"You said 'earned'—what sort of work was he doing?" Charlotte knew that she was getting close and had to tread lightly.

"That's the great mystery. The only way I know any of this is because he'd been depositing weekly checks made out to 'cash' in varying large amounts."

Cash. Trying to remain secretive I suppose.

"That is curious. Where there any notations on the checks that might give you a clue?"

Margaret shook her head.

"Only the account the payment came from. Something called 'KB Holdings,' but I haven't been able to find out any more about that organization."

Charlotte's wheels started spinning.

Horse appeared to have found whatever he'd been looking for on one of the two scarred and well-worn wooden rocking chairs beside the front door of Linc's farmhouse. He used his nose to push the chair sideways, and when he uncovered a knothole in the porch flooring, he tried to make it bigger with his hoof.

"Horse! Stop that, and come here now." Charlotte's voice was stern and powerful. She also gave Horse a squint-eye look that left no room for misinterpretation. He dropped his ears down and walked slowly back to Charlotte.

"What are you planning to do with this house? Raze it like the barn?"

"I'm still weighing my options. It is very rundown, but the realtor says that with a few coats of paint, it might be better to leave it for the new owners, who can use it as an onsite real estate office. I just wish we could close the book on my great-grandfather's murder—that would be the biggest boost toward selling the property." Margaret's chest heaved, and she let out a long breath.

"Oh well, even if that remains a mystery, I'm glad that you're able to get out from under this farm and still have a bit left over for yourself. One more question: Do you know if Linc had any existing medical conditions?"

"I'm ashamed to say that I don't know. But I've got all his files, and I just need a moment to read through them. If I find anything, I'll let you know. Will a text work?"

"Perfect. I'll see you at the restaurant opening."

"I'm looking forward to it. Bye, Horse. You're a cute pig."

Horse trotted over to Margaret and gave her hand a kiss.

"And a flirt I see."

Charlotte shook her head and Margaret giggled.

* * *

Back on the road, Charlotte talked freely out loud to Horse and herself.

"So, Linc had gotten himself into some lucrative business venture that was putting fast money into his bank account. But what could it have been?

"His skills, as far as everyone has told me, were growing strawberries, selling fertilizers and pesticides, and riding with the Rancheros Visitadores. Maybe the last two items were connected somehow?"

Charlotte looked in her rearview mirror at Horse, who uncharacteristically was paying no attention to her words at all and was taking in the passing smells with his head hung out the window.

"You know something, don't you, Horse?"

He remained in the same position, with his eyes closed and his ears flopping in the wind. But Charlotte could have sworn that she saw his corkscrew tail wag.

Chapter Fifteen

"Since you won't give up what you were sniffing on Linc's porch, you've just given me another chore to do, Horse. I hope you're happy, and you will be coming with me on this job."

Horse hopped up and down at the prospect as Charlotte drove up to her farmhouse and parked.

A crowd was gathered out in front of the restaurant. Charlotte saw Diane talking animatedly to Samuel and Alice, and Joe was pacing while talking on his cell phone. The work crew had taken a break and was gathered around one of the picnic tables under the shade of a Chinese elm tree. Charlotte and Horse headed down there.

"At last, there you are." Diane's voice trembled. "They took Danny."

"What happened? Did he collapse? I knew they let him out of the hospital too soon, and he's been really pushing himself to get the restaurant ready."

"No, it was nothing like that," Diane managed to say between hyperventilating breaths. "This is just too surreal to believe."

"The cops came by about twenty minutes ago," Joe explained. "He's been arrested as a person of interest in the murder of Linc Pierce."

"On what evidence? This can't be right." Charlotte looked at the faces of the group.

"They said that they have a couple of eyewitnesses who claim they saw him riding his horse on Linc's farm that day. They heard a heated argument and then silence," Diane said, trying to gather herself together. "With all the other circumstantial evidence like Danny threatening to set Linc straight after fighting with Beau and my statement that he came to our dinner date without having changed clothes, the Chief believes that they have enough for the DA. There's also something to do with the Rancheros Visitadores, but I stopped listening when I realized Danny was going to jail."

Charlotte could see that Diane was laying the entirety of blame for Danny's arrest on her shoulders.

"This is far from a done deal, Charlotte," Samuel gently spoke. "They have to make a solid, convincing case using all the evidence. And I suspect that you have your own theories on that subject."

"You bet I do—more by the minute."

"Be careful Charlotte Finn, I don't want to have to visit you in jail too. I prefer you here on the farm." Diane was gaining her strength. "And if it's okay with you, I'd like to borrow Joe for the next couple of days to take over with the crew and finish this restaurant for opening."

"I think the restaurant will be a sorely needed wonderful distraction for the whole of Little Acorn, Diane. And please put me to work as well. I have something to do starting late this afternoon," Charlotte continued, "but as of tomorrow I am all yours."

The two BFFs embraced, and everyone went back to work.

* * *

After discussing a departure time with Samuel for their "mission," Charlotte walked with purpose to the farmhouse with the goal of taking a nice, long shower to help wash away the bitterness of the day. And steel her for the night to come.

Charlotte entered the foyer just as Alice was coming up from the root cellar, where she stored canned and jarred fruits and vegetables. Her eyes and nose were red, and it was clear that she had been crying.

"Alice, what's the matter, dear?" Charlotte pulled her close and gave her a hug.

"It's nothing. I'm fine."

"You're not fine—you've been crying."

With a quick reflex, Alice's hand went up to wipe her eyes.

"I feel so sorry for Diane and all the restaurant crew. They've been working so darn hard, and they're so proud of what they are building," Alice said, sniffling.

"That crew includes you—you have every right to be upset. Don't keep it bottled, though. we're all experiencing deep disappointment, but we'll get through it easier together."

Charlotte threw an arm over Alice's shoulders and they walked into the kitchen. Alice instinctively put the kettle on for tea.

"I've been with Danny virtually every day for the last month, and I have to tell you I just can't imagine him killing or even hurting another person. I'm aware of what happened to his family and the scars he bears for it. I've lived through my own injustices in the past, and Danny and I have shared stories and comforted each other from time to time." Alice took a deep breath.

"Oh no! I'm so sorry. Sit down, please—I'll make the tea." Charlotte ushered her to a stool at the kitchen island.

"I'm fine. Like with Danny, it was in my family's history and just another example of greed versus good sense." Alice was up again and retrieved a couple of mugs from the cupboard.

"Were members of your family also victims of deadly pesticides?" Charlotte asked, answering the squawking teakettle.

"When my ancestors moved down from San Francisco, seeking sun and job opportunities, working in the fields picking strawberries was the cost of entry. At least five members of my family died way too young." Alice dropped her head down and went about the business of adding milk and sugar to her tea.

"It was a travesty how long the chemical companies were able to continue distributing pesticides that had already been named lethal. I just don't understand it." Charlotte ignored her tea and put all her attention and sympathy into Alice.

"As the philosopher said, 'Wealth is like seawater: the more we drink, the thirstier we become.' Those greedy people were never satisfied. They had a complete lack of empathy and loved playing the manipulative games. We've all met someone like that. They take and hoard what they have and will do anything to prevent others from acquiring it." Alice took a deep breath. She'd delivered quite a speech.

"Alice, you are a very wise woman and I admire you," Charlotte said as she got up to go to her suite, all the way mulling over what Alice had said.

Just before going into the shower, Charlotte couldn't resist turning on her laptop and initiating another search for Agripharm, the company that Danny's family had filed a lawsuit against for wrongful death. The first results that came back were mostly about the company, from Bloomberg, Forbes, and other financial reports. Charlotte learned that in the early years, about 1945, the company's profits came mostly from selling their pharmaceutical products overseas.

I wonder if they were also testing formulations in a less regulated market recovering from a world war.

Charlotte did a deeper dive into the owners and shareholders of Agripharm but made little headway. She decided to try a little reverse engineering and added the name "Barclay Pharmaceuticals" to the search string. After delving down several more layers, Charlotte finally found what she was looking for. Agripharm was a private company licensed in Litchfield, Connecticut, and spearheaded by a Lyon Barclay, great-grandson of the late Nigel Barclay of London, England.

Didn't Ford Barclay tell me that his family traced back to England? And didn't Alice tell me that Ford headed west to California the moment he was eligible to claim his share of the trust fund? Litchfield, Connecticut, is certainly east of Little Acorn.

Charlotte downloaded some of the articles and documents and sent off a quick note to Chief Goodacre.

I hope that she'll run with it.

Just as the sun was sinking into the horizon, Charlotte slipped out of the farmhouse and quietly made her way down to the paddock. She encountered Gary, one of Danny's crewmembers, coming toward her from the direction of the restaurant.

"Have a good night, Gary—you deserve it." Charlotte nodded to him and then stopped in her tracks. "Quick question, is someone looking after Danny's horse while he's, um away?"

* * *

"I brought extra flashlights and batteries. You can never have enough," Charlotte said to Samuel while opening the passenger door to his truck.

They were both dressed like seasoned farmers under the pretense that if they were spotted, they could claim to have been collecting snails for the geese. Samuel had brought along an extra-large empty coffee can and had put a couple of slugs inside as a start. Charlotte was dressed in denim overalls and, at Samuel's suggestion, had tucked her trademark red locks under a dark baseball cap.

"Horse, come on," Charlotte called to her pig, who, at the sound of her voice, came running.

"Oh no, this is a human mission only," Samuel said, starting the engine.

"But I need him for part of it. He made it clear when we were at Linc Pierce's farm earlier that there was something important under the house porch. We need to bring Horse back to the farm to retrieve it."

"How do you know that the pig wasn't just smelling some piece of discarded food? In case you haven't noticed, the animal likes to eat."

"I know my pig. Horse, get in. Plus it's perfectly logical to bring a pig on a snail collection mission, so he's supporting our alibi."

Horse jumped up into the cab of the pickup and wedged his way between Charlotte and Samuel.

"This is a bad idea, I just know it," Samuel muttered, putting the truck into reverse. "What do you propose to do with Horse when we get to our planned destination? We can't drag him along on a spy mission."

"He'll sit quietly in the truck and wait for us to return," Charlotte said with false conviction.

Samuel looked into her eyes. "And what are the chances of that happening?"

Charlotte looked at Samuel and smiled.

"You want me to answer, Charlotte? About as likely as seeing—"

"Okay, I'll think of something. Just drive. Linc's farm is our first stop."

Chapter Sixteen

They rode in silence and in darkness. This rural road had no streetlights, and any farms that were still functional had set their houses far back from the road. Charlotte thought about what Linc would have done with himself all alone at night out here. It was clear that he wasn't spending time on the phone talking to siblings or nieces and nephews. He didn't seem like the type to want to tackle *War and Peace*. Maybe watch a game if one was on TV? A feeling of sorrow and empathy washed over Charlotte as she thought about this.

"This is the turnoff, right?" Samuel asked, bringing Charlotte back to the present.

"Yep, maybe cut the headlights just in case there is somebody on the site?" Charlotte suggested.

"I was just about to," Samuel replied, clearly not happy with all Charlotte's orders. "Have you done something like this before?"

"You mean breaking and entering? No, of course not!" Charlotte gave Samuel her "how dare you" look. Shoulders back, chest out, and glaring eyes.

"We, or at least I am, not going to break and enter. Worst case, I may trespass a little." Samuel straightened his posture as well.

"Define 'a little'?"

"As a kid there wasn't much to do after dark around Little Acorn. The movie theater wasn't built until I was in my late teens, so we'd sneak around farms and see what kind of trouble we could get into. And by 'trouble,' I mean minor mischief like tipping cows and stealing fruit. We knew how not to get caught," Samuel said, ignoring Charlotte's question.

"School me: How do we get in and out of these farms unnoticed?"

"Let's start with the obvious ones. Have you muted your cell phone? I assume that you're carrying yours."

"I was just about to," Charlotte said, getting a taste of her own medicine.

"Are you wearing anything that wouldn't support the story that we're out at night collecting snails? Jewelry, watches? What shoes do you have on?" Samuel looked down at her feet, but it was too dark for him to see.

"My red high heels of course. Do you think that I'm an idiot?"

"Of course not. I'm just looking out for you, for us."

"How many times do you need to hear 'I can take care of myself' before it sinks in?"

"Understood." Charlotte could see how agitated Samuel had become.

"I know you mean well, and I really do appreciate it," she said, and meant it. "I don't see any lights on around the property, that's a good thing."

"Guard dogs don't need them they can see in the dark," Samuel said with a half grin.

"If you're trying to scare me, it's not working. Besides, the hounds would be no match for my guard pig."

Samuel parked the truck behind two robust oak trees so it couldn't be readily seen. And because it was well worn, most would assume that it belonged to the farm.

"There's the front porch. Hopefully there's an opening around the side that leads under the stairs so Horse and I can squeeze in for a look," Charlotte said, hopping out of the pickup, with purpose.

"Whoa. I think that I should go in with Horse. There could be all sorts of nasty critters under there—snakes, rabid raccoons, you name it," Samuel warned. "How are you going to make your case if you're holed up in the hospital for the next month?"

"I'm not afraid of things lurking in the dark, but I suppose you have a point. Being laid up right now would be mightily inconvenient, not just for the case but for the restaurant opening as well."

"Good, you can hide just to the side here and keep watch. The pig's already raring to go, so this shouldn't take long." Samuel turned on his flashlight but mostly doused the light by keeping it inside his jacket. "Okay, Horse, show me what's got your tail in a curl."

Horse dove in through the broken wood trellis on the side of the steps, and then Charlotte watched Samuel's long legs disappear as he slid in after the pig. She was tempted to follow them under the porch, wanting a chance to look for any evidence that Samuel might miss.

Charlotte crouched down to peer into the dark space. She could hear snorting and dirt being push around as Samuel must have been following Horse's trail. Charlotte got down on her stomach and dug her elbows into the ground. She used her boot toes to get a strong purchase so that she could launch herself forward with her legs. Her left foot slipped out of the dirt and kicked into something that sounded like metal. The sound echoed several times. Charlotte slithered back out from under the porch steps to see what she'd hit. Just before she pulled her head out, she heard Samuel whisper, "Damn it."

Charlotte crawled over to the side of the house and risked shining a light on it. She could see that she'd kick a large piece of rusted, corrugated tin roofing. She tapped it with her boot again and heard the same echo. There was some kind of open space behind the old metal. Charlotte stood up and tested the weight of the roof piece. It wasn't too bad, and because Linc had long since stopped watering and taking care of the hedges around his farmhouse, the roofing was standing on dry dirt, making it easy to slide to the side. Once she'd done that, a small version of root cellar doors, standing ajar, came into view. The opening was about the size of a car door. It was unlocked, Charlotte listened in silence for any communication from Samuel, and when she heard nothing, she stuck her head into the space and took a look around, using her flashlight.

"Charlotte! What are you doing, woman?"

Samuel's voice startled her so much that she tried to stand up and hit her head on the top frame of the root cellar doors.

"Geez, Samuel, isn't one of your rules for getting away unnoticed that you don't sneak up on your partner in the dark?"

"My main rule is don't break and enter," he whispered to Charlotte.

"I haven't broken anything. The doors to this cellar were open, and all I did was stick my head in. There could be an animal stuck down there."

"And I assume this piece of roofing just moved to the side by itself?"

"Maybe. You're not going to believe what's down there."

They both got on their hands and knees and squeezed into the doorway. Samuel used his flashlight to scan the cavern.

The light revealed a crude chemistry lab setup. The old door that rested on a couple of sawhorses served as a table and was covered with glass bottles and jars, plastic tubes, razors and knives, clamps, matches, measuring cups, and candles. Also on the table were a number of bottles of liquid labeled with masking tape and a marker, but Charlotte and Samuel were too far away to make out the words. Last, they saw what looked like a camping lantern that had been modified and embellished.

On a tall bookcase next to the table, Linc had stored glass medicine droppers, beakers, Brasso metal polish, pliers, scissors, a glue gun, and some kind of jerry-rigged test tube holder that had been fashioned out of wire hangers.

"What do you think all this was used for? A meth lab or down-home moonshine?" Samuel asked.

"We won't know for sure unless we go down there." Charlotte used her flashlight to locate a fold-down fire escape ladder.

"Oh no, you don't. So far, we've done nothing worse than a little harmless trespassing. Once you enter the property, it's a whole other story. I can't let you do that."

"Alright, alright. At least let me take a couple photos of the lab. That way I can research these items online." Charlotte didn't wait for permission. Horse tried to squeeze in next to her, but Samuel quickly pulled him away.

"Not you too, pig."

When Charlotte was satisfied that she had covered the evidence in photos, she pulled back out and stood up.

"How did you initially find this secret lab?" Samuel asked, looking around the area.

"I accidently kicked the tin roof and heard the noise echo, which led me to believe that there was an open space behind it. I slid the roofing to the side."

"We're going to have to tell the Chief about this," Samuel said, shaking his head.

"Not necessarily. We just have to let people know that it exists."

"I don't like where this is headed."

"Samuel, we can't leave it open like this. It's clear that someone moved the roofing to the side. But it's completely plausible that a wind could have gotten in behind it and sent it crashing forward. If we have a part of metal hanging off the stairs, it will look even more believable."

Samuel thought about this for a moment before saying, "Let's toss some dirt down into the lab as well. It is pretty common in farmland out this way to get sudden bursts of strong winds that disappear just as quickly."

"And then tomorrow when the workers arrive, they'll discover it. Great idea, Samuel. I'll make a second-story man out of you yet."

"What?"

*   *   *

"This next stop is going to be a lot trickier. I have no doubt that Boyd Hoover has set all kinds of security traps around the perimeter of his farm." Charlotte was thinking out loud. "I almost forgot, what did you and Horse find under the patio?"

Samuel snarled.

"It was a damned wrapped peppermint candy. Like the kind they have in a bowl when you pay your check at the diner."

"Really? Horse may be a pig, but he wouldn't lose it over one little candy. There was nothing else down there?"

Samuel glared at Charlotte. Horse shook his head.

"In either case, it got us nowhere." Samuel looked at Horse as he said it.

"I'm not so sure. I'd like to keep it if I may?" Charlotte said, and Samuel handed over the mint.

"Knock yourself out," Samuel said.

"You know the discovery of that lab puts another big target on Danny Costa's back." Charlotte opened the truck window to let some air in and perhaps calm her worrying.

"Danny's never been into drugs, and he does fine as a contractor. He'd never need to sell them."

"I don't think that lab was used to make illegal substances Samuel, at least not the ones that are ingested. I think that Linc was making homespun pesticides using banned substances."

"That's an interesting thought, and it would explain why he suddenly had a nice income deposited into his bank account." Samuel nodded.

"I still have to research the photos I took to confirm it, but I suspect that by the time I do, the police will already have found the lab and confirmed its purpose."

The terrain surrounding Hoover Farms was a stark contrast to that around Linc's place, even during the dark of night. Everything was neatly trimmed and well maintained. It was also very lush with plant growth, making jumping the fence very uninviting. Below, the hacienda-style houses were brightly lit and most certainly protected by set alarms.

Samuel pulled over and off the side of the road and parked in the middle of two thick trees. He doused the lights but remained in the truck.

"Charlotte. You said you'd come up with something, so what is your plan to keep your pink friend quiet while we go exploring?"

"Yes, about that." Charlotte looked deep into Horse's eyes. "My dear friend, I need you to do something very, very important for me. It is vital that you obey. I want you to stay in here and remain completely silent until we return. Do you understand?"

Horse returned Charlotte's gaze and when she was done speaking, he moved closer and began licking her face.

"He understands alright, but that doesn't mean that he's going to obey. That's the best you've got?"

"You have another idea Mr. Smarty Pants?"

"Matter of fact, I do." Samuel got out of the truck and retrieved his backpack from the flat bed and then walked around and stuck his head into the passenger-side window. "You two are going to stay here and let me do the sleuthing."

"Oh no," Charlotte said, reaching for the handle to open the car door.

Samuel pressed on it to keep it closed.

"You know this is the best way. I know what we're looking for, and I can be in and out quickly. I used to play and hunt around this land as a kid, so I know where to go and where there are openings to sneak in and out."

"But this is my—"

"No *buts*. I'll come back and tell you what I've found, and then if you're still not satisfied, you can go in and I'll sit with Horse. Deal?"

"Deal. But not one of my better ones."

"Keep an eye on your phone in case I text you. It's still on mute, right?"

Charlotte flared her eyes at him.

"Of course it is. Stupid question. I'll be back soon."

Samuel turned quietly and disappeared into the brush around the farm's perimeter.

"Be careful," Charlotte whispered, but doubted if he'd heard her.

"You heard the man, Horse. We sit here and wait."

They looked at each other, and Charlotte burst out in laughter.

"Come on, buddy."

Charlotte turned and went in the opposite direction from Samuel. She wasn't sure where she was going or what she expected to find, but she couldn't just sit in the car and do nothing. Especially with Diane so upset about Danny being arrested. Charlotte wanted him to have at least a fighting chance.

Far up ahead she saw faint lights that looked to be coming from the middle of the road.

"Horse, you need to stay right close to my leg as we walk and try not to make a sound."

He closed in the ranks and trotted in step with Charlotte. "Good boy."

As they drew nearer to the lights, Charlotte could make out that she was looking at the back end of a small cargo van. She immediately crouched down in the Mexican sage growing wild along the side of the road.

Better sense got a hold of Charlotte, and she decided not to risk getting any closer and being caught. Anybody out at this hour was most likely doing something that they didn't want other people to see.

But a pig roaming around farmland would seem perfectly normal . . .

Charlotte got an idea and looked around the area where she had squatted for something that she could fashion into a kind of sling. She located a piece of stray barbed wire, but she immediately ruled that out. She let herself sink all the way to the ground, closed her eyes, and thought hard.

"I'm afraid that this part of the mission might be a bust," she whispered to Horse.

The night air was cold, and Charlotte put her hands under the bib of her overalls to warm them up. She felt a lump and realized that there was something in the bib's front pocket. She'd borrowed the overalls from Beau, so she couldn't even imagine what he'd stuffed in there. She removed one hand from the warmth and reached into the pocket.

Charlotte pulled out a pink paisley bandana.

Perfect.

Charlotte removed her ball cap and removed two of the elastic hair bands that she'd used to keep her hair in place and hidden under her hat. She then laid out the bandana into a full square and then folded it in half, one corner to another. Charlotte took her cell phone out of her pocket, went to the Camera app and tapped "Record." She placed the phone on top of the flat side of the bandana until only the camera lens was sticking out. Charlotte then folded the pointed end up covering the screen of the phone. She then fashioned one hair band tightly over each end of the bandana all the way up to the edges of the phone to hold it in place. In essence she'd made a sling.

"Okay, Horse, listen to me very carefully," she whispered as she tied the bandana around his neck so that the phone camera was nestled on his chest and pointed outward. "I want you to trot up closer to that van, but not all the way. When you're there, lift your head up, maybe walk around it a little, and then pretend to be rooting for something. You don't need to stay long, and I'll give you a signal when it's time to come back. You got that, Horse?"

He'd been watching Charlotte intensely during her briefing.

"Oh, and you sense any kind of danger, you run away from there as fast as you can. Got it?" Charlotte asked, scratching his nose.

Horse gave her a wide, apple-cheeked smile, turned around, and set out on his mission. Charlotte watched from behind her blind of Mexican sage and tried to dispel thoughts of anything happening to harm her beloved friend.

Horse followed her directions closely. She saw him alternating from rooting and grunting to trotting. He looked like he didn't have a care in the world.

"What the hell is that?" Charlotte heard a man's voice yell. She was then almost blinded by a strong flashlight that was pointed in her direction. She crouched down even deeper into the brush, closed her eyes and said a little prayer for Horse. Another voice joined in and now lights were bouncing all around her. "There's somebody out there!"

Charlotte risked a quick peek and saw that the lights were moving closer in her direction. If she got caught, not only would she blow her cover and Samuel's, but they'd probably both be arrested for trespassing. Boyd Hoover would have a field day.

"Who's out there?" Charlotte heard another male voice call out.

Think fast, Charlotte.

Before she could make a move, Horse stood up on his hind legs and let out a series of loud, sharp "groinking" barks. It sounded like an angry hippo was protecting her calves. The men both screamed, and Horse made a show of grunting and rooting before quietly trotting back to Charlotte.

Moments later Charlotte saw the van's lights illuminate and heard the motor turn over. Soon after the van's wheels spat out dirt as it revved up. In the moment before the van disappeared down the other side of the hill, the headlights caught the dark shadow of a figure standing at the side of the road. There were boxes stacked on a platform near the person, but what chilled Charlotte to the bone was the fact that the figure was facing in her direction with an outstretched arm that was clearly holding a gun. She dared not breathe and hoped that Horse had seen her quick signal and had frozen in place.

She'd spent some time recently going on hikes with her local friend, Karen Hubbard, who owned a wonderful lunch restaurant in town that also served brunch on Saturdays and Sundays.

Karen had little time off, but when she did, she loved to go out and work on field training with her pair of Labrador retrievers. She didn't plan to hunt with them, but she enjoyed the teaching exercises, as did her dogs. Charlotte would bring along Horse, who loved learning as well, but putting it into practice was a horse of a different color.

Charlotte hoped that she'd remembered the hand signal correctly but had to make some adjustments for the darkness. Samuel had once told her that pigs did not have very good night vision, but they have an amazing sense of the vibrations in the ground, so they can tell with a great deal of accuracy where you are, purely on sound and ground vibrations and smells, and so be able to "see" in the dark. Charlotte held her hand out flat in front of her chest with her palm pointed downward and then slapped it flat on the ground.

She waited, unmoving, and listened.

Silence.

After what seemed like forever, Charlotte saw a light coming from the area where the person had been standing. She prayed that someone wasn't coming searching for her and Horse. Then she heard a noise that sounded like a strong gust of wind had just passed her ear, followed by a soft humming.

Golf cart?

The lights were in motion, first backing up and then moving forward toward the fence around the field. When Charlotte thought that it had been driven inside the perimeter, she started to stir, but then froze. The cart had stopped, and she could faintly hear the sounds of boots walking on gravel. Then came the screech of rusty metal being moved, followed by the clicks of what Charlotte suspected was a large padlock being deployed.

Another silence followed, and Charlotte held her breath.

Finally, the lights from the vehicle disappeared into the darkness. Charlotte released a long breath and patted her palm twice on the ground. In the faint moonlight peeking out from behind the marine layer, she saw a pink head pop up from the tall grasses with a pink bandana tied around its neck.

"Oh, thank god, Horse, major treats are coming your way when we get home. Come!" she whispered.

Charlotte stood up and had to limp back to Samuel's truck. Her foot had gone to sleep after sitting on it for so long, cutting off its circulation. Horse came out of the brush looking all proud and exhilarated, his head held up high and his curly tail twirling like a pinwheel in a windstorm.

"Charlotte?" she heard Samuel's voice whisper. Charlotte quickly loaded Horse back into the cab of the pickup truck and slipped her cell phone into the pocket of her overalls. The pink bandana had been a tight fit when she fastened it around Horse's neck, and it was now damp, and the knot wasn't budging. Charlotte hopped into the pickup and threw an arm around Horse's shoulders.

"I thought I heard voices, yelling—what was going on?" Samuel asked, dropping his gear into the flat bed. He hopped up behind the wheel and looked over at Charlotte and Horse.

"I didn't hear anything. Did you, Horse?" Charlotte asked, playing with his ears.

Samuel looked at the pig and noticed the addition of a pink bandana. He gave Charlotte a wide-eyed, raised eyebrows, questioning look.

198

"We got bored, so we decided to play dress up. I tried some different hairstyles and Horse explored neckwear. Shouldn't we get going, Samuel? We've been lucky so far, but I'd hate to push it."

Samuel started the truck. "I don't know exactly what part of your story isn't true or if you've left a whole chunk of it out. But I do know that you've been up to no good, Charlotte Finn. Sure as I'm sitting here."

"Why, whatever do you mean Farmer Samuel Brown?"

Charlotte grinned but her insides were in knots. She had dodged a bullet.

Literally.

Chapter Seventeen

"Well?"

"Well, what?" Samuel asked Charlotte on the drive back to the farm.

"What did you discover during your spy mission around Hoover Farm?"

"Boyd's crops are healthy and full, just like you suspected."

Charlotte let that fact settle in her mind.

"He's been lying this entire time," Samuel continued. "Why? He could have just told everyone that somehow his crops had escaped the blight. By not telling the truth everything points to Boyd sabotaging the other farms' crops."

"I think that Boyd's definitely lying about something—maybe many things," Charlotte said, clutching Horse dearly by her side. "But I'm not sure that he'd take the time or effort to go about ruining all the strawberry crops in Little Acorn. Plus he'd need help to pull that off, and as everybody says, he trusts no one."

"That's true," Samuel said, nodding. "We know that Linc Pierce and Boyd Hoover were on again, off again buddies, and it's very possible that they were in cahoots on something illegal."

"Maybe Boyd let down his guard and trusted Linc for a while, but then that fell apart. Linc might have threatened to betray Boyd. That's a pretty good motive for murder. A lot will hinge on what's in the lab in Linc's cellar. I guess tonight we took two steps forward and one step backward." Charlotte sighed.

"Are you thinking again that Linc's murder and Little Acorn's sabotaged crops could be two separate crimes?" Samuel pulled into the drive up to Finn Family Farm.

"I sure hope not. That would mean that we've got two nefarious individuals roaming around our properties. I'd hate to even think about that." Charlotte shivered. "I guess we'll just have to do what they do in crime shows."

"What's that?"

"See where the evidence takes us." Inside her pocket Charlotte clutched her cell phone.

*   *   *

"Charlotte, my honey, are you alive in there? I'm coming in." Beau gave her bedroom door a few more sharp knocks and then entered the room. "Hello, sleeping beauty."

Charlotte opened one eye and then quickly closed it again. Beau had opened the first set of drapes covering the French doors leading to the fields, and sunlight was spewing in like a volcano had erupted.

"Hi, Beau. What time is it?" came a muffled voice from under a pillow.

"About a half an hour from lunchtime."

Upon hearing that, Horse flipped over and stood on all fours. He hopped off the bed and raced out of the room. Charlotte slowly pulled the pillow away from her face.

"Did Horse miss breakfast? I must be mistaken." Beau pulled back the last set of drapes and then sat down on the bed next to Charlotte. "Did you participate in some sort of hootenanny last night, girlfriend? You look like you were riding a mechanical bull that suddenly turned into a real one and took off with you. Although I like the messy hairstyle—very Anna Nicole Smith."

As Charlotte regained more and more of her faculties, the bed, her room and the memory of last night came to the forefront.

"My phone! Where's my phone?" she shouted.

"Right there by your side. And your laptop is just there, wedged between two pillows. You're starting to worry me." Beau felt her forehead with the back of his hand.

Charlotte grabbed her cell phone and tried to bring it to life. "Dead. Rats!"

"I'll start the charge. But then you've got some 'splaining to do." Beau took both her phone and her laptop to the desk and plugged the devices into their power cords.

"It's not at all what you think, Beau. I lead a very innocent life if you don't count my chasing murderers. I've got to get in the shower. I'll be out shortly."

"Okay, honey, but brace yourself for bad news when you do."

"What, Beau?"

"Overnight it seems that someone delivered hundreds of snails to the strawberry plants. Hungry snails."

"Give me five minutes!" Charlotte moved to the bathroom, but on her way, she saw that her cell phone now had enough juice to illuminate the screen. There was a notice that she'd received a text message. Charlotte shook her head in hopes of clearing her mind. She finally remembered whom she'd reached out to last night, and quickly read the response.

Forget the shower!

* * *

As soon as Beau slowed the electric cart by the first field, Charlotte was out and running over to her strawberries. Both Joe and Alice were bent over the plants, with buckets, plucking away the slimy interlopers. She saw Samuel pacing, with his head dropped down.

"How many crops were hit Joe? Do we know?" Charlotte put a hand above her eyes, to shield the sun, and surveyed the farmland in front of her.

"I think it's contained to these four plantings. The Tristars, the Albions, and a couple of hybrids, including Miss Fern's third-grade class's white strawberries."

"Oh no! Alice, I'm so sorry."

"Me too, but we'll tend to whatever is still alive and start more." Alice's hands were a blur as she quickly snatched off snails and tossed them in her bucket.

"If we work fast, we should be able to minimize the damage," Samuel said, picking up a bucket and tossing another to Beau.

"Should we bring some field hands in? I'll pay double today, if necessary," Charlotte said, getting to work herself.

Joe nodded. "I've got calls out, but for those guys the day's already half over, so if they're not already on a job, then they could be anywhere, taking a much-deserved rest."

"I've been gone for a week or so, and it's clear that I've missed several important acts of this play." Beau had paused for a moment to remove his striped rep tie and relocated it on his forehead to act as a sweatband. "Who would be so cruel as to deliberately and blatantly execute this kind of destruction? And why?"

Charlotte and Samuel exchanged a guilty glance.

"What on earth?" Diane asked, out of breath from running down to the field.

"Snails, dear Sis, and not the kind you enjoy with aromatic garlic butter. Charlotte was just about to tell me what led up to this act of defiance." Beau tossed Diane a bucket.

Charlotte gave Beau a recap, careful to leave out any incriminating evidence. Samuel filled in some of the blanks when needed.

"Wow, you all have been busy. Do you think that these snails were dropped here as an act of vengeance and as a warning by someone to stop snooping around and asking questions about the strawberry blight?" Beau asked.

"And Linc's murder," Samuel chimed in. "But it must be someone who doesn't know Charlotte very well."

"Why is that?" Alice asked.

"Because something like this will only serve to light a fire under her, with a higher flame!" Samuel grinned and the rest chuckled.

"There is now one thing that we know for sure." Charlotte silenced the group, who collectively looked to her. "Danny isn't responsible for any of this, including Linc's murder. He's been in jail for the last two days."

"That explains the crop destruction, but how can you be so sure about Linc's killer? Don't misunderstand—I desperately want you to be right, Charlotte." Diane gave her those pleading, wide brown eyes.

"Because I happen to know for a fact that on the day Linc was murdered, Danny's horse was being reshod by a farrier at the stables where he's kept. Gary, part of Danny's crew told me about the stables, and I contacted the owner to ask about where the horse was on that date." Charlotte adjusted her posture up to stand tall, proud that some of her detective work had finally paid off.

"One step ahead of you Charlotte," said Chief Goodacre, appearing on the scene. "We released Danny Costa this morning, but he needs to stay local until the case is closed. I also had my deputy press the eyewitness to the person on horseback that day, and he admitted that the sun was in a spot where he could only see shadows and now wasn't so sure that it was Danny."

"Oh, thank goodness. Is he with you, Chief?" Diane asked.

"No, I dropped him at his home to shower and change and then, I assume, get back to finishing that wonderful restaurant of yours, Diane. I've been on a fast for the last few days in anticipation, so he'd better hurry up."

Diane pulled her cell phone out of her pocket and stepped away from the group, presumably to call Danny.

"Honey—I mean Chief—are you taking supplements while you're doing this? You want to keep your electrolytes up." Beau made a caring gesture of patting her shoulder.

"Don't worry, dear, by *fast* I mean I give myself ten minutes for each meal and then push myself away from the table. It works for me."

"I'm the one that called Chief. Overnight someone unloaded about two hundred hungry snails on our crops of strawberries. It may seem a bit trivial compared to murder, but it is an act of

205

sabotage all the same, so I thought that you'd want to take a look." Joe stepped aside to show her the invasion.

"You thought right, Joe—good job." The Chief took a quick look into some of the filled buckets and quickly stepped back. Clearly snails weren't her favorite things. "Has anything happened in the last day or two that could have escalated someone's anger?" The Chief looked directly at Charlotte and waited.

Wide eyed, they all shook their heads slowly. The Chief had a way of making people feel reprimanded when she spoke, even if they'd done nothing wrong.

"Charlotte?" Chief Goodacre walked over to her.

"Nothing that I know of. Except that thing that I sent to you."

"What thing?"

"The email I sent you with research and articles I'd found on Ford Barclay's family and their business with pesticides," Charlotte reminded her.

"That's what that was? The subject line said something about news on banned pesticides, so I forwarded it to deputy Elmwood. He handles those things." The Chief was now staring at Charlotte.

"Is it possible that the deputy could have contacted Ford Barclay after reading the material?" Charlotte asked, her breathing getting faster.

"Illegal pesticides are his area, so I would imagine so. I'll confirm with him." The Chief's cell phone rang, and Charlotte heard her say three things after she answered, "Where?" "Has anybody touched anything?" and "I'm on my way."

The Chief turned on her heels and broke into a run up to her car.

"Forward me that email again," she shouted over her shoulder.

Chapter Eighteen

"Beau!" Charlotte whispered to him. They'd finished the snail cleanup, and Charlotte had found Beau enjoying a glass of lemonade in a swing bench on the porch.

"What?" he whispered back. "And why are we whispering?"

"I need help with something, and you are the perfect, trust-worthy candidate for the job. Follow me." Charlotte went into the farmhouse.

"I'm doomed from the start, I just know it." He followed her into her bedroom suite with Horse by his side. As soon as they were in, she locked the door.

"Charlotte! We're like siblings!" Beau said in a mock shocked voice.

"Silly," she said, and giggled. "Pull up that chair to my desk. Horse will want to sit on your lap."

"Someone needs to tell Horse that he's getting a little too old and a lot too big to be sprawled out on anyone's legs anymore," Beau said as soon as Horse climbed up onto him and gave him a kiss.

"Be serious. You are not going to believe what I did, along with Horse."

"Is it legal? I've only just hopped off the house arrest train."

"I've broken no laws that I know of," Charlotte said while booting up her laptop and plugging in her now charged cell phone.

Charlotte found the movie file from her phone and opened it up on her laptop screen. The video that came up was dark and blurred, punctuated with intermittent splashes of light.

"What am I looking at? Have you been spelunking again?" Beau asked.

"Very funny. This is no cave, and hopefully this image will become clearer very soon."

Sure enough, it did. What filled the screen showed something moving, with the bottom half of the image made up of brown surfaces with occasional vertical splashes of green filling the picture and then disappearing. The top half of the image was more revealing. It showed a light in the distance that got larger and closer with the forward movement of the camera. Thin white strands that moved with the pace of the camera often interrupted the view.

"Okay, you attached a miniature camera to Mrs. Robinson and made a movie titled *The Flight of the Aphid*, which you plan to put to the music of 'Bohemian Rhapsody,'" Beau concluded.

"You know, you're not so far off the mark," Charlotte said between laughs. "It's video taken from my cell phone that I had strapped to Horse's chest with your pink bandana."

"I expect it returned washed and pressed. Where was this taken, and is the location what required the subterfuge? And why are we still whispering?" Beau was getting impatient.

"This was taken late last night outside the perimeter of Hoover farm. Samuel and I had gone on a recon mission to confirm or deny Boyd's claims that his strawberries were also suffering from this terrible blight."

"That explains my first two questions, sort of, but what about my third?" Beau turned his attention back to the computer screen.

"While Samuel used his boyhood recon skills to slip onto Boyd's farm, I was to stay in the truck with Horse." Charlotte paused, also watching the video play out.

"After a year Samuel hasn't learned that the minute you're told not to do something—"

"Shh, let's listen to this." Charlotte and Beau could now hear faint voices from the screen. Charlotte turned the sound as high as it would go.

"What the (unintelligible) that? You got wild bears (unintelligible)." This was followed by some shouts and the sounds of heavy footsteps. Light beams were scattering illumination across the screen like a laser show, letting images come in and out of focus in seconds. Next came the slamming of van doors and the start of an engine. In the half minute that the vehicle was put into reverse and the rear lights went on, Charlotte could vaguely make out a name painted on the back doors. She quickly paused the video.

"Come on—it was just getting good. I take it that Horse made it out okay; he seems just fine to me." Beau petted Horse's head as he was gently dozing on Beau's lap. After all, Horse had seen this movie.

"Okay, I'll continue, but then I need to go back to this frame and try and make out what the sign says on the truck." Charlotte noted the place in the filmstrip and then started the video up again.

They watched the van stop, the reverse lights went out, and then it sped forward, kicking up dirt with its tires. The scene went silent and dark except for one bright light shining into the camera.

"Can you see anything besides the light?" Charlotte asked with her nose almost touching the screen. Beau shook his head and moved closer as well.

The peace was violently interrupted by guttural cacophonic sounds that ranged from growls to screams, to demonic wails. Charlotte and Beau jumped back so fast that they nearly fell off their chairs. The bright light then shone to the ground, and just before disappearing, they could make out a person standing with their arms hanging down. In one hand was a flashlight, and in the other was a gun.

Charlotte noticed that Beau was hyperventilating. She also saw that Horse was sleeping soundly on his lap with a big grin across his face.

That's my boy.

"Calm down. Horse was just doing his job and following my directions. Although the appearance of a gun on the film was a surprise to me too. Somebody really wants to keep their business private."

"You mean like Boyd Hoover?" Beau was vigorously petting Horse's head and belly as if to show how relieved he was that the little man had survived this ordeal.

"Maybe, or it could be one of his henchmen that was posted on guard duty. I need to rewind to that shot of the sign on the van. That's our best chance at a clue." Charlotte rewound the film slowly, frame by frame, until she reached the spot that she'd been looking for. The name was a blur and impossible to make out. Charlotte tried adjusting the focus and enlarging the image, but it still wasn't readable. "Rats."

"How about you let me drive for a while," Beau said standing up and motioning for her to give him her chair in front of the computer. "I've been using graphics programs since before I had my permanent teeth. I may just know a trick or two."

"By all means, and Godspeed, Beau Mason." Charlotte stretched and headed out the French doors to the patio, with Horse at her heels. She needed some fresh air to clear her head and relax her tense body.

They ambled in between two beds of strawberries, their feet occasionally crunching on some dried soil. Charlotte paused for a moment and crouched down to inspect a few of the plants growing out from a hole in black plastic mulch. They looked like they were healthy and thriving.

So how does a plant go from this to wilted and dead overnight? Uniformly across an entire row?

A soft humming sound coming from high above the field made Charlotte look up. It was a small plane flying by overhead, probably from the little municipal airport nearby that offered flying lessons and served as a spot for firefighters to land and refuel during wildfires.

I'm back to drones, aren't I? That's what could spray and contaminate an entire field in a matter of hours. "On tonight's run, the drones are spraying liquid nitrogen for maximum growth"—*that's what Ford told me. He must have another fleet somewhere on his property, and I will need to find it and hope that these drones are white.*

Charlotte got up and continued walking, deciding to include Horse in on her musings about the crime.

"Let's assume, Horse, that whatever was applied to all our strawberry crops to damage or kill them was administered by drones." She looked at him for agreement and thought she saw a nod.

"We have evidence that leads us to believe that these drones are white in color. I have samples to prove that, in fact, but the thorny issue is how to introduce Chief Goodacre to it without getting me thrown in jail for withholding evidence? I may require your services on that one."

They were approaching the far perimeter of the Finn Family Farm, a destination Charlotte had not realized that she'd had in mind. Horse, on the other hand, had broken into a brisk trot, knowing full well where they were headed. His pace turned into a run, and Charlotte followed suit.

They raced all the way along the path until they reached the apple orchard at the end of the farm's property line. To one side of the orchard was a clearing that was covered with grass except for a small pond.

"Here we are at this beautiful sanctuary again." Charlotte took in the view.

In front of them stood a wooden structure that was built low to the ground and was about the size of a small tool shed, only it wasn't more than three feet high. A small ramp led up to an entrance for the enclosure, and perched on the threshold, proud and vigilant, sat "Mumsy," the name she'd given this beautiful snow goose, mother to the gaggle of energetic goslings that were waddling around and eating blades of grass.

Horse gently trotted into the center of them and lay down on the grass. The goslings wasted no time exploring this new pink attraction and were soon walking all over his back. A couple discovered his tail and appeared to fall over laughing every time they played with it. Charlotte lowered herself to the grass and giggled as she watched the frolicking.

"Just what the doctor ordered, don't you think, Horse?" He gave her a giant apple-cheeked grin in response. On the other side of the fence, Charlotte watched a couple of horses from the neighboring farm, running free. A young farmhand walked alongside them for a ways but mostly watched from a distance. This was their time.

"Horse, assuming that we are close to solving the method, and hopefully finding the perpetrators involved in the great strawberry blight, how do we tie that to Linc Pierce's murder? If there even *is* a connection?"

Charlotte watched the horses on the other side of fence, so happy, so free. One of the animals took a rest from frolicking and turned her attention to the stable boy. The mare nuzzled her nose onto his shoulder and then lifted up her head and licked his cheek. The boy responded with a wide smile and a series of gentle tugs on both of the horse's ears. It was such a tender moment that Charlotte was almost embarrassed to be watching. She looked to her side and saw that Horse was transfixed as well.

"How lovely," Charlotte whispered, pulling Horse in close to her side. The affectionate scene continued for another minute until the horse pulled back and touched the boy's hand with her nose several times. The boy reached in his pocket and returned his hand fisted and held it out to the horse. She once again nudged his hand with her nose until he opened his fingers and held up an open palm to her, filled some small red and white discs. The horse instantly gobbled them up and trotted away with glee.

"Are those pieces of apple?" Charlotte asked Horse, and he shook his head.

Suddenly Charlotte jumped to her feet. "I know what that is—come on Horse, we've got to go."

They both took off in the direction of the barn.

Chapter Nineteen

"Samuel?" Charlotte shouted, racing into the barn. Her voice echoed but did not receive a response. The goats were outside, alternating between sunshine and shade as they played some kind of wrestling match involving head butting, kicking, and rolling around on the ground. And Pele the horse was not in his stall, which explained where Samuel was.

"Darn. Let's go, Horse—time to check my purses."

The dynamic duo was on the run again, tearing up the hill and bursting through the French doors to Charlotte's bedroom suite.

"I was just about to call you," Beau said, standing up from her desk and laptop.

"Beau, help me get all my handbags out of the closet. We'll lay them out across my bed," Charlotte barked, flinging open her large closet doors.

"Ooh, are we playing dress-up? You know my position on the shoes matching the bag?" Beau asked.

"Yes: unless you're in prep school, the military, or an aspiring mime, don't do it. I know, Beau—it's what's in the bags that I'm looking for," Charlotte explained, tossing purses across the room.

"What exactly are you looking for?"

"Mints. Like the type you get with your check presenter at some restaurants."

"Like this?" Beau asked, producing a wrapped red and white peppermint from his pocket.

"How did you know? Where did you get that?" Charlotte asked, exasperated. She snatched it out of his hand.

"I stopped at Neptune's Net on the drive up here. I can never resist their fried clams. But in order to politely be able to get within kissing distance of other people, it's imperative to freshen one's breath."

"I love you for being so considerate. Now we just have to wait until Samuel and Pele return, and then I'm hoping that we'll have a major break in the case." Charlotte beamed. Horse suddenly took an interest in the candy item as well.

"Okay, I'm both excited and intrigued. Want to see the progress I've made on clearing up the words painted on the back of the van?" Beau teased.

"Yes! I almost forgot, things are getting so crazy around here. Do you have a company name for me?" Charlotte sprinted to her desk and woke up her laptop.

"I have a partial. I think some of the letters have been worn away. Here's the best I could do:" Beau opened the enhanced image on Charlotte's laptop and stepped aside so she could get a closer look.

"Wow, I can't believe that you recovered that much detail from that dark, blurry movie frame. Good job." Charlotte opened a side drawer of her desk and pulled out a pad of paper. "This is what I see—tell me if you disagree."

Charlotte wrote the letters *r y o—e s h*.

"Not much to work with. The two missing letters in the middle are so difficult to read because there's a big dent in the back of the van. I can keep working on it, though. The first letter is just scraped away except for a few small black marks," Beau explained.

"It's a start. Too bad Horse never got a good shot at what was being delivered." Charlotte grew silent and slipped into deep thought.

"Maybe you should ask him." Beau grinned and looked at his pink friend. Horse's ears popped up and he cocked his head.

"That's not as crazy as it sounds." Charlotte glanced out the French doors and, in the distance, saw Samuel riding Pele into the paddock. "They're back! I've got to go. You're welcome to tag along if you hurry, Beau."

"You report back while I continue working on optimizing this image. And I've got to work on my table flower designs for Diane's restaurant."

"Sounds good. Get a move on, Horse—we need to talk to Samuel before he heads to his cabin for a nap. You're having a really aerobic day, little man!"

* * *

They burst into the paddock, startling Samuel, who was busy removing Pele's saddle.

"Pele! Just the man I wanted to see." Charlotte ran over and hugged his neck.

"Well, technically he's still a boy. What's got you so riled up that your hair's even curlier than usual, Charlotte?" Samuel asked, turning his back to her as he carried the heavy saddle with both hands into the barn. Charlotte quickly followed him.

"Does Pele like candy?"

"I wouldn't know. His only source of sweets is natural fruits and vegetables like carrots. He's more than happy with that." Samuel grabbed a grooming brush from a shelf and headed back outside.

"Okay, maybe not *all* candy, but what about peppermint?" Charlotte persisted. Her hand was fisted around Beau's breath freshener in her pocket, but she wouldn't dare try to feed it to Pele without Samuel's permission.

"Like I said, Pele doesn't—I see where you're going with this. That mint I salvaged from under Linc Pierce's front steps." Samuel thought for a moment. "I do know people who give their animals peppermint to help with their digestive system, which, on a horse, is very fragile. Perhaps the horses know by instinct that it's good for them, because once you introduce mint to the horse, they will do pretty much anything for it. With Pele I've found that as long as he gets plenty of exercise and a balanced diet, all his parts work just fine."

"But someone who went to see Linc could have had mints—in a pants or jacket pocket, say—and one fell out and slipped through the spaces in his steps to the patio right?"

Samuel nodded. "Or Linc could have had a spicy Mexican dinner and needed something to settle his stomach so he could sleep through the night."

"Boo," Charlotte said, thinking again. "Except that Horse was intent on finding that particular peppermint, not because he wanted to eat it, but because it captured his interest in another way. Watch."

Charlotte pulled Beau's mint out of her pocket and dropped it to the ground. Horse watched her do this and then looked up to Charlotte and then to Samuel waiting for something else to happen.

"See? Do you still have the rescued peppermint? Can you get it?"

Samuel loped over to his desk in the barn and after what seemed like an eternity returned with the specimen. He was clearly hesitant about humoring Charlotte in this experiment.

"Great. Now set it next to the one I tossed on the ground," Charlotte instructed, crouching down to hold onto Horse for a moment. When Samuel was done, she let her pink friend loose.

Horse immediately trotted over to the mint that Samuel had placed on the ground and let out a series of grunts before looking back over his shoulder at Charlotte.

"He identifies that mint with a person and/or a place, but most likely a person, since it was sitting under those steps for a while. Who owns a horse around here who knew and would plausibly visit Linc's farm?"

"Like I told you, I haven't been to his place in years, so it wasn't me."

"I would never have thought so, Samuel."

"Well, Danny has a horse but the Chief has let him go. I'd hate to see him run back to jail on something so circumstantial. He's been with horses since before he could walk. I doubt that he needs candy to get a horse's attention."

"Easy enough to find out," Charlotte said, looking around for Diane and Danny. "That leaves Ford Barclay and Martin Ross. I believe that either one of them would use any trick necessary to get an animal to do what he wanted."

"So do I." Samuel nodded.

"But Horse has only ever met Martin when he came to the farm. And I could tell that he had mixed feelings about that new stranger."

"I'm firmly in Horse's camp on that one." Samuel's eyes squinted as he thought about it.

"But why would Martin ride over to Linc's instead of taking his way-too-cool car?" Charlotte asked, frustrated.

"Because it's much quicker. On horseback Martin could cut across a couple of neighboring farm fields and shave about thirty minutes from what it would take to drive there. He could come and go totally inconspicuously, which he couldn't do in a flashy sports car."

"As always, you are right. My head is spinning, though."

"It might be all those curls," he said, grinning.

Charlotte giggled and did a self-conscious run of her hand through her hair. "I'm going to find Danny and at least clear up one mystery. See ya!"

Charlotte and Horse were off running again.

* * *

Charlotte was excited to see Danny's truck parked under the trees in the shade when she arrived at the farmhouse.

"He must be at the restaurant—one more dash, Horse!"

He looked up at her and plonked down on his bum in defiance.

"Okay, we can walk. Will that be acceptable?" Charlotte asked, but got no reaction.

"We'll walk *slowly*—deal?"

Horse agreed and they ambled down to the almost finished restaurant.

"There you are! Come and see the lighting over the tables. I think it's magical. And Danny's back." Diane beamed; all was right with her world again. Charlotte followed her into the restaurant while Horse went for a lie-down in the waning afternoon sun.

"This is so warm and cozy, guests will never want to leave. Especially when you have a roaring fire going in the winter," Charlotte cooed.

"That is exactly why I had Danny build a library, or den, alongside it. People can relax there in soft club chairs over drinks or grab a book off the shelf and immerse themselves in a great story while sipping coffee, tea, or hot cocoa. There's even a bamboo screen that acts like a pocket door if the dining room gets too rowdy." Diane demonstrated by pulling at one end of the bamboo.

"Diane, the painters are circling around the space, doing touch-ups. Then I'm going to need you and any staff you want to listen in, to go over the lighting and HVAC systems," Danny told her. He looked like he'd lost weight but was otherwise unscathed from his stint in jail.

"It is so nice to have you back, safe and sound, Danny." Charlotte gave him a big hug.

"Diane tells me that you helped establish an alibi for me. I am indebted to you for that." He held her hand as he spoke.

"Nonsense. I know that you'd do the same for any one of us, Danny. Unfortunately, there is still a killer out there, and I do have one question that may help clear up some things and point me in the right direction."

"Sure, ask away."

"What's your thinking on giving horses those round red and white peppermint candies as treats?"

Danny let out a long exhale. "It's true that horses like peppermint, although I'd never give candy to my horse. Neither would most of the old-timers in the Rancheros Visitadores. You've probably seen cowboys feeding sugar cubes to their animals in movies, but what you don't know is that in real life it's done very sparingly. The problem is the sucrose can lead to an elevated level of insulin in the horse's body. There are sugar-free peppermint treats made especially for horses, but I prefer to treat them with what grows around us, and lots of verbal praise."

"But a horse owner who is not as considerate of the animal's health might carry a supply of peppermint candy 'atta boys'?" Charlotte asked.

"Sure, especially if the horse is getting fussy and you need him to be calm and quiet. It's like giving a baby a pacifier."

"You've been extremely helpful, Danny. Thank you! I'll send Diane over to you in a sec." Charlotte gave him another hug.

"See? He is a good guy after all," Diane said, hooking arms with Charlotte as she walked her to the door.

"I did have a question for you too."

"Okay," she said warily.

"There are my girls," Katharine said, meeting them at the door to the restaurant. "Diane, your restaurant is simply breathtaking. I can't imagine it being anything but a monumental success from the first time you open the doors for service. Don't you agree, Charlotte?"

"As lovely as it is, it will be Diane's scrumptious food that will send them off to bed with a smile."

"To be sure, to be sure. Diane I'll need some manpower to bring the cases of wine in. I want to thank you both so much for giving me this opportunity to showcase my wines to the Little Acorn community. As you are well aware, I've had a big uphill climb in making my winery a viable business, especially since the family resources are prioritized and applied heavily toward strawberry production. I've been waiting my turn patiently, but you know how obstinate my father can be about becoming the biggest grower in the county. With my wines on your menu, I'm sure the restaurant will be an overnight success. I now have a much-needed leg up." Charlotte could see Katharine's eyes grow moist, and her heart went out to her.

"Right back at you—your beautiful wines immediately elevate and complement our food." Diane gave her a hug, and Charlotte joined in as well.

"Thank you, dear friends, and if I may, I'd like to use your 'little girls' room before I get started with the offload?"

"Of course. You know where it is." Diane pointed her in the right direction. Suddenly Horse was up on his feet and about to cross the threshold of the restaurant as well.

"Oh no you don't, mister. From now on the only four-legged creatures allowed in or out of here have to be too full and drunk to stand erect." Charlotte blocked Horse and turned him around by his shoulders.

"I'd better get the wine in. There's so much more to be done, and if I stop, I'm sure that I'll forget some of it. Late-night cup of tea in your room, Charlotte?" Diane winked.

"I'll wait up for you. And Diane? Breathe—enjoy every instant of your dreams coming true." Charlotte blew her a kiss, and she and Horse made one final trek for the day up to the farmhouse.

Chapter Twenty

When Charlotte returned to her room, she saw that Beau had gone, but he'd left a note on her desk beside her laptop.

I hope that he's solved something. I'm getting tired of uncovering clues that lead to nowhere.

"My beautiful Charlotte," the note began. "I have worried my pretty little head over that sign on the van so that you don't have to worry yours. And guess what? Success! At least partially. You'll recall that the letters we could make out were *r y o—e s h*. I was able to zoom in and enhance more of the word and I'm about ninety percent sure that the word is *r y o f r e s h*. All you have to do is figure out the first letter. And here's the best news: I'm pretty sure that there are only twenty-six possible solutions. I'm off to work on surprise signage for Diane's restaurant. Happy trails, darling!"

I guess I'll run through the alphabet and search online for each word until I get a match . . .

Before Charlotte could start, her cellphone rang. It was the Chief.

225

"Hi, Chief. How are you this evening?"

"Forget the sweet talk. You are in deep trouble. At least Samuel is, and I'm throwing you in for good measure."

"In trouble for what?"

"Boyd Hoover called me, ranting and raving. He claims that he had a trespasser on his farm, stealing all his secrets. He got a license plate number off a truck, and he insists that I find the owner and make an arrest. Well, guess whose truck that plate sits on? Your boy farmer, Samuel Brown."

"He had nothing to do with it," Charlotte lied. She was determined to keep him out of any issues with Boyd. He worked too hard for that. "Have you had dinner?"

"Is it that time already? I need to wrap this up so I can get home. I've got a series I'm binging on."

"How about I treat you to dinner, and I'll tell you everything? I've been wanting to try that Crab Shack in Little Acorn."

"Hmm . . . cheddar cornbread. You've got yourself a deal. Twenty minutes?"

"Grab a table and order yourself a beverage of your choice, and I'll be right there," Charlotte said, grabbing a cardigan and her laptop as she raced out the door. Horse looked up from the bed and then dropped his head right back down. If there was more running involved, he was sitting this one out.

* * *

On the drive into town, Charlotte thought about what she should and shouldn't tell Chief Goodacre. She should definitely keep the midnight visit to Linc Pierce's farm and the discovery of the chemical lab to herself. Hopefully, she could coax that nugget on the case out of the Chief, along with what her team had found on closer inspection of the cellar. More canisters of liquid nitrogen?

The filming outside the gates of Hoover Farm and resulting footage was harmless enough. She hadn't committed any crimes, and the Chief might get a kick out of it.

Then there was the research she'd done, linking Ford Barclay and family with a company that made fertilizers and pesticides. He certainly had the means to spray and kill Little Acorn farm crops, but what was his motive? Just for fun? And was it a coincidence that not long after the Chief had contacted him about the pesticides, it had rained snails all over her crops? Probably not. She knew firsthand how much Ford hated to lose at anything.

The Crab Shack was just that, an oversized trailer with outdoor picnic tables, string lights overhead, a large trough of live crabs, and a walk-up window where you order on one side and pick up your food on the other side when they call your number. Charlotte found the Chief comfortably ensconced at a corner table, chosen most likely so that they were away from prying ears. Since she was still in uniform that wasn't such a difficult task. No one wanted to be seen being "overserved."

"I took the liberty of ordering for both of us. It can get very busy at this time of day. I paid, but you can leave a tip in the jar up there. I figure I'll be invited to yours and Diane's restaurant opening, so we're square. That's your beer." The Chief pointed to the bottle of Mexican brew with a lime wedged into the top.

"Thanks. See? I remembered," Charlotte said, and tipped her bottle toward Theresa's. This place is just what I was hoping for. Are the crabs local?"

"Rock crab caught in traps on the reefs right offshore. So sweet and divine. I tried to persuade them to let me do the cracking—you know, get out some aggression—but they have some rule about handing out wooden mallets to guests. Last time they tried, it didn't end well, I heard."

"Pick up number fifteen," they heard someone shout.

"That's us." Theresa said, looking at her receipt.

"I'll get it," Charlotte said. "In the meantime, watch this, and I'll explain when I get back."

Charlotte handed over her cell phone, all cued up to the video Horse had gotten.

When Charlotte reached the window and waited for their tray to be passed through, she looked over her shoulder and saw that Theresa had a smile on her face.

A good sign.

"This smells so good," Charlotte said, returning with the crab meals.

"That's all you're going to do is smell it until you explain what I'm looking at here," Theresa said, and dragged the tray over to her side of the picnic table.

"Please, that is inhumane," Charlotte begged.

In response Theresa buttered a piece of warm cheddar corn bread and took a torturous bite. Charlotte watched her chew with delight, eyes at half-mast and crumbs bathed in melted butter clinging to her lips.

"Okay!" Charlotte said, and she told Theresa about her recon mission to Hoover Farm, leaving out that Samuel had been with her and had been the one to confirm that Boyd's strawberry crops were healthy and prospering. When she was done, Theresa slid the tray of crab meals back to the center of the table.

"One more question," she said, and Charlotte nodded in between bites of sweet crab and coleslaw.

"How the heck did you get that camera on Horse?"

Charlotte giggled and explained.

"I may have to change your name to McGyver. I could use someone like you on the force if you ever get tired of farm life. Were you able to make out the name on the back of the van?"

"Not entirely. I've been able to confirm some of the letters, but not all." Charlotte held back info about all the letters Beau had confirmed. She knew that she just needed a bit of time to get the first letter, and she wanted to know what she was dealing with first.

"Have you spoken to Margaret, Linc's great-granddaughter lately?" Theresa asked.

Charlotte shook her head. "I've had no reason to, but I did invite her to the restaurant opening if she's still in town. Why do you ask? Is she okay?"

"She's fine. The contractor made a discovery on the Pierce Farm today. It seems that a large piece of roofing that was leaning against the outside of the farmhouse next to the front steps fell forward, revealing a kind of root cellar."

"I'd never have taken Linc Pierce as a fruit and compote preserver, Theresa." Charlotte tried to sound as nonchalant as possible.

"He wasn't. Turns out that he was hiding a lab filled with chemicals and remnants of experiments. Bunsen burners, the whole nine."

"What? Like a meth lab?" Charlotte asked.

"Doesn't appear to be, from the powders and solvents we found. It looks more like Linc was in the home fertilizer business. Using banned substances such as methyl bromide. So sad."

"You remember that his great-granddaughter said that he was a salesman before he became a farmer. He sold fertilizers and pest control products. Maybe he held onto some of the solutions and was trying to replicate the recipe?" Charlotte guessed.

"Very possible, so now we've got to conduct an audit of every farm in the county to make sure that there are no supplies of dangerous chemical cocktails being used in the fields. It will be days and days of canvassing." Theresa shook her head at the thought.

"Margaret also told us she'd had a surprise windfall when she learned that Linc's bank account showed a significant influx of cash in recent months? If I recall, she said that the account name on the checks was KB Holdings. Were you able to trace the owners of that enterprise?"

"Not without a warrant, and I don't have nearly enough to go to a judge with. From the registrar, all I could learn is that it is most likely a shell corporation."

"That's a shame. I need to take a moment to tell you just how delicious this crab is. Thank you for joining me for dinner." Charlotte could feel melted butter sliding down her chin but didn't care.

"Someone had to make the supreme sacrifice, and I guess it was me." Theresa laughed.

"Do you do much cooking? I know that you bake, and I've heard your peach cobbler is legendary."

"When I have the time I love to cook, but my skills are at a home-kitchen level, nothing like Diane's gift. I was born on a farm—not around here, but in the South—in a suburb of New Orleans. So, I do roast chicken and biscuits, shrimp boils, gumbo, glazed ham, and pork chops. Nothing that would help me keep my girlish figure, so I only indulge about once a month."

"Whatever the next day is, I'm available!" Charlotte said, and they both chuckled. "How'd a good ole southern girl get all the way across the country and find her way to Little Acorn?"

"You are going to laugh your head off." Theresa paused before continuing, as if thinking about the best way to tell this story. "I was the only girl in the family with four brothers. As you can see, I grew up being kind of a tomboy. Still am. If I wanted to be included in what they were doing, then I had to learn to play like them. Their sport of choice was baseball, so that's what I learned, and I was good at it. So much so that after I graduated, I looked for professional teams that I could join. I hadn't played any competitive games and had no score record, so I was forced to take what I could get. Which was a women's professional softball team based in Stockton, California. I played catcher, and we had a glorious first year. I was hooked. The next year, not so much. We lost all sixteen games we played and lost our qualification for the National Pro league. I'd gotten hooked on the pleasant temperatures of California and the low humidity, and decided to enter the police academy. When I finished, there was an opening down here, and the rest is history."

"Wow, what a story. I think that's very cool. I just got on a path and stayed in my lane until I inherited the farm. Do you ever wish that you'd tried to pursue a softball career somewhere else?" Charlotte asked.

"Yes and no. Like most young women, I was looking for a job that really meant something to me. I loved playing, but I could also face facts. Women were always going to play second fiddle to men and their baseball prowess. And in law enforcement I actually make a difference. I sleep well at night, and there's a police baseball league and I'm one of two women on it. And each time we're on the field, we're kicking ass and taking names." Theresa's mouth turned into a devilish grin as she thought about it. Charlotte gave her a high five.

Going back to Linc's lab for a moment," Charlotte began, "I remember you saying that there were canisters of liquid nitrogen found in Linc's barn. Did you find similar ones in his cellar?"

"No, we think that what was in the barn was the finished product. I've sent it out to be analyzed. What we found in the lab were the ingredients to make the liquid nitrogen mixture, powders, chemicals, etcetera"

"So, he'd fill the canisters in the lab, pressurize them there, and bring the liquid nitrogen up to the barn to sell?" Charlotte was trying to visualize the steps.

"Possibly, minus the pressurization. The canisters we found were not vacuum insulated," Theresa said, getting up to bus their tray and eaten-clean plates.

Charlotte turned her head so that the Chief couldn't see how far her jaw had dropped.

I've been thinking about this all wrong.

Charlotte joined Theresa at the pickup window and left a generous tip in the jar.

"This is the last time that I'm going to warn you: stay away from this case. The next time you have a hunch, call me day or night, and I'll promise to give it serious consideration. You saw the gun that person was holding outside Hoover Farm. If it had gone off, I'd have been hard pressed to see that as anything more than protecting private property. I always enjoy your company, Charlotte, and I hope that we can have many more delectable meals together. But for that to happen, you need to stay alive. I need a promise from you."

"Understood, and I promise. You're a good cop, Chief Goodacre."

With that they walked to their separate cars. The Chief was headed home to continue watching her series on TV. Charlotte was racing back to the farm to talk to Diane as soon as possible.

Chapter
Twenty-One

When Charlotte arrived home, she heard music from the opera *Carmen* coming from the living room. She followed the inviting sounds into the room.

The fireplace was lit and offered amber warmth to the room. Two leather club chairs had been turned to face the hearth. When Charlotte walked around to the front of the chairs, she saw Beau curled up in one of them and Horse doing the same in the other.

"You two look comfortable." Charlotte smiled at them.

"Who knew that the little man was such a fan of the rhythms of flamenco music?"

Charlotte looked over to Horse. He rested, supine, on the soft leather, and she could swear that he was moving one hoof with the music.

"Is Diane around?" Charlotte asked. "I desperately need to talk to her."

"Sorry, Char, she's out on a date with Danny, and if I were a betting man, I'd wager that we won't see her until the morning." Beau winked at her.

"Oh no!" Charlotte's shoulders dropped.

"Will another member of the Mason family do? I am a blood relative."

"Not unless you know all about this liquid nitrogen freezing technique that she's using with some recipes."

Beau raised his arms in a "surrender" pose. "I'm afraid not. Too much science for my left brain. But Alice might be able to help out—she seems mesmerized by the process."

"Great idea, Beau!" Charlotte turned on her heels and ran out of the living room, to the orchestra playing the "Toreador Song."

* * *

Charlotte tapped softly on the Wongs' cottage door, just in case they'd gone to bed. Alice and Joe lived in a house below one of the strawberry fields, and recently Charlotte had sold it to them for one dollar so that they'd know that they were part of the family. The relief it gave them was greatly appreciated and won their hearts.

Charlotte saw the white shutter slats open on the window beside the door, and then Joe welcomed her in.

"I hope nothing is wrong. You never know as long as there is still a murderer loose in Little Acorn," he said.

"Everything's fine, Joe, and I hope I haven't come too late, but I needed to ask Alice some questions that could be important to the case. You could help as well."

"You're not disturbing us at all," Alice said, appearing in the doorway as well. "We're working on a thousand-piece jigsaw puzzle that is driving us crazy."

"I love jigsaw puzzles. As kids Beau, Diane, and I used to work on them during rainy days at the summer cabin on the lake. What's the subject of this one?" Charlotte asked, stepping into the living room of their exceptionally clean and beautifully decorated home.

"I'm guilty of picking it, but I didn't realize that it had so many pieces when I bought it," Joe confessed, and pointed to a white, painted, wooden side table.

"Candy wrappers." Charlotte looked at the picture on the box lid. "Lots and lots of candy wrappers."

"I've gained three pounds already while working on it, and we just started," Alice complained.

"Are you sure it wasn't due to your and Diane's cooking?" Charlotte wondered.

"That too, I'm sure. I heard you say that you had some questions for me. Please make yourself comfortable. We're having a glass of wine—would you like one?"

"I'm good. I just gorged myself with food and drink at the Crab Shack."

"One of my favorites." Joe sat down in what Charlotte could see was clearly "his chair," a light tan corduroy-covered armchair accompanied by a wooden side table where books, including the *I Ching*, sat. Joe often cited quotes from the work.

Alice brought over their wineglasses from the puzzle table and settled on the sofa next to Charlotte.

"I wanted to ask you about this liquid nitrogen food freezing that you and Diane are working with. Something came up, and Diane is out for the evening."

"Sure, we can tell you what we know, but Diane is really the authority," Alice said.

"Specifically, I'm interested in the kind of liquid nitrogen you use and how it's packaged."

"I've still got a cylinder left—let me go get it quickly." Joe rose from his chair and went to the back door.

"I can tell you that Diane learned this technique from a coworker in Los Angeles and was excited to experiment with it on her own recipes. We've had fun playing with it, but Diane doesn't think that it will be used after the opening, except maybe on special occasions."

"Why is that?"

"Diane says that it's too expensive for just a 'wow' factor."

"Expensive? How can all these farmers afford to use it on their crops?"

"Those are entirely different products, Charlotte," Joe said, bringing in a cylinder like the ones she'd seen before. "This is what they call 'food-grade' liquid nitrogen. It's delivered in cryogenic cylinders that are insulated, vacuum-jacketed pressure vessels like this one. It will quickly freeze fruits and vegetables just after they're picked, to maximize freshness."

"That's what we're doing because I don't have the time just now to make jams for the Farm Store," Alice said, jumping in.

"This isn't what the farmers are using?"

"Not at all. They're using nitrogen to promote the growth of their crops. This product comes in a number of packaging, when we used it in the past it was delivered in what they call Dewars containers. They're non-pressurized and hold about a liter. Many farmers then use liquid nitrogen in fertigation, the application of fertilizers through their irrigation systems."

"These two different packaged liquid nitrogen products are used for quite different uses and presumably by very different people. One more question: Could the blight on our strawberry crops have been caused by applying food-grade liquid nitrogen to them?"

Joe thought for a moment. "It's possible, but the question is how would it have been applied to the fields? It needs to be delivered by a pressurized cylinder."

"I think the owls know the answer to that."

* * *

It had been an awfully long day, and as tired as Charlotte was, she couldn't get to sleep. That night she was the one leaving their warm bed to go outside and watch the owls perform their magic. Horse was in a deep dream and didn't even change his soft, even breathing when she left.

When Charlotte reached the field with the occupied owl house, she sat down and turned her attention to the sky. It was a clear night, and the stars were actively winking at her. It didn't take long for Charlotte to spot Fred swoop out of his house and cruise across the field, looking for dinner. Ginger watched on from the porthole of her roost.

"I wish that you two could tell me what you've seen going on to harm my strawberries," she said to the raptors. "I want to make sure that this farm is safe for you to bring your babies into the world."

"You've still got about a month before they arrive," she heard Samuel say before he joined her on the ground. "I was doing rounds and heard you. I'd hoped that you were talking to another person." He grinned.

"I was talking to Fred and Ginger—same difference." Charlotte looked into his warm, almond-shaped green eyes and saw concern.

"You think I'm on a fool's errand, don't you? That I should leave this to law enforcement and move on? The attack on our crops seems to have subsided except for it raining snails last night, so the worst is over? You think that I take this personally because Beau and I found poor Linc Pierce's body?"

Samuel looked surprised at first but then smiled. "As you, Beau, and Diane like to joke, those words you've put in my mouth number more than I'm known to say in a month. But more importantly, they are not what I think at all. I've never made a secret of my concern for your safety every time you start dealing with people who are no strangers to criminal behavior. The farm—all of us—would be lost if anything happened to you. Sure, I wish that you'd leave these cases to the cops, but I know that's not in your nature. You have an insatiable appetite for keeping balance in the world and correcting wrongs. That's what makes you such a good farmer. All I ask is that you keep me involved as your wingman, so speak. I'll run interference and try to keep you safe as best I can." Samuel blinked and his salty, teary eyes turned a brighter, neon shade of green.

"You're wrong." Charlotte paused, and he dropped his head. "What you just told me amounted to more words than we've heard you say in one go ever!"

They both laughed, and Charlotte let her head rest on his shoulder. He reached for her hand, and they sat in silence for a while, enjoying the owls' flight.

"You're a wise and kind man, Samuel Brown, I don't care what anyone says.

"Thanks—I think. You're not so bad yourself, Charlotte Finn." He kissed her head.

"*Cryofresh!* That's what the sign on the back of the van said! Of course, why didn't I think of that sooner?"

"Er, I can't answer that question because I have no idea what you're talking about."

"Come on, Samuel—we've got to get to my room right away."

"Are you sure?" Samuel asked, hyperventilating a bit.

"Positive. It's all on my computer—I'll show you. And then we can get to work!"

Charlotte took off running, leaving Samuel standing there stunned. He thought for a moment and then followed closely behind her.

The sun had one foot out of its bed, ready to rise with the chickens.

Chapter Twenty-Two

"I'll make some coffee," Charlotte said, opening the door of her suite about an hour later. "Since neither of us got any sleep last night, we're going to need it." Samuel followed her out into the main foyer of the farmhouse.

They both stopped in their tracks when they noticed Diane staring at them as she closed the front door.

An awkward silence hung in the air.

"Diane, just the person I wanted to see! I have a couple of questions for you that could really point to Linc Pierce's killer," Charlotte said, marching into the kitchen.

Samuel and Diane were still frozen in place.

"It's not what you—" Samuel gave up trying to explain and walked out the back to the barn and his cabin.

"I'll be down in a little while," Diane shouted to Charlotte in the kitchen, and then took the stairs, two at a time, up to her room.

When Charlotte reemerged from the kitchen, coffee mug in hand, the only one in the foyer was Horse doing a downward dog to stretch out his sleepy muscles.

"Where'd everybody go?" She watched Horse trot out to the back porch, stick his snout in the air, and smile. Breakfast was being served, and he scampered down to the paddock.

I know that I'm going to crash at any minute, Charlotte thought, walking back to her room and computer. *I'd better write down my thoughts before I sleep them away.*

She sat at her desk and grabbed the nearest thing that she could use as paper, which happened to be one of the sale receipts for the farm's produce that Samuel had used to write down some of the car parts he needed for his vintage truck restoration. The other side was blank. Charlotte found a pencil and got to work.

*   *   *

When she was finished, Charlotte picked up the knife ring bag and tossed it up and down in her hand.

What am I missing here?

She put the ring on her index finger and tried it out in the air. Suddenly she had an idea and reached for her cell phone.

"Hi! Are you swamped? Because I've got some downtime and would love to take a tour of your operation."

Charlotte listened and nodded.

"Got it. I'll be there in about forty-five minutes!"

After being up all night, Charlotte needed a shower and a change into fresh clothes before she could politely be in front of anyone.

*   *   *

Carefully following the directions she was given, Charlotte had the feeling that she was driving her Buick Roadmaster into familiar territory. The terrain got really familiar when she passed a double-wide gate in the fence around the farm that Charlotte was sure had been the site of Horse's recon mission. But everything looked so much different in daylight.

The road she was driving on was deserted, just like it had been before, and it was difficult to see much of the farm on the other side of the fence because of the tall stalks of milkweed, pampas grass, and the dagger-sharp leaves of yucca plants growing all along the perimeter. Still, unlike in the dark of night when everything looked sinister, today the atmosphere was brimming with vibrant life and the floral and musky scents of nature.

Charlotte slowed just briefly as she passed the gate, but couldn't see anything out of the ordinary. Whoever had been there, accepting a delivery and holding a gun, must do this regularly, or surely she would have seen some signs of disruption.

Soon the road curled downward, indicating to Charlotte that Katharine's winery was separated from the strawberry fields of her father, Boyd, not just by name but by tons of immovable soil as well. The road up ahead was paved, and as described, Charlotte came upon a wooden and wrought iron gate with the name shaped into the top in iron script: "Holy Terroir Winery."

Kind of creepy and I notice no mention of the name Hoover . . .

The gate was open, so Charlotte drove in and parked outside a one-story building with a sign that said "Tasting Room." The grounds were well kept, and as Charlotte took in the scenery, she admired the vineyard in clear view in the back. It was not very large, but the vines looked to be healthy and growing. She watched a worker on horseback riding between the rows and inspecting the grapes. Charlotte spotted Katharine talking to a man at the wheel of an old, rusted truck that was being loaded with wine barrels.

"You found us—yay!" Katharine said, giving Charlotte a warm hug.

"Your directions were impeccable, as is your vineyard. Just beautiful. Well done!"

Katharine spoke to her workers. The men nodded at her command, and Charlotte watched as they switched to adding large, sealed plastic buckets to the remaining space on the back of the truck.

"What are those?"

"My frozen grapes that I sell in bulk. And the barrels are going to the bottler I use."

Charlotte raised her eyes to the sky, trying to think through the process that Katharine was describing.

"I see you're confused, and rightly so. All the wine production, from stem to bottle, should be done onsite. But Boyd keeps a tight rein on the family business purse strings, and I have no choice but to find ways to keep costs down. It's much cheaper to ship wine in barrels versus bottles. The total weight is a fraction of what it would cost to send all that glass."

"Ah, that makes sense," Charlotte said, following Katharine into the tasting room.

"And the frozen grapes I sell because I don't have enough capacity to make wine from all the harvest, so this is a way to supplement the loss of income." Katharine recorked a bottle of pinot noir from a previous tasting and put it down below the counter. "None of this is ideal. It's like trying to tie your shoe with one hand tied behind your back. Meanwhile, my dad is off experimenting with all sorts of things, from fertilizers to automating some of the processes in bringing strawberries to market. Just so he can strut around telling everyone that he's the biggest grower in the county." The thought made Katharine so angry that she grabbed a used tasting wineglass up and threw it hard onto the floor, where it shattered into hundreds of pieces.

Charlotte jumped back in fear.

"I'm sorry, girl—I don't know what came over me. It's just that I've struggled for so long that I just reach a boiling point. You see my field hand riding out there? He's all I can afford on a daily basis, and he can't possibly inspect all the vines in one day."

"I get it. Look what you've already done, though. Your wines are wonderful, and no doubt once more people have sampled them, you'll be able to upgrade your entire process based on large purchase commitments. This is hard to understand right now, but you're almost there. You just need to hang on and keep doing what you do. The rest will come, I'm sure of it."

"How can you and Diane always be so positive? I'm starting to hate that." Katharine half grinned as she spoke.

"Are you kidding? We each have days when we've thought about smashing a full shelf of wine glasses to the floor. But the only thing that comes of that is the mess you'll have to eventually clean up. When Diane was working at one of the most popular restaurants in Los Angeles, she had a coveted job that most chefs, especially women, would crawl over hot coals to land. For a long time she let that thought get in the way of her happiness. Her hours were insane, her pay was pitiful, and she was always going to be standing in the shadows of their lead chef and management.

I had a similar situation at the advertising agency I worked for in Chicago. I was only as good as my last ad."

"So what changed?" Katharine asked, using a dustpan and broom to sweep up the broken glass.

"We talked it over and over and over. Every night we'd be on the phone for hours. It was Diane, as astute as she is, who finally put her finger in it. She said, 'I'm tired of hitting the pillow every night with this empty feeling that I've wasted the day. Sure I'm working hard, but it feels like I'm watering a dead plant. I want to fall asleep thinking about a day that makes me smile, and looking forward to tomorrow.'"

"Wow. Maybe Diane should start an inspirational greeting card company next."

Snide sarcasm from Katharine? I haven't seen that side of her before.

"But you don't have Boyd for a father. Nothing is ever good enough, big enough, and rich enough. And I had the bad luck of being an only child, so he dumps all his frustration on me."

"Isn't that why you started the winery? To strike out on your own?"

"What the hell is she doing here? Get off my property, or I'm calling the cops." Boyd Hoover had driven in on an electric cart and now had his cell phone out of his pocket, ready to dial. Charlotte saw a rifle resting on the back seat.

"I invited her, Dad, and last time I checked, this was my land too."

"I was just leaving," Charlotte said to both of them.

"I'll walk you to your car," Katharine said, giving Boyd a very nasty, squinty-eyed sneer.

"Can't you benefit from using some of the materials that he uses in his strawberry fields? That should save you some money. Like sharing the liquid nitrogen, for example?"

Katharine laughed. "Dear Charlotte, sometimes I have to laugh at your naivety. The nitrogen that he uses to promote growth is cheap and easily mixed with water. The liquid nitrogen that I use to flash-freeze the fruit is a much higher grade and comes in expensive cylinders. So once again I lose."

Charlotte and Katharine heard and saw Boyd fire off his shotgun into the air.

"I'm going." Charlotte quickly slipped into the driver's seat and started her car. "We'll see you at the restaurant opening in two days. This will be your debut as well, and you're going to shine, Katharine Hoover!"

As Charlotte drove out of the winery, she kept her eyes on the rearview mirror just in case Boyd took aim on her. And she was still feeling the sting from Katharine's snarky and condescending words.

Chapter
Twenty-Three

After arriving back at her farmhouse, Charlotte marched directly into the kitchen, looking for Diane. No one was in there. She searched the ground-floor rooms and patio, and then decided to knock on the door to Diane's room on the second story. But after climbing the stairs, she found Diane's door open and her room vacant. Even Horse was nowhere to be found.

They must all be at the restaurant, putting on the final touches.

She jogged down there, and sure enough, the place was buzzing inside and out. Beau, Samuel, and Joe were huddled together to the side of the restaurant, working on something that sat on a makeshift table of plywood and sawhorses. Alice and a helper from the farm shop were washing all the windows of the restaurant to a transparent clean.

Still no Horse . . .

Charlotte wandered inside and then stopped. What she saw took her breath away. On a back wall adorned with white subway tiles, Diane had hung wooden planter boxes with different stains and lengths, all filled with growing fresh herbs. In front of it sat a marble-topped, narrow side table with a wood plank base that showcased the fruits and vegetables being featured on the menu. Descriptions of each were written in chalk on small black slate signs. Aged tin dome pendant lights illuminated the display with soft amber bulbs.

Charlotte next looked to her right. The glass, roll-up garage door that took up the wall facing the lake was open, and tables and chairs spilled out onto the patio. Inside, the wall on the side of the entry was lined with built-in benches covered in charcoal-gray fabric and cushions. Dark, rectangular tables separated the benches from two aluminum and wood patio chairs for each party. The middle area of the dining room was filled with four-top farm tables with the same patio chairs. And in front of the produce display was a long community table lined with bamboo patio side chairs. Charlotte now looked to the left where the white, subway tiled open kitchen was bustling.

And at the helm she finally saw Diane. They waved to each other, and Diane walked toward Charlotte, removing her apron on the way.

"Have you seen Horse?" Charlotte asked Diane, who beckoned with her finger for Charlotte to follow her. They walked around to the outside patio, where Charlotte found Horse munching on a bowl of fruit salad. He was barricaded in the corner of the patio by tables turned on their sides.

"This is my fault. I should never have let him roam free in the restaurant while we were in build-out. It's hard to unring that bell now, and all I need is for a health inspector to drop by unannounced and catch Horse in the kitchen, waiting for scraps." Diane sighed.

"Have you tried just telling him he can't go in there anymore?" Charlotte asked while lifting the tables around Horse up to their proper position.

Diane laughed. "As if that will work."

Horse smiled and trotted happily over to Charlotte.

"Hello, little man," Charlotte said. "I need you to do something for me, okay?" Horse sat back on his hind legs and cocked his head at her. "Promise me that you won't go inside the restaurant again. I need you outside, welcoming the guests. Can you do that?" Horse stood and gave her a smile and what looked like a nod.

"He appears to have understood. The question is whether he won't be tempted by the food aromas coming from inside."

"I'll keep an eye on him as well. Pigs need jobs, and now that Horse has one for your restaurant, I'm guessing that he'll perform his duties admirably."

They continued walking and Horse followed.

"Let's go sit on the dock over the lake, shall we?" Diane suggested. "I suspect that we both have things to tell each other."

"If I could get the words out in the proper sequence, I'd tell you that your restaurant is jaw-dropping gorgeous and perfect in every way," Charlotte said, hooking arms with Diane as they walked.

"Bravo! You have mastered the English language." Diane giggled. "Do really mean that?"

"Absolutely. We never lie to each other."

"Okay, explain this morning."

"I went to visit Katharine Hoover's winery. I would have asked you to come along, but I knew that you were busy, Diane."

"No, before that, when I watched you and Samuel come out of your room. This is very exciting!" Diane squealed as they sat down on the end of the dock.

"Oh, that. It's not what you think."

"Funny. Samuel said the same exact thing."

"Because it's true. Oh wow, did you think that we slept together?"

"Not exactly. You went to make coffee because you both had been up all night." Diane leaned over and nudged Charlotte's shoulder with her own. "Come on, 'fess up."

"Replaying it in my head, I can see how you could come to that conclusion—I wonder if anyone else surmised the same!"

"I don't think anyone else was up but the two of us, sneaking around."

"Okay, I need to set the record straight. Last night I couldn't sleep, so I went down to the field to watch the owls. Samuel was on patrol, saw me, and sat down to keep me company."

"That's what you want to call it?" Diane winked.

"That's what is was. Suddenly I had a breakthrough on the case, and we both ran back to my computer to do some research. And before you say it, that's also what I call it because that's what we did. The sun was almost up anyway, and Samuel was only in my room for maybe a half an hour. You, on the other hand, toots, were out all night." It was Charlotte's turn to wink.

"If I told you that Danny and I were up all night talking, would you believe me?" Diane asked.

"No."

"You don't want to think about it for a minute?"

"Nope."

"Fine. Then we agree to disagree. Now what was so urgent that you wanted to ask me the second that I walked into the front door this morning?"

Charlotte brought Diane up to speed on the finding under Linc's front stairs, the scouting of Hoover Farms, and Horse's debut as film director Alfred Hitchcock.

"Now that's a movie I've got to see. So did anything eventful happen at Katharine's place?" Diane asked.

"I'll get to that in a sec, but I need to ask you: Those cylinders of liquid nitrogen that you've been using in the kitchen? Where did they come from?"

"Katharine shared them with me. She only gave me three of them. I know they're expensive, and I would never want to use it on a regular basis. Too gimmicky."

Charlotte nodded. "A long walk for a short drink of water. Do you know of anyone else around here who would need food-grade liquid nitrogen?"

"No, and Katharine checked. She was hoping she could tag on her order with a large farm's request and take advantage of a bulk discount."

"I feel sorry for Katharine. There's a lot of anger going around Hoover Farm. In fact, Boyd chased me off with a shotgun.

"What?"

Charlotte recounted her visit to Katharine's Holy Terroir Winery in detail.

When she was done, Diane and Charlotte looked at each other. As best friends, they always knew what the other was thinking.

"Okay, here's what I need you to do as soon as you have the opportunity." Charlotte turned to Diane, all business.

Chapter Twenty-Four

"**I**'m turning myself in, Chief," Charlotte said into her phone while packing up her laptop for transport. She looked around her room and gathered a few more items, including the envelope that she'd scribbled her clues on, and tossed everything into a tote bag.

"Do you want to tell me what you've done first? It will help me decide if I need to call in the SWAT team," Chief Goodacre teased.

"Very funny. You'll see when I get there. And I'm bringing Horse with me, as he was an accomplice. Besides, I've got to keep him out of Diane's restaurant while the health inspector does his thing."

"I'll put on some coffee for us and cut up a couple of apples for my pink friend."

About twenty minutes later, Charlotte and Horse walked into the police station. Since farms surround Little Acorn, no one gave a second glance to a pig marching by them. Horse strutted through like he owned the place. *He isn't even a taxpayer . . . ,* Charlotte thought, and laughed to herself.

"I figured that this was going to be our 'you show me yours and I'll show you mine' meeting, so I'm prepared to share up until the point when it is no longer quid pro quo on your part."

They'd settled in the station's small conference room, where Chief Goodacre had files and boxes scattered across the table. Horse settled into a chair at the head of the table.

"What if you run out of *quos* before I've finished my *quids*?" Charlotte asked with a smile.

"We'll just have to see about that. Okay, what's your first piece of evidence and theory?" the Chief asked, getting right down to business.

"What kicked this all off was the fact that our strawberry crops were dying an unnatural death. No one could find the cause or a way to stop it. The thing is that everybody complained, but we didn't know for sure whose strawberries got hit and whose didn't." Charlotte hesitantly took a sip of her coffee, prepared for the worst. Police department brew was notorious, but she was pleasantly surprised.

"From my own stash," Chief Goodacre said, then nodded. "Please continue."

"We've later learned that Linc Pierce's crop and Barclay Farm's and Hoover Farm's berries are thriving."

"How did you—"

Charlotte held up her palm to stop the Chief from continuing. "Let's save all my infractions until the end, please. Then you can try and convict me."

The Chief squinted her eyes at Charlotte but didn't persist.

"So the obvious suspects, since we've established that this was sabotage, are Linc Pierce, Ford Barclay, Martin Ross and Boyd Hoover," Charlotte concluded.

"Correct, but then Linc went and got himself killed, and the murderer tried to disguise it as a suicide," the Chief said, taking up the story. "At the scene we found canisters of liquid nitrogen on Linc's workbench that appeared to have been used recently. Most everything else was covered with dust. When we later discovered a secret chemical lab under Linc's house, it became clear that Linc was making liquid nitrogen, which he stored in his barn and presumably used on his own strawberry crops to promote growth."

"Do you think that's where the extra money in his bank account came from? Linc was selling beautiful, plump strawberries year round?" Charlotte asked, and then shook her head.

"He didn't have the amount of acreage to earn the consistent checks that had started coming in." The Chief opened one of her folders. "I still can't convince a judge to authorize an investigation of KB Holdings, but hopefully after we compare notes today, I'll have a stronger case."

"Was your team able to recover any other evidence out of Linc's chemical lab?" Charlotte asked, her brain going a mile a minute.

Chief Goodacre shrugged. "Some latent prints that we've sent out to the lab, but I'm not very optimistic. The slab of roofing that was hiding the entry blew off during the night, and the scene was compromised when we discovered it."

Charlotte looked at her shoes, hoping to hide the guilt before she spoke. "Maybe this will help?" She held up a plastic baggie carrying the knife ring.

"Where did you get this?" the Chief asked, snatching the evidence out of Charlotte's hand.

"It's a knife ring. It's used for cutting through stems when harvesting fruit." Charlotte hoped that she'd recited this correctly from Alice's explanation.

"I know what it is. I asked you where you got it."

"Around Linc's barn."

The Chief stared at her.

"Okay, *in* Linc's barn. I found it by accident . . . I stepped on it. I didn't think that it was important."

"Then why did you preserve it in a bag? This is withholding evidence, and you're in deep trouble. Was this what you were looking for when you said that you'd seen a cat run into the barn?"

Charlotte slowly nodded.

Chief Goodacre took a blank piece of paper out of a folder and started writing. "Withholding evidence, lying to a police officer. We'll just start a running tab, shall we?"

Charlotte swallowed hard. "Look at the diameter of the ring part, Chief. Unless Linc would wear this on his pinkie, which would seem odd and not very effective, this could have belonged to somebody else."

Chief Goodacre examined it closely. "How soon did you bag this?"

"As soon as I got home. You'll find my prints on it, of course, but no one else touched it after I picked it up."

The Chief nodded and thought for a moment. "Next let's talk about this strange scarecrow that you found hanging from a tree in your orchard." She produced an eight-by-ten photo of the effigy and slid it across the table to Charlotte, who shivered when she saw it again.

"What makes that so creepy is the 'Hello, my name is' label stuck on the scarecrow's shirt that read 'Pretty Boy,' the name Linc called Beau in front of the Garden Center," Charlotte said.

"Can you remember everyone who was in that crowd and would have heard the name-calling?"

She nodded and the Chief got ready to write.

"Beau and myself. An angry Linc Pierce, Martin Ross from Barclay Farms. And Boyd Hoover, accompanied by two of his farmhands. There were other onlookers, but they weren't actively involved in the discussion, and I can't attest to how much they heard."

"Why did this effigy turn up on your farm? Just after you and Beau discovered Linc's body? It's an odd way to scare Beau if that was the intent."

"Very strange. If someone trespassed onto my farm to give us a warning, why hide it way back in the orchard where it could have been days before it was discovered?"

"I've been meaning to ask you, Charlotte, what made you wander over there?" the Chief asked again, staring deep into her eyes for some sort of confession.

Charlotte cleared her throat. "In the middle of the night, I noticed that Horse had gotten up and escaped through the French doors out to the fields. I had a hunch where he'd gone and made my way down to one of the strawberry crops. Samuel had erected some owl brooding houses on tall poles, hoping to attract the beautiful birds and encourage them to feed on the ample rodent supply that was attacking our crops. I found Horse mesmerized, watching the birds in flight."

Chief Goodacre looked over to Horse seated at the head of the table. He was happily munching on apple slices set before him on a paper plate. "So you're a fan of raptors, are you, my friend? I agree, they are beautiful and do us a great service."

Horse gave her an enthusiastic grunt.

"While we were out there, I heard some footsteps and rustling of leaves coming from the orchard. We followed the sounds and that's when I found the hanging effigy." Charlotte's eyes grew wide, remembering.

"And why didn't you call me until the next morning?"

"Joe was on patrol that night and heard my scream. I didn't see the label on the shirt pocket at that time of the night, and Joe suspected that this was probably kids playing a prank. It wasn't until I went back in the light of day that I realized that this was no joke."

"So you tampered with another crime scene?" the Chief asked, adding to her list.

"I didn't know that it was a crime scene! I still don't, really." Charlotte was losing her patience.

Chief Goodacre motioned with her cocked head to the tote bag that Charlotte had placed at her feet. "What else is in there?"

Charlotte shook her head. "Quid pro quo, remember?"

The Chief scowled and then looked over the table at her closed folders. "You asked about Ford Barclay's family businesses and the possibility of their entity being involved in selling deadly pesticides in the past." She pulled out a stack of printouts as she continued. "Because the pharmaceutical company that the Barclays run is public, there is a lot of information available, going all the way back to when the founder, Nigel Barclay, began selling product in London, England. Numerous lawsuits plagued the enterprise; they were spending more money defending than they were marketing their drugs. So they moved the operation to Litchfield, Connecticut. There were lots of pharmaceutical companies located there, so the Barclays hoped that they would get lost in the shuffle. Which they did for years."

"And did Ford Barclay start working in the family business when he was old enough?" Charlotte asked.

"Deputy Elmwood did a great job digging up background information on Ford, but this is where it gets tricky. He was raised as an aristocrat—private schools, a stable of horses, summer months spent in Europe—but there is no indication of him ever being on the payroll for Barclay Pharmaceuticals. Which doesn't mean that he didn't shadow his father and ancestors learning the business." Chief Goodacre shuffled the folders in front of her, finally finding what she was looking for. "He did leave the East Coast and settle in Northern California just after he turned twenty-one and the purse strings were loosened on his trust fund. But again, there is no record of employment history on Ford until he started Barclay Farms."

"Maybe he was too busy being a playboy and buying everything and everyone he wanted." Charlotte had a bitter memory.

"Did he do something inappropriate to you?" the Chief asked, steely-eyed.

Charlotte shook her head. "Nothing that I couldn't handle."

"You'd tell me, wouldn't you? Because I'd lock his privileged butt up faster than my split-finger pitch. Which has clocked in at about sixty miles per hour."

"Duly noted. Does it seem like a coincidence to you that Barclay Pharmaceuticals, clear across the country, would suddenly be interested in developing agricultural pesticides and fertilizers?"

"Coincidence? What's that? There's no such thing, and I will keep Deputy Elmwood on this trail to its conclusion. I have no doubt that Ford Barclay was involved and shared in the insane profits until California finally shut down the use of lethal, banned chemicals and enforced that law. But unfortunately it will take time to prove." Chief Goodacre sat down and poured herself a glass of water from a pitcher on the table. "Okay, Charlotte, open your bag of tricks and show me what you've got."

Charlotte complied and started with the white carbon drone parts that Horse had found on her property. Horse got down from his chair and trotted around to where Chief Goodacre sat. He was up.

"These pieces were found in the field where Samuel built one of the owl houses, after it was occupied with a couple I've named Fred and Ginger. The house was a success, and they're now brooding." Charlotte smiled and puffed out her chest, proud.

"Congratulations. Please keep me informed about the date and time of the baby shower," the Chief said, deadpan. She picked up one of the fragments and took a closer look, turning it over in her hand.

"It was Martin Ross who identified what these pieces are from. They're made of carbon and are broken parts to a white drone. We found more under the apple tree where the effigy of Beau was hanging." Charlotte had hoped to slip in the second part of her statement unnoticed.

"You found drone parts at a crime scene and didn't report it?" Chief Goodacre retrieved the infraction tally she'd been keeping on Charlotte and added another to the list.

"Once again, I didn't know it was a crime scene at the time, and I had no idea what those pieces of metal were. The point here is who owns white-colored drones? Martin Ross said that the fleet that Barclay Farms own are all black and have the farm logo on them." Charlotte hoped to refocus the Chief.

"That makes sense—Ford Barclay wants his name everywhere."

"True, but he has the resources to have a duplicate set of drones that Martin Ross knows nothing about. Which other farms in Little Acorn use drones? Does Boyd Hoover?"

"Good question." The Chief picked up the internal phone and passed along this assignment to her deputy. "What else is in that tote bag?" she asked.

"Nothing." Charlotte turned it upside down and shook it to prove so. "But I do have one more discovery."

"Go on."

Charlotte shook her head at the Chief. "Quid pro quo was the deal, correct?"

The Chief let out a frustrated sigh. "What do you want? I've shared everything we've got."

Charlotte pointed to the sheet of paper that the Chief had been using to keep track of each time Charlotte had broken the law. "Tear that up and I'll tell you."

Charlotte could swear that she heard Horse giggle.

The Chief thought about it for a good minute and finally tore the paper into pieces.

Satisfied, Charlotte proceeded to tell Chief Goodacre the story about the different kinds of liquid nitrogen and their properties.

Chapter
Twenty-Five

When the meeting concluded, both Charlotte and Chief Goodacre left with assignments that would put them on the path to conclusively solving this case.

Charlotte had held some things back and suspected that the Chief had done the same, but all in all, combining resources had been fruitful in her mind. There were a few crucial loose ends that needed to be tied up, and frustratingly every new piece of evidence could possibly be attributed to the same suspects: Ford Barclay, Martin Ross, and Boyd Hoover.

Which one killed Linc Pierce?

Charlotte let out a howl of pent-up energy as she pulled up to her farmhouse, and Horse, thinking she was starting an a cappella group, did the same. But when Charlotte saw the frenetic pace everyone on the farm was taking, she remembered that there was one day left before the restaurant opening. This case had to be put aside so she could focus all her attention on helping Diane.

"Horse, please remember that I don't want you going inside the restaurant anymore. You need to stay outside, or Diane won't be able to run her new restaurant. Understand?"

Horse gave Charlotte an emphatic nod of his head.

"Good. Now go play while I get to work."

He scampered off, and Charlotte saw Beau driving up from the barn in a cart with a large piece of rustic metal riding in the back.

"Whoa, cowboy. Wherever you're going I want to go too," Charlotte said hopping into the passenger seat when Beau came to a stop. "Whatcha got back there?"

"You'll see momentarily, and I think you'll be pleased. It involves you too." Beau gave her a conspiratorial smile and wink. Today Beau was in blacksmith attire, or at least his interpretation of it. He wore a mauve chambray shirt under a well-broken-in leather blacksmith's apron. *I wonder where he got that?* For the bottom of his ensemble, he'd chosen skinny yellow chinos, and although he was no longer welding, or perhaps never had, protective eyewear rested atop his head.

"Are we getting close to being ready to open?" Charlotte asked, concerned by all the activity she was seeing around the restaurant site.

"I'm not sure, but it doesn't matter. By tomorrow afternoon the cars will ascend Finn Family Farm hill, park in the designated patron area, and enter the doors of my dear sister's masterpiece to have the meal of their lives. They'll have an experience to tell their grandbabies and their great grandbabies about."

"Has Diane settled on a name for her restaurant? I keep forgetting to ask her."

"Ah! The answer rests behind you. She didn't want a separate name for the restaurant since it's on the Finn Farm property, but I think that she'll accept this compromise." Beau reached behind him and tapped the metal piece.

"Of course she should name her restaurant whatever she wants it to be. That's ridiculous. As soon as I see her I'm going to have a word."

"Hold your ponies; just give me and the fellows a few minutes to put this up." Beau stopped the cart around the backside of the restaurant building. They were greeted by two of Danny's workers and shown the brackets that the men had affixed above the double doors of the entry.

"Perfect, boys. My sign should fit nicely there and, with some outdoor spotlight curating it, will become a beacon for all to see. Can you guys help me with the sign?" Beau asked.

When they lifted the large metal plate off the golf cart and carried it around to the entry, Charlotte could finally get a good look at it from the front. Raised lettering in a warm script rested about four inches from the base of the sign, which looked like polished but rustic brass. Etched into the back were rows of rolling lines that looked like crop fields. The wrought iron letters read:

THE FINN-MASON
BOUNTIFUL FARMSTEAD

"Oh, Beau, I love it! I'm feeling my cheeks burn, and I can't wait to see Diane's reaction. You are a genius," Charlotte oozed.

"I can't take all the credit. You need to thank that tall-drink-of-water farmer standing behind you as well."

Charlotte turned to see Samuel admiring the sign with a lopsided grin. Charlotte felt her heart do a little flip.

"Where's your leather apron, Samuel?" she teased.

"Beau grabbed it the minute he saw it, and threatens never to take it off."

All three of them watched as the sign was anchored into place.

"It's official, Sis," Beau said as Diane joined them and read the words.

She stood in silence, a little teary-eyed. Samuel, Charlotte, and Beau watched as she took in the momentous meaning of this event. Diane let out a slow, long breath before saying, "You couldn't put my name first?"

They all broke into first nervous and then bellyaching laughter.

"It's in alphabetical order, Sis—you know how I am about propriety."

"Yes, I do. To you propriety is disingenuous and a hackneyed stand-in for kindness."

"That's right!"

Charlotte and Samuel giggled at their exchange as they headed up to the farmhouse.

"You know who would be beside himself with excitement right about now, Charlotte?"

She nodded. "My great-uncle Tobias."

"First of all, he always said that spring was his favorite time of year because that's when the farmland came alive with a preview of the new and wonderful plant life for the year," Samuel told her. "And he thrived on having lots of people around to share it with."

"Just from spending that one summer here with him, I could see that. Between the friends and the crops, he was like a kid in a candy store, a store that stretched for acres in the rolling hills." Charlotte smiled, remembering.

"You really are just like him. You get that same fierce twinkle, if there is such a thing, in your eyes when you talk about the land. I miss him, even though I was a kid for most of the time I knew him. The whole of Little Acorn does. That's probably why he sent for you."

"You think that it was Tobias's master plan to leave the farm to me? Was he the optimistic rainmaker, hoping to lure me back to carry on his legacy?" Charlotte asked.

"I don't know for a fact, but I do see that the apple doesn't fall far from the tree." Samuel looked into her eyes and smiled.

"When the restaurant is up and running and the crops are on their way, perhaps you could give me a tour of this glorious farm country, I kind of hit the ground running and never had a chance to explore it."

"I'd be delighted, Miss Charlotte." Samuel tipped his hat and walked away.

Charlotte bit her lower lip and enjoyed the view.

*   *   *

Charlotte was exhausted from all the day's events, the brain-scratching and hard thinking with the Chief and the emotional tug at the heartstrings with Beau, Diane, and Samuel.

She wandered out back and onto the patio that surrounded the farmhouse. Beau, always wanting to please, had put up a hammock there and was in it, gently rocking in the late afternoon breeze. It was too inviting to pass up, and Charlotte got in and let it envelop her. Soon a ladybug with one bright yellow spot landed on her hand.

"Mrs. Robinson, how are you, beautiful lady? You've been doing a fantastic job with your troops, keeping the aphid population down. Are you as tired as I am? Let's just close our eyes for a minute."

When Charlotte opened her eyes again, hours must have passed, because it was now dark outside. She was no longer in the hammock but walking along a dirt road at the top of the hill.

Is this outside the fence of Hoover Farms?

"Horse?" Charlotte called out, but got no response. A chill ran through her body, it was a cold night and she'd forgotten to bring a jacket. She looked around for her station wagon or Samuel's truck and saw neither.

How did I get up here?

Charlotte felt the earth rumble before she heard the clopping of running horses. The sounds were getting nearer. The clopping turned into louder and louder rumbles, and by the dim light of the stars Charlotte could see a large dust cloud approaching.

How many horses are there?

Charlotte didn't want to wait around to count them and broke into a run. If she could reach the silvopasture up ahead, then maybe she could find safety behind the big trees on the left bank. She picked up speed and ran like her life depended on it, which it most likely did. Her fatal mistake was taking one more look over her shoulder. The noise was getting deafening, and as the dirt kicked up by racing horse's hooves swirled, she saw something pink trying to stay ahead of the stampede.

"Horse! Run off to the side and let them pass! You're going to get trampled!"

He either didn't hear Charlotte or chose to ignore her, which he was prone to do when he was having fun.

"HORSE!"

Charlotte pivoted and raced back toward him, flying over tall grasses and shrubs along the way. But unfortunately she couldn't see the boulder on the other side of a fledgling coyote bush in the dark and landed hard on it with her right foot. She felt herself flip head over feet in midair before she landed with a hard thud on the dry chaparral. She tried to look for Horse, but a curtain of dust blocked her view.

Which direction have I fallen?

Her answer came seconds later when she was surrounded by horses speeding past her. Charlotte tried to roll back and forth to avoid being trampled, but she couldn't see her hand in front of her face. There was nothing she could do but flatten herself down on the ground and hope for the best.

Above she heard voices commanding their horses to run faster. She thought she heard Danny Costa and then Martin Ross. A group of men yelling in Spanish.

Rancheros Visitadores?

Ford Barclay flew past, and she heard him yell his horse's name. Then came a group led by Boyd Hoover. Charlotte could recognize his snide, condescending voice anywhere. Following him, she heard the weathered sound of an old man attempting to be heard over the thunder.

Charlotte tried to tune everything out and focus on her last thoughts. The people she loved, Horse, the farm, and all its animals. The sunlight that helped living things thrive and grow every day.

She began to feel an on again, off again pounding on her back each one more fierce than the one before. She couldn't take much more . . . Charlotte felt herself drifting out, losing awareness of her presence on the earth. Just as she thought she couldn't take anymore, a shower of hard pebbles pelted her. She reached out and dug her fingers into the hard soil, wanting farmland to be the last thing she saw. One of the hard pebbles landed on the back of her hand and bounced to the ground right before her nose.

It was a red and white striped peppermint. She let out a silent scream and tried to roll away from it.

Charlotte landed with a thud and remained still, waiting for the end to come. She soon realized that the horrendous noise had subsided, replaced with the swoosh of a gentle breeze and the rhythm of cicadas drumming out their songs.

And a soft, low, bellowing series of grunts coming from just outside her ear. When she stirred, she felt something cold and wet try to bury itself between her neck and shoulder. Finally she heard a series of unmistakable squeals.

"Horse?" Charlotte asked, slowly opening her eyes. Her pink little man was dancing around her. She looked up and saw the hammock still swinging from her fall.

Charlotte worked to piece together the elements of the dream that she must have just had. It made her shiver.

That was horrifying . . . but also enlightening!

Chapter
Twenty-Six

"Hello, my name is Bernice, and I handle the accounts payable for KB Holdings, and I'm checking to see if we have any outstanding invoices with *Cryofresh*. I need to get everything settled before the end of the month." Charlotte tried to sound efficient, impatient, and unfeeling.

"Are you kidding me?" came a man's voice on the other end of the line. "I must have told your boss at least five times that there will be no more deliveries until you settle the balance on your account."

"That's why I'm calling. Can you give me the amount that is owed?" Charlotte smiled to herself. This might just work.

"I'll need a check for $4,217 before we can ship again." Charlotte could hear the sound of papers being shuffled and the click of a keyboard and mouse being manipulated. "And another $250 for the drop-off that was made a few days ago. My partner took that order—I would never have approved it. And for the next couple of months, we're going to require payment in advance. Tell the owner that this is not the way we like to do business, but she has left us no choice."

"I will pass that along and I'm issuing the check as we speak. Thanks." Charlotte ended the call and pushed her chair away from her desk. She'd hardly been able to wait until morning to make this call, and she couldn't have been more delighted with the results.

I'd better go see how I can make myself useful to Diane on her big day.

Charlotte wandered into the kitchen, but once again it was empty. She checked the counters for a basket of freshly baked rolls but found nothing. She opened the refrigerator, hoping to see a bowl of fruit salad, perhaps some yogurt, but no such luck. Horse trotted in, licking his lips in satisfaction, clearly after just having devoured *his* breakfast. Charlotte put on the kettle, opting to settle for a nice cup of tea. When it was ready, she took it out to the front patio, ready to jump into work when anyone asked.

Charlotte watched the people rushing in every direction and ultimately ending up at the restaurant. Wagons of produce, just harvested, were being brought up from the fields. This was truly farm-to-table. Danny's construction crew kept walking past Charlotte on the way to their trucks, packing up their tools and any unused supplies. Horse sat beside her, watching the action.

Charlotte took the small notebook that she'd started carrying around with her out of her back pocket and ran her hand over it. She'd found it among her great-uncle Tobias's things. It fit in the palm of her hand, and it was bound in worn, soft leather and looked to be quite old. She'd seen that he'd taken some notations in it about early plantings, weather predictions, and so on, but abandoned writing in it after about ten pages of entries.

271

Charlotte loved seeing his handwriting and would hug the notebook close to her chest when she needed some inspiration from the magical Tobias Finn. Now was one of those times.

I'm so close, Uncle, so close to solving this crime that has turned Little Acorn on its ear.

Charlotte opened the book and skimmed through the pages. She stopped when she came to the notes that she'd taken from her case review with Chief Goodacre. She checked the open questions and learned that they'd uncovered the answers, together and separately, to all but one or two. Charlotte also saw that she had a way to acquire perhaps the biggest and most damning piece of evidence.

Charlotte reached for her phone, looked up a number, and pressed "Call."

"Hoover Farms and Market, Suzie speaking. How may I help you?"

"Suzie, hi! This is Charlotte Finn, Katharine's friend. Do you remember me? We met about a week ago."

"Yes, hi."

She sounded a little wary, Charlotte needed to think fast of something to say to put her at ease.

"Are you ready for your prom? I remember you telling me that you were saving up to buy a dress. It's not too far away now, is it?"

"I know! I have my eye on one I found online, but I'm not quite able to afford it yet. I hope that I'll make it in time."

"Maybe I can help with that a little. Would you like to do a bit of research for me? See, I'm interested in purchasing some drones for fertilizing on my farm. I can't believe how our crops have grown. I was wondering if you could find out what they use on Hoover Farms? I'd ask Katharine, but she'll be too busy with our restaurant opening this afternoon. You and your family are joining us for the party, aren't you?"

"Wow, I didn't know that we were invited. Thanks. Everybody's talking about it."

"Great, four o'clock. Back to the drones: I'm just curious about the brand your farm uses, maybe a model number, type, color? Just the basic things so I can be informed when I go to buy them. I'd be happy to pay you fifty dollars for your time and effort. As you may have guessed, I can't really ask Mr. Hoover in his present mood."

"That seems pretty straightforward, I should be able to do that. I think that the paperwork is filed somewhere in this office. I'll just need to find it."

"So long as you won't put yourself in a position where you could get in trouble, that would be great! I'll pay you in cash when I see you this afternoon. Thanks, Suzie!"

Charlotte made a few notations in her notebook and then closed it with a sense of finality.

Today is Diane's day.

* * *

Charlotte found her, surprisingly, taking a break out on the patio that faced the lake. Diane was sipping a lemonade and admiring the restaurant's outdoor seating.

"I figured that you'd be in the kitchen, frenetic or fussing with the napkins and the place settings on the tables. I never thought that I'd find you relaxing under one of these whimsical market umbrellas with your feet up."

Charlotte had loved them the minute they arrived. Brick red, these umbrellas had ruffled edges that reminded her of a fun

French parasol. They were just large enough to shade each patio table and chairs.

"You know what? I couldn't be more calm and at peace. This is where I'm meant to be, and this is what I was born to do."

"That must be an incredibly satisfying feeling, I can only imagine."

"Who are you kidding? You're in exactly the same place. You've got maybe two fingertips clinging on to your cosmopolitan past—let go. This farm, this land, this life, it's in your DNA. You were born with chlorophyll running through your veins. You have many reasons to call the Finn Family Farm home, and one reason that you're not going to able to ignore forever." Diane nodded over Charlotte's shoulder.

She turned to see Samuel, who was following behind Beau with a box of solar lights that Beau was strategically placing along the path to the restaurant.

Charlotte sighed and smiled at Diane.

"I'm so proud to be your friend." Charlotte gave Diane a hug.

"Right back at you."

"Chef, the servers are ready for the tasting and to be walked through the menu," Alice said with a big grin when she stepped out onto the patio.

"On my way," Diane said, giving Charlotte's shoulder a squeeze.

"Charlotte?" Beau called, appearing on the lawn on the other side of the patio fence. "I have three outfits, and I need another pair of eyes to advise."

"A fashion show—this day gets better and better!" Charlotte hopped over the fence and followed Beau and Horse to the farmhouse.

Chapter
Twenty-Seven

When Charlotte emerged from her suite a couple of hours later, she immediately noticed that the parking lot that had been constructed for the restaurant was beginning to fill up.

This is so exciting!

The problem was going to be Horse. After today the pace would slow, and everyone wouldn't be arriving at the same time, so she was fairly certain that she could keep him away. But with all the activity happening in the restaurant now, even if she locked Horse in a room, she couldn't be positive that he wouldn't find a way out. She needed a plan.

Charlotte thought about Beau and the attire that they'd chosen for him: light tan suit, white button-down shirt, and a denim vest in a vibrant blue. He'd settled on a straw pork pie hat with a blue and orange ribbon.

Charlotte had an idea. All she needed to find for Beau were sunglasses and a camera. And he'd make the perfect staff photographer.

"Beau!" Charlotte shouted up the stairs.

"Coming! I just need to apply my favorite cologne for the season, Spring Eternal," he shouted down to her.

When Beau met Charlotte in the foyer and she shared her plan, Beau thought that it was genius.

"We'll need some props, and I'll have to rely on natural light, but I can fix all that in postproduction. While I gather the items we need, how about you set to making a sign?"

"Perfect, I'm on it. I think that I have what I need here. I'll work on it out on the patio."

The two parted ways and got down to their tasks. Charlotte had left Horse locked in her room, but she knew that this pink Houdini could easily escape.

"Ready?" Beau asked when he appeared at the farmhouse door, arms loaded with blankets, an array of hats, and a bag of Horse's favorite pig treats.

Charlotte held up her sign.

"Love it. Where's the man of the hour?" Beau asked.

"I'll get him. This might just work!"

When the three amigos neared the restaurant, they saw that the staff had lined both sides of the path leading to the entry and were greeting the guests. A line had formed.

"Perhaps over here? Under the Chinese elm tree? The leaves are still sparse enough to let a lot of light through."

"I'll make it work. Need help getting that sign posted?" Beau asked.

"I think that I just spotted a helper. You just worry about setting up and explaining to Horse that he's going to have a starring role."

Charlotte caught up with Samuel, chatting with a few of the farm's neighbors waiting their turn to get a table. He looked very handsome in light blue dress pants and a white shirt and striped tie.

I wonder where and why he acquired more formal clothes?

"Hi, gentlemen, and welcome," Charlotte said, hooking her arm through Samuel's. "I wonder if you would mind me borrowing Samuel for a quick task? I promise to return him to you in one piece." She laughed.

"I wouldn't hold your breath," Samuel told his friends. "You look beautiful," he said, admiring Charlotte.

She had chosen a white spaghetti-strap dress with a ribbed bodice and a periwinkle floral print. Charlotte had put her flowing red curls up in a loose bun and wore yellow espadrilles. She thought that she'd been going for comfort, but by Samuel's reaction she might have added a little flirt appeal as well.

When Charlotte arrived back at the tree, Beau had spread out the picnic blanket and basket and had set out an array of fruits and a bowl of Horse's crunchy snacks. Horse sat proudly in the center of the blanket sporting one of Beau's bow ties.

"We need this sign put up where everyone can see it. This is our master plan to keep Horse busy and outside the restaurant— in his starring role, posing for photos with friends." Charlotte said the last bit in a louder voice and nodded to Horse. He grinned back and moved his head from side to side to show off his profiles.

"Got it. Have a picnic and get a free photo with Horse, the amazing pig." Samuel gave Charlotte a nod of approval. "And might I say, Horse, you look dashing," Samuel said, and winked at him.

*   *   *

The guests started arriving in larger groups, and Horse was enjoying a brisk business in his modeling career.

Charlotte blew a kiss to Beau for his stellar job as fashion photographer and joined the reception line to welcome everyone. The turnout was amazing. Charlotte saw several groups from her neighboring farms, dressed in their Sunday finest, follow the line into the restaurant. The town doc, mayor, and fire chief had perhaps carpooled, because they were all clumped together as they made their way to the entrance.

"Quite a hungry crowd gathering. Diane and Alice will have their hands full," Samuel said, taking his place next to Charlotte.

"She's got this. Diane's had to deal with aggressive paparazzi in Los Angeles, so today will be a piece of cake."

Charlotte stiffened when it was Ford Barclay and Martin Ross's turn to pass by.

"You are a gracious, wonderful host for inviting me in spite of our misunderstanding. I am humbled and grateful," Ford said, taking Charlotte's hand.

"You are also delusional, Ford Barclay. There was no misunderstanding. Please enjoy your meal, gentlemen and leave the wait staff a healthy gratuity for all their hard work." With that Charlotte gave them a big smile, and Samuel ushered them past her.

"Looks like the local press has arrived," Charlotte said, watching several photographers snap photos while a reporter interviewed guests.

"That should help Diane, don't you think?" Samuel asked.

Charlotte nodded.

Next came Boyd Hoover and a couple of his men, along with his daughter Katharine. This time it was Samuel's turn to brace himself. They were so busy arguing about something that they completely missed seeing Samuel and Charlotte.

"You never did tell me the history between you and her. What happened to make you both visibly ignore each other whenever you meet?" Charlotte figured it was now or never for getting an answer.

"It was just a misunderstanding—" Samuel caught himself before continuing. "No, it wasn't that. We were oil and water. We had one date our senior year in high school, and when it ended, we couldn't get away from each other fast enough."

"You're going to need to tell me more than that, Samuel. What you've said isn't even enough for the book flap copy."

He looked at her and chuckled. "Okay, it seemed inevitable that we should date. We were both working on farms, loved being outdoors, we're both tall. That's about it, but at the time it seemed to be enough. There was the strawberry festival going on that weekend, so I invited Katharine to join me. We'd play games, eat strawberries made every way imaginable, and maybe hop on the Ferris wheel at night."

"You dog, you!" Charlotte laughed.

"We couldn't agree on anything. First she insisted on driving. She didn't want to be seen riding in a truck on a date. So we went in her Honda, the same one she still gets around in today. Only it was new then and her graduation present from Boyd. She thought that she was 'all that' at the wheel of that car."

"She's had it that long?" Charlotte's wheels started spinning.

Samuel nodded. "Katharine insisted on choosing the booth games we played. I could see her cheating whenever she could get away with it. She harassed the other farmers about the lack of flavor in the strawberries they were selling, and she complained about the food I bought her. It was miserable."

Suzie from Hoover Farms waved to Charlotte and approached. It looked like she'd brought her parents and cute, younger brothers. Charlotte reached in her pocket for the envelope that she'd placed there.

"You made it! I'm so happy to see you and your family." Charlotte gave her a hug and placed the fifty dollars that she'd promised Suzie into her palm.

"I just texted you the information you wanted." Suzie smiled. Charlotte could tell that she was proud of her accomplishment.

"There's a table waiting for you inside. Enjoy your afternoon!'

Samuel had watched this entire exchange with confusion. He had no idea who Suzie was or why Charlotte had been so excited to see her.

"Did I just witness an exchange of some kind?" he asked.

"What about the Ferris wheel?" she asked, ignoring his question. "That was when you planned to make your big move, wasn't it, Samuel?"

He laughed dryly. "We did do that, but I insisted that we ride in separate passenger cars. She didn't argue."

"There's the Chief and Linc's great-granddaughter Margaret. I need to talk to them for a minute—I'll meet you inside," Charlotte said, and made her way to them.

"Hi, you two—welcome! I hope you're hungry. Chief, could I have a brief word with you before we go in?"

Chief Goodacre nodded and motioned Margaret to go ahead and be seated at their table.

"I've got news," Charlotte said as she took a look at her text messages.

"I do too, but you first," the Chief said when she was sure that they were out of earshot from the guests.

"If you have even a small amount of what we discussed at the station, then you may just have enough evidence to make an arrest. I'm going to have to warn Diane, but she wants this crime behind us as much as anyone," Charlotte said, looking around for prying eyes.

"Okay, shoot—what have you got?"

Charlotte and the Chief talked for several minutes and compared notes. When they next looked around, the last of the guests were walking into the restaurant.

"Showtime. I'm going to call for reinforcements."

They entered the restaurant full of happy, excited, chatting people, and Charlotte looked for Diane. When she spotted her, she mimed that they needed to talk.

Diane nodded, held up her hand, and opened her fist. In it were four or five red and white peppermint candies.

Charlotte made her way over to Diane.

Chapter
Twenty-Eight

A makeshift dais had been constructed just on the other side of the open kitchen facing the main dining room. As soon as the presentation was over, it would be removed and replaced with tables and chairs for the Finn-Mason family and friends.

Beau was the first to take the stage.

Charlotte wondered where he'd left Horse, but it was too late to do anything about it.

"Dear guests, welcome to the Finn-Mason Bountiful Farmstead restaurant!" Eager applause erupted all around. "My name is Beau Mason, brother of Her Excellence—as you will soon agree—the fabulous Chef Diane Mason."

More applause.

"Since she was a little girl," Beau continued, "Diane's had a passion for making people happy with her specially prepared food. Even when she only had access to Silly Putty, lip balm, and grass." The crowd laughed. "Hey, don't knock it if you haven't tried it."

Beau grinned. "When our dear childhood friend Charlotte inherited her great-uncle's farm, it was a chance for each of us to work on making our dreams come true." Charlotte looked up and caught Samuel staring back at her with a smile. "I couldn't be more proud of my sister than I am today. She's poured her heart and soul into the Bountiful Farmstead, and you will feel and taste the love with each bite. It is my honor to present to you the head chef and founder of this exquisite restaurant, Diane Mason." Beau motioned for her to take the stage and handed Diane the mic.

The room gave her an extended standing ovation, led most vigorously by Danny Costa, who was standing by the double doors at the entry.

"Thank you, thank you," Diane said when the cheering started to die down. "Some of you know or may have read that my last restaurant job was with a very popular, ultimate California cuisine showcase in Los Angeles. The atmosphere was electric, and you were bound to see a celebrity or two dining there any day of the week. It was a great learning experience, but it was not how I wanted to make my mark in feeding people." Diane motioned to the wall displaying all the fresh fruits and vegetables being served today. "In my restaurant the celebrities are on display for all to see and admire. And to taste. The point of opening a restaurant on my dear friend Charlotte's family farm was so that you could eat the way we do every night. Enjoying bounty grown with the utmost love and care and harvested at its peak. That is my promise to you each time you dine with us. Nature actually decides what we eat, and I have the privilege of being able to prepare and serve your meals, showcasing the absolute best ingredients. We're starting off today with a chilled green gazpacho soup served with roasted cashews and lightly fried zucchini blossoms.

As you enjoy, my BFF and mentor, Charlotte Finn, would like to say a few words."

Charlotte was hesitant to take the stage and ruin such a magic moment, but she wouldn't have a better chance than the present. She had all the suspects and most of the witnesses in one room. She had evidence to unveil. As the Chief had said, it was "showtime."

Charlotte receive vigorous applause as well. The crowd probably thought that she would have equally exciting news to share.

"Thank you all for coming and supporting this magnificent new restaurant and the most inspired chef I know, Diane Mason. I promise not to take up too much of your time, and I certainly don't want to throw a wet blanket on the jubilant mood in the room, but Chief Goodacre and I have some updates on the murder of fellow farmer Linc Pierce," Charlotte began, and a hush came over the room. "We also believe that this case is linked directly to the blight that has been destroying many of our new season strawberry crops. We have learned that this was an act of sabotage." Low murmurs could be heard among the tables. "With help from all of you, we believe that there is enough evidence for the Little Acorn Police Department to make an arrest today and bring the person responsible for both crimes to justice."

Charlotte paused for the weight of her words to sink in and noticed that the guests were now eying each other with suspicion.

I better make this quick before a fight breaks out.

"Chief, would you like to start?" Charlotte asked, making room for her on the dais.

"Good afternoon, everyone, and trust me when I tell you that I am as anxious as all of you are to get back to this delicious meal, so I'll make this quick." Charlotte stepped up to the

Chief and whispered something in her ear. The Chief nodded. "For those of you here with children under ten, you may want to encourage them to go outside, where they can have a picnic with the Finn Farm's lovely pig, Horse." The Chief waited for a moment while some gathered their young ones and left the restaurant.

"Here are the basic facts of the case," the Chief continued. "Charlotte Finn and Beau Mason made the gruesome discovery when they visited Linc Pierce's farm and found him in his barn, hanging dead by a rope. Suicide was suspected but that conclusion was soon converted to homicide after the coroner's report was issued. Several pieces of evidence found at the crime scene and later around the Pierce property got the ball rolling in establishing a viable suspect." The Chief held up Charlotte's notebook to read from. "There were a number of canisters filled with liquid nitrogen in Linc's barn, and it was determined by the absence of dust that they had been recently added. Subsequently, and after Linc's great-granddaughter took possession of the property, my deputies discovered that an underground chemical lab had been crudely built under his farmhouse." More talking was heard going around the room.

Holding up her hand, the Chief added, "The more you interrupt me, the longer it's going to take to conclude this." That silenced them. "My CSI team found all the elements necessary to make this liquid nitrogen in the lab. They also found samples of methyl bromide and other illegal substances that were used to make the dangerous pesticides and fertilizers that were banned in this country years ago. Apparently, Linc Pierce was now making the stuff that he used to peddle for chemical companies before the government stepped in. Which explained why his crops were in such beautiful shape. But someone else was bankrolling this illegal operation. Linc had very little money to speak of, but after he was killed and his granddaughter Margaret took over the estate, she learned that he'd had a sudden windfall in the last six months, depositing into his bank account checks that totaled over fifty thousand dollars."

This time it was more difficult to control the crowd's reaction. Charlotte took over in the hopes of turning their attention in another direction.

"Along the way and with the assistance of a number of people and one very smart pink pig, I was able to gather pieces of evidence that helped to narrow the field of suspects." Charlotte reached for a small bag that she'd hidden by the side of the kitchen before they'd started. She held up the knife ring. "This item was found in Linc's barn. It's supposed to make harvesting fruit easier, but the old-timers wouldn't touch what they considered nothing more than a novelty item. Note the small size of the ring portion, which led us to believe that it was worn by someone with smaller fingers." Now everyone looked at one another's hands.

"We also found this under the Pierce farmhouse steps." Charlotte held up the mint candy. "Sure you say, 'Linc could have picked this up when leaving any number of restaurants.' It would have to have been recently because the candy wrapper was still in pretty good shape. The only problem with this theory is that Linc was diabetic. It is doubtful that he would have risked his health on such an average sweet. But you know who loves these? Horses love these. Not my pig—he found the candy but had no interest in eating it. But riders have been known to have a pocketful of the mints to keep their animals calm and under control."

"This was of interest to my department," Chief Goodacre said, picking up the narrative again, "because we'd gotten a tip from a witness that they'd seen someone on horseback riding across the field and away from the Pierce Farm about the time that Linc was murdered. At first, they thought they'd seen Danny Costa, but then couldn't be sure. Danny's horse was getting new shoes that day, so he was dismissed as a suspect." The Chief made a crossing-out gesture with her arm. "Let's get back to the sudden income that Linc was receiving. It came in checks made out to 'Cash' drawn from a private bank account with the name 'KB Holdings.'"

Charlotte took a subtle glance at the Hoover table, where the group was suddenly listening intensely.

"We couldn't get more on who was behind the company without a court order, and at the time we didn't have enough evidence to convince a judge. But we do now, and I have one of my deputies paying a visit to his Honor as we speak. Charlotte?"

"The Finn Family Farm strawberry crops also fell victim to this strawberry blight." Charlotte made air quotes when she said those last two words. "On several occasions, we heard someone trespassing at night on the grounds, and during one visit a crudely made scarecrow mocking Beau was found hanging from a tree in the orchard. We also found these scattered around the fields." Charlotte extracted the pieces of white drone and held them up for everyone to see. "These are parts of a drone that broke off during some sort of crash while flying over one of my stricken strawberry fields. This is what ultimately led us to believe that what was actually killing the berries was liquid nitrogen being sprayed from a pressurized cylinder attached to a drone flying overhead. And in the shadows, the drone was being directed by a human operator."

A group of angry farmers who had suffered loss from this act of sabotage began pointing fingers and yelling at Ford Barclay and Martin Ross.

"Whoa Nelly," the Chief said, stepping down from the dais, ready to intervene. Charlotte saw the doors to the restaurant open, and three of her deputies stepped inside and made their presence known. "Before fists fly, you need to know that we're ready, and we won't tolerate any acting up in here. You also need to know that these drones did not belong to Barclay Farms. Theirs are black, marked with their logo, and an entirely different and more powerful piece of equipment."

"Also, each time someone was on our farm at night," Charlotte continued, "I heard a car engine start up and watched its shadow as it drove away. Both Ford and Martin drive Teslas. Say what you will about them, but one thing is for sure. They don't make a sound." Charlotte was no longer playing coy, and stared directly at the Hoover table.

As if on cue, Diane sent out the next appetizer with the servers. It was a fresh crab salad served on a bed of arugula with breaded goat cheese and adorned with balls of mango juice that had been frozen with liquid nitrogen. Diane took a moment to demonstrate the technique from behind the kitchen counter.

"To do this kind of flash freeze with fruits and vegetables, you need to use food-grade liquid nitrogen like I have here in this cylinder. It's pressurized before being dispensed and is quite different from the solution that you farmers use to encourage growth of your crops," Diane explained.

The Chief got back up on the dais. "In Linc's secret lab, we found one other set of prints on a lot of the items being experimented with. They belonged to our friend Boyd Hoover."

The deputies had quietly gathered behind his chair. Charlotte saw Katharine try to suppress the smirk that was spreading across her face.

"Oh come on, Chief. Linc and I were experimenting on our own crops, that's all. We didn't go out and sabotage those other farms. I was focused on finding ways to get the highest yield in the county. Make it to number one," Boyd explained. "Anyone could see that."

"Boyd, you can't be that stupid. These chemicals were banned for a reason. They've been known to cause cancer, tear up our ozone layer, ruin our soil. And what were you planning to do once you'd grown these beautiful strawberries? Send them out into our food system? Loaded with deadly poison?" Chief Goodacre nodded to her officers, who pulled Boyd up from his seat and cuffed his hands behind his back.

"That's why this was an experiment, Chief. Once we'd gotten the mixture right, then we were going to find ways to replace the poisonous ingredients with safe ones," Boyd said, hanging his head down. "She's the one you need to talk to." Boyd nodded toward Katharine, still seated at the table.

"Oh sure, throw me under the bus for your bullying and ego. You always have to get your way, Dad, and you don't care who you stomp on along the way."

"You're the one who cut off the payments to Linc, Katharine. We were going to get this right, Chief—you have to believe me. None of the crops that we'd been experimenting on were going to leave the farm," Boyd pleaded.

"That money was supposed to be both of ours, Dad. And I needed every penny I was entitled to so that I could get the vineyard up and running. All the profits would have gone back into the account," Katharine reasoned.

"You were against the testing that Linc and I were doing from the beginning, Katharine. You were constantly badgering Linc—that's why I ended up going to his stinky, dirty lab to meet. He was afraid to be around you and your lousy temper." Boyd spat at the floor.

"My temper?" Katharine kicked back her chair as she stood. One of the deputies tried to restrain her, but she was too strong for him.

Charlotte remembered that Katharine had been in charge of security at Hoover Farms for several years.

"Now I'm being made out to be the bad guy? Because I couldn't stand by and watch you drain the farm's entire capital?" The Chief moved in, and they finally got cuffs on Katharine. "What's this for, Chief? I didn't do anything wrong!" Katharine shouted.

"Except for sabotaging other farms' strawberry crops Katharine. That wasn't very nice." Charlotte looked her in the eyes. "You were hoping that Hoover Farms would come out ahead of the competition without investing in more fertilizer experimentation?" Charlotte asked.

"What the hell are you talking about, Miss Perfect? Stay in your lane, Charlotte, whatever that is." Samuel moved up to Charlotte's side and gave Katharine a stony stare.

"The berries were killed by someone using food-grade liquid nitrogen. Just like the kind you'd been having delivered by Cryofresh before they cut you off for not paying your bills."

"How dare you, Charlotte!"

"You needed the liquid nitrogen to freeze your harvested grapes to sell in bulk to distributors. And you probably used one of these to cut samples of grapes in the field. The more bulk orders you got, the closer you'd be to affording to buy the equipment to start your own winemaking."

"So what? I bet lots of farms around here are doing the same thing."

Charlotte shook her head. "No, I checked. You might have gotten away with it, Katharine, except for your temper. Linc Pierce discovered what you were doing and threatened to blow the whistle, didn't he?"

"Now you're babbling and making an even bigger fool of yourself, Charlotte. Let me go," Katharine said to the deputy beside her. Then to Charlotte again: "I'm done with your pathetic excuse for a restaurant."

"Afraid we can't do that Miss Hoover, and by tonight you'll be kicking yourself for not partaking of this delicious food. The boys at the jail are pretty good at opening cans, but that's about the extent of their culinary skills." Chief Goodacre gave her deputies the signal to take the Hoovers out.

"Good luck proving any of this, Chief. All you've got is silly circumstantial evidence."

"Which when looked at together builds a pretty strong case against you." Charlotte consulted her cell phone. "And to seal the deal, we know that the pieces of white drone match the brand, model, and color of those used at Hoover Farms. You brought them in when you were head of security for the farm, didn't you? But Boyd wouldn't go for the expenditure of adding a computer control system to fly them remotely. That's why you needed to be present at my farm to perform the sabotage."

"It was your damned owls that interrupted my plans. They bombed my drone and tried to fight it to the ground. It spiraled, hit a tree and broke into pieces. I heard you and that pig, and grabbed as much of the drone as I could find before running back to my car. And I hung that effigy, hoping to shine the suspect spotlight onto Beau."

"But you still had Linc Pierce nipping at your heels, didn't you?" the Chief asked, putting her hand up for the deputies to stop walking. "So you rode your horse over to the Pierce Farm, taking a shortcut across farm fields? We'll show the witness a photo of you on your horse, Katharine, and I bet this time we'll get confirmation that it was you they saw. I've already compared the description of the horse to yours, and they match."

"I went to his farm to knock some sense in the old man, warn him that he'd better back off. But the cranky geriatric put up a fight. No wonder Linc and my Dad were friends. Both could hold a grudge into eternity," Katharine said.

"So you killed him." Charlotte waited for a confession.

"Lucky for me I'd been trained in self-defense when I worked with our farm's security team. He actually wore himself out trying to fight me." Katharine laughed. "Once Linc was dead, I got the idea to make it look like a suicide. People would believe that. Nobody liked Linc Pierce."

You could hear a pin drop in the restaurant.

"Take them away," the Chief ordered, and the deputies moved them out.

As they were going through the doors, Charlotte raised her hand full of mints and loudly said to Katharine, "I think you dropped these. They fell out of your purse."

Once again the room erupted in applause.

EPILOGUE

D iane had to adapt the menu a little bit as it was now approaching dinnertime, and she sure didn't want anyone going home hungry.

Thanks to her great staff, led by Alice, they were up to the job, and Joe and Samuel were sent out to the fields to gather some additional fresh ingredients.

"I'm sorry that you had to sit through that," Charlotte said to Margaret Pierce, joining her table along with Chief Goodacre. "It must have been tough to hear the details of your great-grandfather Linc's murder."

"I'll admit it wasn't easy. I kept thinking that if maybe his family had spent more time with him, he might have developed a gentler disposition."

"No use looking back. It's the future that counts," the Chief said between bites of freshly baked bread and churned butter.

The waitstaff were visiting tables and pouring glasses of Katharine's Holy Terroir wines. The irony wasn't lost on Charlotte, but she had to admit that the pinot noir tasted pretty good.

By the time dessert was served, everyone was in fine spirits, and several tables had burst out in song.

Charlotte approached Diane, who was watching the atmosphere in the restaurant give off a warm glow. "Is this how you pictured your opening?"

"In a way, yes. Peace has been restored to our world, people are mingling, and enemies are making up and becoming friends. Look at us. Who would have thought that two girls from the suburbs of Chicago would so organically embrace farm life?"

"I would have, that's who," said Beau, coming toward them. "A bunch of us have gathered on the patio. Care to join us?"

Arm in arm, the three childhood friends walked across the room to the outside tables overlooking Finn Lake.

Someone had lit the firepit, and Charlotte saw Alice sitting next to Joe, who was telling the group Uncle Tobias stories. Samuel and Danny were listening intently and adding their two cents when needed. Charlotte, Diane, and Beau joined the group, and another bottle of wine was passed around.

And just like at any family gathering, there was a kiddie table off to the side. But this one was occupied by geese, goats, a horse named Pele and a pig named Horse. Mrs. Robinson preferred to remain in her warm perch behind Horse's ear.

Every family has a rebel.

And out on the farm, under a cerulean sky with twinkling stars, Charlotte could almost see owls Fred and Ginger tripping the light fantastic . . .

Acknowledgments

Like Diane's menu, this was a labor of love inspired by nature. As Aristotle so aptly observed, "In all things of nature there is something of the marvelous."

I must thank the grebes, herons, cormorants, buffleheads, owls, geese, ducks, and pelicans that inhabit my world just outside. And also the dogs, cats, raccoons, possum—all furry members of the animal kingdom. I can't forget the insects that keep the natural world spinning. And, of course, pigs of all shapes and sizes.

Thank you to the inspirational molders of this story, Jenny Chen, Ella Marie Shupe, and Sharon Belcastro, as well as all the wonderful people at Crooked Lane Books.

I am grateful for the assistance I was given on fertilizers and drones used in farming from Suzannah and Craig Underwood of Underwood Family Farms, and to Raymond for his extensive knowledge of liquid nitrogen.

Thanks to my dear friend Mary Beth Hickey for always being there and for showing me all the wonderful farm life on the North Fork of Long Island, New York; and to my real-life

Acknowledgments

BFF, Diane Desrosier: we met when we were twelve and have never stopped inspiring each other.

Lastly, thanks and unending love for my mom, Doris, lover of nature and known for saying, "They are all God's creatures. Except for flies. I hate flies."